Moments of Livvy

Regitze Ladekarl

© Regitze Ladekarl 2020

ISBN: 978-1-09830-769-1

eBook ISBN: 978-1-09830-770-7

All rights reserved. This book or any portion thereof may not be reproduced or used in any manner whatsoever without the express written permission of the publisher except for the use of brief quotations in a book review.

For Lisa

with gratitude

Moment 0

Calabasas, CA
Thursday, November 25th, 2010, 10:30 AM
I am 65 years old

"Mom, we've decided to do an intervention for you!" Lily says and checks my reaction.

The words strike me like lightning, and I am stunned. I can feel the buzz of electricity travel down through my body to the nice beige carpet they had put in when they renovated the house three years ago. My ears are burning as if my second-grade teacher, Mrs. Taft, had scolded me, and the rush of emotions are the same—shame, guilt, shock, confusion, discomfort, and above all, regret and disappointment. Regret that I didn't see this coming and disappointment that Thanksgiving has just been ruined.

"We think you drink too much. It has to stop!" Maya says.

Maya looks relieved that she delivered her line to perfection. She always did get nervous at school plays, which threw her timing off.

I wait for Ben to chime in, but the girls must not have trusted him with a speaking part. All I get is a wordless apology as he joins the other two in their expectant stare.

"Why?" is the only response that comes to my mind, but I don't say that out loud. Instead, I look at my hands. They are wrinkly with spots, but the nails are still healthy and right now, polished bright pink by Anabel, Lily's nine-year-old daughter. In hindsight, that must have been an effort to keep me off the bottle last night. The polish will chip off when I get home and pick up my needlepoint again. I miss that right now. I could also do with a drink, but I guess that's out of the question.

I do a mental head slap because I walked right into this trap. Of course, Lily wouldn't just invite us back on a whim after my little mishap on her birthday in April. I should have known something was up when she called out of the blue two weeks ago. There is no such thing as a free turkey. There is only pretense turkey, bait-and-switch turkey, and gotcha turkey that I now have to pay for.

Lily mistakes my silence for agreement and presses on,

"We think it's best if you get into some sort of rehab program, so we're going to look up the AA meetings around here so you can get started right away."

Always so efficient, so considerate, so right. Lily has this whole thing wrapped up with a bow and ready to go. It is well thought out and generous of her to offer to help, but as usual, it is more for her convenience than mine. She wants to tie up her loose ends. She wants me not to be so difficult, not be so disappointing, not be so…me. She wants me to fit into the standard box of grandma, so she doesn't have to worry about me, but I have never fit into anything, and now I am tired of trying. I want to be left alone.

"I also think it'd be good if we set you up with a therapist to talk you through this process," Lily continues. She seems to forget I don't live in L.A. Here, everyone has at least a handful of shrinks and coaches and spiritual guides to tell them how to live their life. In Elko, Nevada, we have the doctor and the church, and neither of them is big on the why.

"Don't you have anything to say, Mom?" Maya asks.

While she is not the most perceptive of the three, she doesn't have Lily's habit of plowing through. Maya needs me to confess my sins so I can be forgiven and by association then her, too. This is our 'Come to Jesus' moment. Who would have thought that she would be my one child to find God? She was so open and creative—much more of a wild one—until she met pious

Derrick at the age of 16. I know Maya is concerned for my soul. She is convinced that if I just accept God into my heart, my life will turn around. God is her magic wand. But no God can erase my past, and then I would rather go without. I don't need the judgment. There is already enough of that to go around.

"I don't know what to say," I lie.

I seem to be the only one to notice that the intervention is not about me. They all want me to change, so I don't reflect poorly on them. Even Ben, my sweet helpless baby. It could as easily be him on the receiving end today. Like his dad, he can't stay out of trouble even though his life depends on it. He is adrift in a sea of bad choices. It is not that he doesn't want to do better; he just doesn't know how. If I were to do this for any of my kids, it would be him. He needs the hope.

But it is too late for me. I know it can be done; I just don't have the strength or the will anymore. I have taken leave of my responsibility. I worked so hard for them for so long that I deserve a break. They don't need me any longer. And me getting sober won't change that. I don't want to take care of their snotty kids or sit at their prayer meetings or make sure Ben doesn't kill himself. My job is done, and I did the best I could. Now I want to do my crafts and enjoy my wine. I don't see what's wrong with that. If they are afraid of me driving, I can get Robert to do that. That is what I married him for. Because he takes care of me.

No, this intervention is for them. It is like when they were kids, and we played doctor, and I was the patient. It was over much faster if I let them cover me in Band-Aids and gauze. They are paying their dues to me, and they can't see I have no interest in their debt. That whatever they think they owe me, I don't want to be burdened by.

"Well, it can hardly come as a surprise for you, Mom," Lily adds another argument to her case. "It hasn't gotten any better since my birthday. Quite the opposite from what I hear!"

Ah, there it is. One point for me. The unexplained invitation. Robert's uncharacteristic eagerness to accept it. His passive aggression hasn't sharpened with age, has it? Still the same blunt force without wielding the hammer himself. I can't decide if I am more impressed or hurt by his cunning betrayal. Getting the chickens to come home to roost. My two chicks and their reluctant brother.

We all have our roles in this script. We have performed it many times, so I don't need any prompts from stage left to know what I should do now. I reach for my forgotten teacup on the table. My hands tremble with anger and whatnot. So much, I have to grab the cup with both hands to not spill. I know they notice. I try to cover it by standing up at the same time but only succeed half as I am out of hands to help me get up from the couch. Results are overall wobbly, but I have not to care. There is no such thing as a gracious drunk. I head for the door like I always do.

BEFORE

Moment 1

Carrizo Plain, CA
Saturday, April 11th, 1953, 6:40 AM
I am eight years old

I see my dad's right shoulder jerk before I hear the shot. It is as if the two things don't belong together. Like the shot doesn't come from my dad's shotgun but from elsewhere that has nothing to do with us. That would be better. The jackrabbit stops dead in its tracks. I do, too. I hope if I stand very still and pretend it didn't happen, maybe it won't have, and the jackrabbit will hop on. But nothing moves. Maybe it is afraid to come out because we are here. Like me.

"Why don't you go get it, Livvy?" my dad says.

It is not a question, just a sign for me to do my part. My dad explained it when we drove here. How we could be a team. How I could help him scare the rabbits out so he could shoot them, and I could bring them back to him. I don't like that last part. I don't like any part of it. I thought about how I could avoid it. I asked my dad if we could get a dog. It seems like a thing a dog could do. And then the rest of the time, the dog could be mine. It would be a little white dog with silky fur. I would name her Bella. She would always be by my side. I would like that.

But my dad saw right through me. He knew I was asking because I didn't want to do it. I could sense he was disappointed in me. He sometimes is. When I am slow or don't pay attention or when I am scared. It is my own fault. I think he would like me better if I were a boy because boys are not scared.

Driving here in the truck, he said, "Don't be such a sissy. You have to be able to handle stuff. I can't take care of you forever."

I guess that is true. He would get tired of it. And I will be a grownup. Some day. Grownups can't have their dads take care of them. But it is hard to figure out. I take care of Mom. I bring her food and remind her when we have to do laundry on Tuesdays and to turn on the light in the kitchen at night, so she doesn't have to sit in the dark. I sometimes wish I didn't have to do that. But then who would do it? I don't have any sisters or brothers. That means I am both the oldest and youngest at the same time. I would like to have an older sister. Now that I am not getting a dog, maybe my sister's name would be Bella. I like that name. A lot.

Dad snaps his fingers to get me going. I drag my feet over to the spot where the jackrabbit stopped. Please run away, please run away, please run away, I say in my head with each step forward.

The rabbit is dead. It can't run away. Dark blood, thick as gravy, has trickled out the pellet wounds in the grey-brown fur. It smells warm and sweet and metallic at the same time. My stomach turns, and my legs go gooey. I kneel down in front of it and think about its family. What will they think when it doesn't come home? Will they be worried? Will they come out looking for it? Will its babies cry?

My dad says it is okay to shoot the jackrabbits because there are so many of them, and they have babies all the time. I don't understand. How can he know if this one had babies? Who will take care of them now? What if it didn't, but was all alone in the world? It is all so sad, and I start to cry. Sad, sad tears roll down my face with no sound.

"Whatya doing over there, Livvy?" My dad calls.

I am supposed to pick it up from the bottom of the ears. That is the proper way of carrying it, my dad says. I don't want to. I don't want to touch it at all. But I also don't want Dad to be mad at me, so I close my right hand around the top of the head and feel the fur against my palm. It is a lot coarser than I thought it would be. I get up and turn around and walk over to my dad with my arm stretched out in front of me.

Dad has spread out a small patch of tarp on the ground next to him and motions me to put the rabbit down there. I lay it down on its back, paws up in the air, and dad folds the tarp around it and gets up from his crouch with the shotgun around his shoulder and the hunting bag in his hand. I get to carry the tarp with the dead jackrabbit.

We walk through the landscape in silence. Red and yellow and lilac flowers in bloom all around us. Insects and butterflies buzz. A falcon circles overhead keeping an eye out for movement like my dad. I trail behind in mourning and thought. Maybe all animals are the same. No matter if we fly or hop or walk, we have to eat. And if there are too many of us, maybe there won't be enough food.

"Is that why you just had me?" I ask, not looking up from the ground.

My dad stops and turns around to me.

"What did you say?" he says, but by the way he says it, I know he heard me the first time.

"Did you and Mom only have me because you don't want there to be too many people?" I ask again. I look up at him towering over me, his brows furrowed and eyes dark. He seems to search my face for the answer. After a while, he says,

"No," and turns around and walks on.

Moment 2

Bakersfield, CA
Tuesday, October 19th, 1954, 4:45 PM
I am nine years old

I sit at the kitchen table and draw dresses for my paper dolls. I have the small table covered in paper, colored pencils, a pair of scissors that don't cut too well anymore, and a pea-sized piece of a red eraser for when I make mistakes, which luckily doesn't often happen because it is pretty hard to use. I am good at not making mistakes. I have to be. If I make mistakes, my mom will be upset and cry, and my dad will yell at her, and I don't like that. So I am careful.

My mom sits next to me at the table, but she doesn't look at what I do. She sits so still that she could be a doll, too. As if I had just propped her up on the chair but forgot to straighten her back, she is slouching a little with her hands in her lap. She looks out the window at the sky. The sun is low and makes the clouds look like giant cotton candy and marshmallows in pink and white and light orange and milk chocolate. I can make light orange with a red, a yellow, and a little bit of white on top. That is a pretty color for doll clothes.

Mom doesn't look like a doll. She looks the way she always does. A bulky black dress with buttons down the middle. Her arms are white like unbaked dough and hanging down her side. Her face is grayer but maybe, that is because of her eyes. She has lines from her nose to her mouth and from her mouth to her chin. Her hair is curly and hard to comb through. I know because mine is the same kind. Just a different color. Mine is brown. Hers is not. And I have brown eyes too. They match, my hair and eyes.

I love my paper dolls. There is the blonde, Molly. She likes fun and colorful dresses with flowing skirts and puffy short sleeves, and sometimes she wears white gloves and a hat when she goes out on picnics or shopping. And then there is the dark brunette Cynthia. She is elegant. She only wears fitted gowns and pearls and attends fancy balls where she meets handsome knights and dukes and dances all night. I hum what I imagine the musicians would play as Cynthia twirls around in the arms of an invisible prince who is about to fall in love with her and sweep her away to his father's kingdom.

I stop my humming when I hear my dad's truck on the side of the house. I look at my mom to see if she's heard it too, but she keeps staring out the window as usual. Sometimes I think she must not have the right feelings because she's never happy or smiles or anything. My dad gets angry about that. He says we are not what he signed up for. I don't like that.

Today could be one of those days because my dad slams the truck door hard. My mom flinches at the sound and sits up straighter as if she is at school, and the teacher just woke her up at her desk. It is just a tiny flinch, and her eyes are still fixed on the clouds.

My dad comes in through the side door and stomps past the kitchen to the bedroom. Mom and I sit frozen in our spots as we listen to him rummage around in there. The big closet is opened, and something heavy is slid down from the top shelf. The dirt from his work boots crunches as he turns around in it. Drawers are pulled out all the way and emptied. He takes four steps into the bathroom and picks up a toothbrush from the water glass on the sink and something from the thin shelf in the medicine cabinet. Then he fills the door to the kitchen, his black hair in disarray and touching the doorframe over his head, his shoulders so wide he could be wearing it and his blue eyes darkened by determination, a suitcase in one hand, and his lunchbox in the other. He looks at my mom and says,

"I can't do this anymore! I want a real wife and a real family."

Then he turns around on his heels and walks out the side door, gets into his truck, and drives off. The house is quiet again. Quiet and empty. We held our breath, and now we have room to breathe out. I look at mom. She looks at her hands in her lap. A tear rolls off her cheek and down on her thumb. She doesn't make a sound.

I don't know what to do. I want to ask her if Dad will come back, but her stillness eats all the air, so I can't say anything. Maybe if I wait a bit. My body is restless. It wants to move around. As if my questions got into my arms and my legs, they are bursting to get out. My chair makes a loud noise on the kitchen floor as I stand up. Too loud. I tiptoe over to the light switch by the door and turn it on. All the light in the room is sucked into the lamp and shines down on the table. Mom is in the darkness outside the beam. Outside my reach.

I sit down again and pick out a dark teal color for Cynthia's new ball gown.

Moment 3

Bakersfield, CA
Monday, December 2nd, 1957, 4:05 PM
I am 12 years old

I stare at the letter on the table to put my dreams in it. I am not even sure what my dreams are. I only know that this particular dream is about my dad.

The letter is from him. I recognize the handwriting on the envelope even if it has been more than three years since he left. It was in the mailbox when I came home from school. It is for Mom, but she isn't home yet.

I almost burned myself on the envelope carrying it in, so I had to put it down on the table. I wonder what he wants. Maybe it is something for my birthday on Thursday. It is light, doesn't seem to have a lot in it.

I don't miss him. At least I don't think I do. What would I miss him for? Family, maybe. It is just Mom and me, and that gets lonely fast. Whatever life mom had in her, dad took with him when he left. Now she's just surviving. For my sake, she says. But I don't know what she does for me. I take more care of her than the other way around.

She misses him. She missed him even before he left. She always just waited for him to come home and tell her what to do. Not in a commandeering way. Just tell her what she should be doing. It's like no one ever taught her how to do it herself. That you have to cook dinner at night. That you have to wash clothes in the morning so it can dry outside. That you have to talk to people to make them like you. Now I have to tell her. Or do it myself.

I wonder what he writes. Maybe he is coming back. Maybe my birthday made him miss us. Maybe the holidays made him think about us, and now he wants to come back. Mom would take him back too. In a heartbeat. There's no doubt about it.

Where has he been? Did he have a place to go? Has he been drifting around from town to town? The postmark says Sacramento. That is far away. I have never been that far away. I have never been anywhere. I am always trapped here.

I hear mom lean the bike against the side of the house. She must have been out to clean somewhere. That's what she does. Sometimes I go with her, but that is hard because we only have the one bike. Then we walk instead. If I am lucky, she will have gotten us something for dinner but probably not.

There is a flutter in my belly as she comes in through the door. I both look forward to and dread showing her the letter. Maybe I will leave it here as a surprise for her.

"Livvy, dear," she says. "I should have worn mittens, but I don't know where you put them."

The world is against her. Everything is beyond her control. It's never her fault. And even if it were, she wouldn't know how to make it right.

She plunks down her purse on the kitchen counter and blows into her folded hands. There is no bag of groceries. Cheese sandwiches again, then. Just like yesterday.

She notices the letter, and I suck in a little air in anticipation. But she just picks it up and slides it into her purse as if she doesn't want me to see it.

"Wasn't that a letter from dad?" I ask before I can stop myself.

Her hand is still in her purse. She fingers the corner of the envelope and looks at a spot somewhere below my chin.

"No," she says with hesitation and a nervous smile. "Was it?"

"You know it was!"

"Oh, it's just the normal one," she says like I should know what that means. She pulls her hand out of the purse and lets it rest with the other one down in front of her. Her eyes retract to the floor.

"What normal one?"

"Oh, you know…" her voice trails off.

"No, I don't know. What is it?"

She fidgets with the nail on her thumb and turns away from me.

"Livvy dear, I'm tired," she says. "I think I'm gonna go lie down for a bit."

"Oh, come on! For once, could you be honest with me?"

She squirms there by the kitchen counter. I can almost hear her thoughts. How little can she get away with telling me? Can she get past me and out the door? Why do I have to bug her? In the end, it seems the least possible scrap of information wins out.

"Your dad sends money," she whispers.

"What?" I don't understand.

"Your dad sends some money sometimes," she repeats a little louder in a broken voice.

It pains her so much to say it that she starts to cry. A silent inward cry. Like a maid being rightfully whipped by her mistress. I hesitate to go on, but I cannot not know.

"Is there a letter too?" I ask.

"No, never," she says.

She sits down at the table, and her shoulders collapse into her chest. She rolls into herself like an armadillo. Once again, struck down by her shame. Once again, exposed for her inadequacy. Once again, reminded of her failure.

I should console her. I should tell her she is doing all she can, and the two of us will be alright. But I don't believe that. We are castaways. We might be stranded here forever since no one is looking for us.

Moment 4

Bakersfield, CA
Thursday, May 12th, 1960 3:35 PM
I am 15 years old

I lie on the bed in my room and read *Lolita* by Nabokov. I like the story, but Lolita is a bit annoying. Why doesn't she use her power over Humbert Humbert? She can have everything she wants, and she chooses to stay ordinary. What a waste!

"Livvy, dear?" My mom calls.

Time for us to go, I guess. I put down the book on the dresser that doubles as a nightstand because it is right next to my bed. I have to sit up on the bed and scoot sideways until I am clear of the dresser to stand up— that's how small my room is. In the kitchen, I grab an apple from the table, and I'm out the door. I get in on the passenger seat next to my mom and take a bite of the apple.

Me eating the apple is the only sound apart from the noises of the old truck. It whines and creaks at every move that isn't just straight ahead. It is a piece of junk that some cousin gave Mom out of pity. Take your family in, and they will mooch on you forever, give them a banged up truck, and they will be somebody else's problem.

Mom keeps her eyes on the road. She's not a great driver. She's not a great anything. She doesn't want to talk to me or listen. Says she does her best. Well, that isn't good enough, is it? And the Chevy can be tricky. It has a mind of its own. Jumps all over the place. Mom won't let me drive. That is so random. Of all the things she has me do, driving is a no? Even this cleaning job she's supposed to do for the Hunts, she brings me along. I roll down the window and throw out the apple core.

The Hunts live in a yellow brick mansion on the rich side of Bakersfield. There is a long driveway that cuts in front of the house. The help should park on the left side of the house at the door to the mudroom, Mrs. Hunt says. There are no other cars in the driveway today. There usually are. Either Mr. Hunt's black Chrysler Windsor or Mrs. Hunt's sporty Ford Thunderbird or the workmen's truck. I get out and find the key in the flower pot next to the door.

We go in through the mudroom to the big kitchen. The house is quiet and seems empty. Mom plops her handbag down on the counter and sighs. I ignore her and get a caddy with cleaning supplies from the cupboard next to the door.

"I'm going upstairs," I tell her and head through the two-way door to the dining room with its polished dark wooden table and glittering chandelier making dots in all colors on the wall and ceiling and continue to the entrance hall in cool light marble and wide stairs. At the top of the stairs, I turn left down the carpeted hallway to the Hunts' master bedroom. I knock on the door and enter.

This is how I imagine my dream bedroom. A light blue gold rimmed bed with matching bed stands. Pillows upon pillows with delicate fringes on the soft blue bed cover. Lush light carpet that goes into the bathroom as well. Gold rimmed mirrors opposite the tall windows. And this room is meant for two, which makes it even better.

I put down the caddy on the floor and walk over to sit down on the left side of the bed. There is a family photo on the nightstand. The Hunt kids Amelie and her older brother Brad when they were small. The dark, handsome Mr. Hunt, the blonde Mrs. Hunt with her curls and a little too wide mouth. What would it feel like to be in a bed like this with someone like that? To lie under the covers naked and kiss and hold someone?

I kick off my shoes and lie down on the bed facing the middle. I pretend Mr. Hunt is there on the other side, looking into my eyes. My fantasy is a little off because I don't know what his first name is. I decide to go with Tom since his smile in the photo reminds me of the cartoon cat. He looks all the way into me, into my mind, into my heart, my breasts, and even further down. I grab a pillow from his side of the bed and hold it tight and start to kiss it. The kiss gets deeper and deeper, and I long to take off my clothes to feel him against my skin.

A door slams somewhere in the house, and I sit up like a catapult. My face feels hot; my breath is fast. Nobody was supposed to be home. Are they coming in here? I get off the bed, put the pillow back, and straighten the bedspread. Then I pick up the caddy and go to clean the bathroom while I try to hold onto the flustered and thrilling feeling inside.

After I'm done in the master suite, I walk down the hallway to Amelie's room. I knock to be sure there is no one in there. It might be because of Amelie taking pity on me at school that mom got this gig, but I am not about to clean her room while she's there. But she isn't, and I enter. Amelie has got the whole world going for her. Her parents give her everything she points to. She even has a riding horse, and there are horse show photos and ribbons on the end wall in her room. She is smart at school. And she will be just as beautiful as both her parents because she has her dad's dark hair and eyes and her mom's curls. A true princess just waiting for her perfect match. That will never be me.

The thought is cloying, and the walls start to close in on me, so I hurry out and down the hall to Brad's room. I listen for a second, but the house is quiet again. For some reason, I open the door without knocking and find Brad on his bed. He looks up at me from what he is doing, and it takes me a second to register what that is. He is jerking off. He has his pants around his knees and is pumping his…thing.

I am too stunned to do anything. Brad must see that because he doesn't stop. Instead, he looks me straight in the eyes as if to say, "Well, what do you think of that?"

My brain yells to get out and close the door, but my body has that nice warm sensation again. Against my will, I step closer to the bed and put my right hand on top of his. He folds his hand around mine and shows me how to do it. Slow motions all the way down, all the way up. I feel myself getting warmer and wet between my thighs. My body wants more. Without thinking, I reach under my skirt with my left hand and manage to wrestle my panties off. Brad takes my hands and pulls me up on the bed with him. He still has that smirk on his face. He challenges me. I do not back down. Instead, I get on top of him and slide him inside me. I hold his stare while I begin to move back and forth, back and forth, back and forth. It feels good. It feels right. He closes his eyes and moves faster and faster and then arches his back with a grunt.

He opens his eyes and looks at me again. He smiles. That same cartoon cat smile as his dad in the family photo. He grabs my arms and turns me sideways and off him. I stand down on the floor and put my panties back on. I can feel his juice running down my inner thigh. Brad swings his legs down on the floor on the other side of the bed and pulls up his pants in one swoop. He picks up his keys and wallet from the nightstand and walks out. As he passes me, he squeezes my shoulder with one hand, and then he's gone.

Moment 5

Bakersfield, CA
Friday, June 3rd, 1960, 3:40 PM
I am 15 years old

I sit at the kitchen table and doodle in my notebook. Intricate filigree and lace. I should be doing my homework, but my thoughts wander off into daydreams. That happens a lot these days. My mind cannot seem to stay in one place for long but makes up storylines and fairytales as elaborate as my drawings.

A maiden so beautiful stylish and clever

A prince comes along who will love her forever

Together united whatever life brings

These are my very favorite things

That is how it should be. People should meet and fall in love and conquer everything and respect each other and share their lives forever. That is what I wish for.

I am pregnant. I know because I am weird every morning, queasy and hungry at the same time. Also, I missed my period. That is not how it should be. It is so far away from how it should be that it belongs in a fairy tale. I look for a silver lining—a possible happy ending.

I search for clues like a nauseous Nancy Drew. Clues that I am a forgotten princess and this, a test of my worthiness of the crown. Clues that Dad left us because he was tasked with defending a faraway kingdom and not because we did not live up to his expectations. Clues that Brad is noble and kind and will stand up for my honor and do the right thing and not a dingbat who doesn't know my name or even care. And even if I've seen no evidence yet, I can't give up, because then, all is lost. I have to believe to succeed.

Mom is the only one who knows. I had to tell her because of the hurling. She looked like I slapped her in the face, but she didn't say much. She never does. She lets life pounce on her.

I am not like that. I am doing something, going someplace, being someone. I have a plan. Not a good one, but a plan. I am going to wait to tell Brad until I am further along. Then he'll have to marry me. He is almost 18, and I heard you can get a special permit if you are too young. I hope the Hunts can take care of that. Maybe they will ask me to move into the house right away and have the baby there. Brad's bedroom is big enough for all of us. And then Mom can see us when she comes to clean.

It sounds too good to be true. Maybe it is. But I have to believe this is not a mistake; that I did not give it away for nothing, that I won't get punished.

I know what they say about girls like me. Except I am not. I didn't do this to trick Brad. I am not a loose girl. And I don't want Brad to take care of me. I can take care of myself. I just want him to be with me, and with time, he will fall in love with me, and we will have a nice family. Like his. I don't cheat. I am not weak. I have patience and skill.

The sound of the truck on the side of the house brings me back to the kitchen.

"Mrs. Hunt says you have to get rid of it," Mom spits out before she is even in. She sounds like she ran the whole way holding her breath not to get infected by the poison of her message.

"What do you mean?" I try to buy myself some time to process.

"She said you have to go to one of those ladies to get rid of it. The Hunts will pay." Mom says as if that makes it all right.

My head starts spinning, and I feel the color of my face change as it is first ice-cold, then flaming hot. All feelings leave my body to give space for the rage, and I jump up with the force of a prodded mountain lion.

"YOU TOLD HER?" I roar.

I don't know what angers me more; that Mom took matters in her own hands or that I failed to see it coming. It rushes through me like a pounding river, faster and faster towards the fall.

"I had to Livvy. Don't you see?" she pleads in a small voice from the corner right inside the kitchen where she cowers. I want to squash her like a bug.

"You ruin EVERYTHING! No wonder Dad left you. You are USELESS!"

She winces and crumbles at every word.

Anger fuels my body, and I have to do something with it. I grab my teacup on the table and smash it into the floor. It helps but too little. I take the butter knife from my plate and step towards her. I want to stab her, break her, burn her into ashes. I realize I want to kill her, and that scares me enough to stop.

A mother should not kill her child. A child is bound to return to the favor. I am both and neither to her. I sit back down on the chair. Disappointment replaces anger. The betrayal stings worse than salt in a paper cut.

"How could you do it?" I ask. "How could you betray me like that?"

"I had to," she claims again. "You can't have a baby on your own, Livvy. What would you do? What would people think?"

"Brad would marry me!" I say, but I hear it's not true. He won't marry me. He hasn't even talked to me since that day. He is 17 years old and does whatever is easiest. And that is not getting hitched to a 15-year-old girl he only met once. He is used to people taking care of him, not the other way around. He doesn't have to be responsible. He has his mom for that.

I am alone with too much responsibility. I cannot carry both a mother and a child. Not by myself. My plan lies broken with the tea leaves and porcelain shards on the floor. Cut short, like the life of my baby will be.

Moment 6

Bakersfield, CA
Tuesday, June 7th, 1960, 8:20 PM
I am 15 years old

I sit on a kitchen table in my underwear. My hands clutch the edge of the table. My feet dangle off the floor. I stare at my knees that are knuckled and milky white-blue in the light from the lamp just above me.

Mom sits on a chair against the wall away from the table. Both her hands hold on to the bag in her lap as if it is a lifesaver and she is lost at sea. She looks like she could barf in it at any time.

Ms. Jane washes her hands at the kitchen sink and dries them in her apron. Then she evens out a kitchen towel on the counter and puts a pair of knitting needles and glass on top of it. She fills the glass half with bourbon, wets a cloth in it, and wipes off the knitting needles. She drinks the rest of the bourbon as part of the ritual.

I know her name is not Ms. Jane. A Jane is a tall blonde woman with wavy curls and spiffy tailored bathing suits with polka dots. This woman is short and stout with dark, flimsy hair. She wears a shapeless brown dress and a big apron that once was white but now is gray with stains on it. I don't even want to think about what those stains are from. She looks more like a Peggy to me. It doesn't matter. Jane is not her name; it is what she does.

A radio plays dance music somewhere in the house. I have heard a chair being pushed over the floor several times, too. It must be Mr. Jane. Ms. Jane went to give him the envelope with the three hundred dollars and the address in Mrs. Hunt's neat handwriting just when mom and I got here.

"Okay, young lady. Take off your panties and lie down on your back with your knees bent and your feet as close to your body as possible," Ms. Jane says to me. "Scoot as far as you can up the table so I can see something in the light." she sounds bossy and kind at the same time.

I do as I am told. The table is long but not long enough for me to rest my head and feet on it at the same time, so my head ends up tilted in a weird angle neither up on the wall nor down on the table. Ms. Jane puts a towel between my legs. I shudder as her hand touches my inner thigh by accident.

I make myself look at the ceiling, but it is hard to make anything out in the dimness above the lamp. I pretend the ceiling is a map. A map of a kingdom with an enchanted forest.

I gasp for air when Ms. Jane forces her whole right hand into me. The pain is all over from the pressure of something about to burst. I want to sit up and punch her, but she must be familiar with the impulse because she puts her left hand on my lower belly and pins me down while she feels around inside.

The pain is unbearable. I have to give up my body and retreat to the forest. I, the fair maiden Olivia, have been banished to the enchanted forest by the evil queen, Mrs. Hunt. Little does the evil queen realize that I feel at home and know how to survive in the forest. The trees shelter me, the soft cushy moss gives me rest, the sun keeps me warm, and the animals are my friends. What the evil queen thinks is punishment is a refuge.

Ms. Jane pulls her fingers out, and my body makes a little sucking sound. I feel myself getting wet and mushy down there. I relax my stomach that has been tight as a rock while I was out. I am a bit confused about being back in Ms. Jane's kitchen but relieved that it is over. Only it is not. It has not even begun. Stupid, stupid, stupid! I am so stupid. Tears start rolling down sideways on my cheeks as Ms. Jane takes one of the knitting needles from the kitchen counter.

I am staggered by the pain. It takes all my strength not to scream out loud. I clench my jaw as Ms. Jane stabs my insides again and again. I yell to the treetops in the enchanted forest. I curse my mom— that weak, wretched woman— for telling on me. I shout in anger at myself for being so thick to think Brad would stand up for me. I wail and I howl. I kneel on the cool forest floor and cry for being alone. For having no embrace to disappear into.

"You can sit up now and put on your dress, dear. You will need to keep towels down there for the blood. It will be heavier than normal."

I open my eyes. Ms. Jane washes off the knitting needles in the kitchen sink. I put my hands flat on the table and push myself up. I feel woozy and close my eyes again. Breathe, breathe, breathe. As I open my eyes one more time, I see Mom trying to hand me my dress. Her hands shake, and I wonder if I let out my rage in the kitchen. For once, I don't care. I can't bear to look at her. She is nothing. A nobody. And she knows it. I yank my dress from her and put it on. I take my time buttoning it down the front. As if now is the time to cover up.

All the while, it feels like my innards are leaving my body through my private parts. Every little movement hurts. I slide down the table and into my ballerina shoes on the floor. Then I shuffle towards the door clutching the towel to my crotch.

Our truck is parked at the curb. It is packed with our belongings. I work myself into the passenger seat while mom hurries to the other side. Once in, she puts on her seat belt and starts the car. We drive off. As we turn left at the end of the street, the headlights light up a sign that says,

FRESNO 109 miles

Moment 7

Fresno, CA
Thursday, October 15th, 1964, 6:30 PM
I am 19 years old

I sell tickets at the Sequoia Movie Theatre. The booth is snug and hotter than hell in summer. In the evenings, it's cooler. Then I like my little pod. The job is not bad, either. I like seeing the moms with their kids and the grandparents and the couples on dates. I have a little guessing game on who will walk out hand in hand and who won't. I am usually right. Tonight is busy. *Send Me No Flowers* just started running after the longest time of no new movies.

"Do you want to go to a party? If you don't, that's okay," he says to me without meeting my eyes. Not what I expected. I already had my hand on the roll of tickets to tear one off for him. I take a look at him. He looks nice but shy. His hair is blonde and tussled. His eyes are bright blue. His lips are on the full side. His nose has a kink on the upper part as if it has been broken. He wears a flannel shirt over a not-so-white t-shirt, dirty jeans, and work boots.

"Do you want me to go or not?" I ask him.

"Yes, yes!" he says.

He looks scared and hopeful at the same time. I decide to let him off the hook.

"Well then, okay."

The people in line behind him are getting restless. The movie is about to start. He must notice because he half turns and begins to walk away.

"When is the party?" I yell after him.

He stops in his tracks and turns towards me.

"Tomorrow. I will pick you up here at eight," he yells back and takes a couple of steps backward. "I am James, by the way."

One more turn and he's gone.

Moment 8

Fresno, CA
Friday, October 16th, 1964, 9:30 PM
I am 19 years old

I am at the party with James. It is not a fun one. I don't know any of the people here. I don't think James does either. James is nice enough. Just not much of a talker. Or a dancer. So we mostly stand around and look at other people talk and dance.

He was late to pick me up. I almost went home. I would have to sneak back in so Mom wouldn't hear me. She wouldn't say anything. She would think I got what I deserved. But then, he showed up. In an old Chevy way older than the one we had when we moved to Fresno. I was afraid it would fall apart before we got here.

I tried to talk to him on the way, but it was like pulling teeth. Only one-word answers. Yes. No. Not much of a conversation. I did find out that he is a mechanic. The body shop is in Edison close to the 180. It is just him and the owner.

James and I stand close to each other in the dining room. He smells clean. We avoid looking at each other. He looks at his shoes. I look at two couples standing next to us. They all know each other. One of the guys has put his arm around his girlfriend's shoulder. The other couple holds hands. That looks nice.

"Do you want another drink?" James asks.

We both got some punch from a bowl in the kitchen when we first got here. It was sweet and sticky, but I drank it anyway. Now we have the empty glasses in our hands. I don't feel like drinking more, but there aren't a whole lot of other things to do.

"Sure," I say.

James disappears through the two-way door to the kitchen. I can breathe a little better. I move back into the living room to see if there is somewhere to sit down. Wearing new shoes wasn't the best choice. Soft yellow and pointy with kitten heels. My toes are squeezed together, the back of my shins hurt.

Just as I enter the living room, the front door flies open, and a whole gang of people make their way in. They talk and laugh. I notice a man in the middle of the pack. He is tall and slender with sleek blonde hair. His face is chiseled. His eyes are green and blue. He has a crooked smile. I wonder if I know him. He senses my stare and locks eyes with me. Something happens. A tickle in the small of my back. My ears go bright red.

He breaks free from his group and steps toward me.

"Hey there," he says.

He is even more handsome up close. I must look like I swallowed a stick of dynamite, and the cat got my tongue. I want it to end right now and last forever.

"Don't be shy," he says.

Easy for him to say. It's all I can do to keep my mouth shut and not look like a complete doofus. James breaks the moment. He is back with a glass of punch in each hand.

"What are you doing here?" James asks the man with the eyes. "Shouldn't you be home with your wife?"

The words hit me. The story I just made up in my head is a lie. He is not a prince. He is not here to sweep me away. He is spoken for. But he still looks at me. Reads my face. Builds us a private bubble. He says,

"Hello. I'm Jonathan."

James lashes out once more.

"I see you have met my brother," James says to me and tries to hand me my glass of punch. "Don't bother telling him your name. He won't remember."

I am just the rope in the tug of war. I do feel sorry for James. Jonathan seems like everything James is not—elegant, confident, well-spoken, charming, paying attention to me.

"My brother is unfair," Jonathan says as he grabs both my hands.

Never once since he saw me staring at him from across the room has he looked away.

"Go away you…cheater!" James sputters.

By now, Jonathan must know every detail of my face. I can't seem to get tired of looking at his. James is a fly buzzing around the outskirts of our feast.

"I am Olivia. I work at the Sequoia Theatre," I tell him.

"I'll find you," he responds.

He squeezes my hands and then lets them go. He takes a step backward and turns to see where his crew is and disappears further into the house.

"We should go!" James says.

Defeat is all over his face. He puts down the punch glasses on a side table and guides me through the door and down the walkway to the street. We walk the two blocks to his truck in silence. We drive through town with our eyes fixed on the street in front of us. As I get out of the truck at our walk-up apartment, James says,

"He is bad news. I'm just saying."

I slam the truck door and head up the stairs.

Moment 9

Las Vegas, NV
Friday, January 1st, 1965, 3:10 AM
I am 20 years old

I arch my lower back backward and yell to prolong the wave of…I don't even know what to call the intense feeling overtaking me. Somehow, orgasm seems too small a word. It's standing in the middle of a fire where the flames kiss every part of my body at the same time. It's flying into space lightning-fast and just wanting to keep going forever and ever, although I will combust in a moment. It's driving at full speed towards a wall knowing the impact of the crash will be so sweet it will make me cry.

I release him from inside me and slide down on my side in the vast sea of the comforter on the bed. Tears stream down my face, and I can't stop them. Tears of relief and gratitude and truth. I want to explain that I am not sad, quite the opposite. But I have no words.

Jonathan moves down to spoon me. We lie together in a drawing of how we were standing up just a few minutes ago. I feel his thing against my buttocks. He reaches his right arm around my back and under my arm to cup my breast. He kisses the back of my neck.

"I bet you liked that!" he says in between kisses, with more than a little triumph in his voice.

"Yes," I whisper, unable to say anything else without sobbing.

I want us to stay like this forever. I have never been this happy. This content. This satisfied. I am not feeling any guilt. No regret. No remorse.

Just bliss. Pure bliss. I didn't know people could make each other feel this way. Now that I have tasted it, I want to do it again. Drink it up. Drown myself in it. I am sure this feeling can cure anything. Why are people not doing this all the time? Maybe it's just for the few. Maybe not everyone can do this. Maybe not everyone will let themselves be like this. Surrendered. Exposed. Giving themselves up to each other. Giving themselves up to the Universe.

Mom and Dad cannot have had this. Otherwise, they would have stayed together. This is a feeling that holds people together. If they share this, they will never want to be apart again. Such a shame. I wish for everyone to experience this.

"Thank you," I whisper to Jonathan.

"Yeah, I was good!" he says.

Silence settles upon us. I feel sleep seeping over me. It has been a long day and a long night. We left Fresno in Jonathan's brand new Cadillac Fleetwood before lunch yesterday. Jonathan, I, Timmy, Craig, and Craig's girlfriend, Desiree. Desiree used to be a showgirl at the Sands and could get us a suite here. I have never been to Las Vegas, let alone a casino before. I have only seen places like this in the movies. I was in the back seat with Craig and Desiree most of the time. They could not keep their hands off each other, so I had to look out the window or sit at the edge of the seat and talk to Jonathan and Timmy on the way. Jonathan insisted on driving most of the way. He had brought a bottle of Jim Beam for the road, but I only had a little because I get car sick. We stopped late afternoon and got a hot dog and a beer. At the Sands, Jonathan ordered champagne to the suite before we headed to the Copa Room to celebrate the new year. Timmy also brought something for the nose. I usually don't like it when Jonathan is high. He gets tense and hyper and combative and rough. For some reason, he paced himself tonight. Maybe we were in sync.

After the party, Jonathan and I came back to the suite and had more champagne. We took it into the bedroom, where Jonathan undressed me and had his hands and tongue and thing all over me. I heard Craig and

Desiree come back a little later, but we were too far into our lovemaking to mind. What a tornado!

As I am just about to close my eyes and drift off, Jonathan slowly disentangles himself from me and leaves the bed.

"Where're you going?" I ask, sounding harsher than I want to.

"Ssshhhh" is all he says as he dresses and slips out the door.

I haven't spent a whole night with him yet. He always leaves after sex. And it is not as if he doesn't sleep. But he gets wired and restless. Maybe it's the drugs. Maybe it's me. I still have no clue why he chose me. I like him. More than like him. I am in love with him. I am swept away by him. I am consumed by him. When I see the other girls who throw themselves at him, I don't know what he sees in me. I am afraid that every day we are together is the last. I am afraid that every time he leaves, I will never see him again. I am afraid that the next word out of his mouth is goodbye.

But it hasn't been yet. We have found a rhythm. A way of being together. An arrangement. We don't see each other every day. We did in the beginning. But I can't keep up with his schedule. I have my job. I have mom to look after. He is out almost every night. All night. He likes to party. He lives in the guest house at his parents'. It is a whole other house next to the main house. It is bigger than our apartment. His dad owns three or four car dealerships around Fresno. That is how Jonathan always has new cars. That's also where Jonathan works. He sells cars. He's good at it. So good he can make his own hours. That's why James knows how to fix cars. Jonathan jokes that if the family had a restaurant, he would be the chef, and James would be the dishwasher. He thinks that's hilarious. I cannot help but feel sorry for James. Not that I have seen him since that night in October. Jonathan and James don't get along.

We see each other when Jonathan wants to. He picks me up after work. Or at home. He has come up a couple of times. He has said hello to mom. Mom has decided she doesn't like him, but she doesn't like anyone and certainly not men I go out with. She says he is a charlatan. A cheater. A philanderer. That is not how it is. It is not like we have promised each other to be exclusive. Jonathan is very free. He doesn't believe in labels like that.

I don't have a claim to him. And he doesn't claim me. Our relationship is based on us wanting to be together. I think. All I know is that it is so amazing when we are. And when we are not, I try not to think about it too much.

We usually hang out with his friends. He has a lot. He is kind of the leader of the group. Of any group. That is just who he is. He knows every bar and club and restaurant owner in Fresno. He knows where the good parties are, or maybe it's just a good party when he's there. And if there isn't one, he throws his own. There's always something going on.

His friends treat me with some respect. More respect than I have had before. They are a little bit afraid of me because I am Jonathan's girl. They are polite but keep their distance. It is a hard group to break into. Many of them have known Jonathan since elementary school. I cannot compete with that. It will get better. Or not.

I will not doubt Jonathan. That is what I've decided. I will not doubt him. We cannot have what we just had without it meaning something. He might sneak off into the night, but it has to mean something. It has to tie us together. It has to make us tighter. Not choking us but making us closer. It has to mean something. It might seem small now, but down the line, it will mean something. Down the line, he will remember this just as I do, and it will make him come back. Down the line, it will separate us from all the noise, and there will just be the two of us. I'm sure of that.

Moment 10

Fresno, CA
Thursday, April 15th, 1965, 11:10 PM
I am 20 years old

"Come on, Livvy!" Jonathan coaxes, "Don't be such a square. Let's do it together!"

I am torn. I am torn between my fear of drugs and desire to be with him always and in everything. I am torn between my mother's voice in my head and my trust in him. And I do trust him. He would never leave me astray. He loves me. He would never let anything happen to me. He loves me. He wants us to experience the Universe together. He wants us to go deeper together. He wants us. He loves me. He would never.

"He's no good for you, Livvy!"

That is what my mother says. All the time.

"I can see it in his eyes. It's not gonna end well for you!"

I have stopped listening to her. What does she know? Look at her miserable life. Alone. Lonely. Depressed. She just wants me to be as miserable as her. She can't stand that I have happiness and love. She never had that, and she will not allow it for anyone else. I can't take it. I have to shut her out. Shut her down. Shut her up.

"Livvy, Love," Jonathan says. "Would I steer you wrong?"

We are on the couch in his living room. Our living room. He is in a purple West African Dashiki and loose linen drawstring pants and with bare feet, which are resting on the edge of the coffee table in front of him. Two small squares of paper with smiley faces are on the table. I have disentangled myself from his arms and moved a little away from him on the couch. I sit with my legs criss-cross-applesauce to his side to give myself room to think. I can't do that when I am too close to him. He takes over my mind, and I can only think about him and how he is not wearing anything underneath. Especially when we are alone like now, and he focuses all his energy on me.

I can decide for myself. I have had to decide for myself since I can remember because my mother wasn't there. Why should I stop now? I have had to trust my instincts all my life because she never helped me out. Why should I stop now? I have only had myself to listen to because she never told me. Why should I stop now?

Only if I am perfectly honest, I can hear a bit of my own voice in there too. But it might just be because I am projecting. Jonathan says I project a lot. The thing is I don't really like the drugs. I am not always sure what I am supposed to feel when I am on them. It is like they don't always work. Or it gets too scary. The things I see. The things I hear. The things I feel: monsters and screams and endless sadness. Jonathan says I have to face that in myself. That I will feel better afterward. But I thought people took drugs to forget those kinds of feelings. And that is the other issue. I don't like to forget. I don't like to blackout. I don't like not being able to remember what happened. I want to remember every minute and every second with Jonathan.

I am afraid that if I don't do drugs with him, there won't be any more minutes with Jonathan. But it's not like he is forcing me to do anything. It's more that he will lose interest in me if I don't. We are meant to be together. He says that. I feel that.

"I want us to go forward together," he says, "for us to experience things together for the first time. I want us to be adventurous together."

I want that too. But...but...I just think we could be together around other things than drugs. There are loads of things we could do together for the first time that is not drugs. Get married. Have kids. Except he is already married. And I sound like such a prude when I say stuff like that. It is just my conventional thinking. It is because I don't let myself dream enough. That is what Jonathan says. That I don't dream enough. And that drugs are good for dreams.

It is tempting. And necessary, I think. He can have any girl he wants, and he chose me. He chose me. I love him so much. I do not want to lose him. I want to be adventurous. I want to dream. I want to let myself dream.

Tomorrow is Friday. I have the day off. I don't have to be at the movie theater until 6 PM. We have time. We have time by ourselves. That doesn't happen often. He is usually surrounded by a whole group of people. I don't know why no one is here tonight. Maybe he planned it that way. Maybe he just wanted us to be alone. He can be sweet that way. It is just that people want a lot from him. He attracts people. Friends. Women. I understand that. He can have whomever he wants.

I look him in the eyes. Search for the answer there. For affirmation. For safety. I want to know that I am safe with him. That he will not let me go. Ever. He assures me with his eyes. I trust him. I love him. He loves me. There is nothing to be afraid of. He will take care of me.

"Okay," I say, "let's do it!"

Moment 11

Fresno, CA
Tuesday, November 2nd, 1965, 6:20 PM
I am 20 years old

"Mom?" I call out as I enter the apartment. It is quiet and stale as if no one has lived here for a long time. I can hear the clock tick in the kitchen, but that is all.

I am checking in on mom. It is a new habit. I am practicing motherhood. Since I found out I am pregnant, I have become a little bit more amenable to her moods. I have become a little bit more forgiving of her passive-aggressive ways. I have become a little bit more understanding of our broken relationship.

But while my surging hormones make me softer, they have not had the same effect on her. There have been no congratulations, no excitement, no embrace of the grandmother role—just the same old whining threats and guilt pushing.

"I don't know what will become of me when you are not here" is a frequent comment accompanied by hand wringing and sagging shoulders. That one is a classic meant to evoke both pity for her and put shame on me. She has always dragged me down into her misery, never tried to lift herself out of the darkness to join the living.

"Well, I don't even know what you are now!" has been my standard reply to that one for years.

"Don't think you can just come back here when that charlatan kicks you out."

This one comes with yelling down the staircase, followed by door slamming. It is filled with anger and jealousy. She has had her mind made up about Jonathan from the beginning and usually lies in wait, just inside the door, for me to admit that it is over between us. The fact that we have been going out for more than a year now, that we live together, and that I am expecting his child has not deterred her at all. As if I would ever want to come back. As if.

"There is nothing left for me in this life when you are not here," is another favorite statement delivered with tears and defiance. Her pendulum swings back and forth between her needs and my faults with no end.

"Mom?" I call again, louder this time as I turn on the light in the narrow hallway and the kitchen and the living room to the left without finding her. My pull-out bed is still there with bedsheets and all. That is yet another one of her jabs at my conscience. It has been five months since I officially moved out, and she keeps the living room intact to remind herself and me of how cruel I am.

She doesn't see that she is the cruel one, which might not be surprising since I didn't see it either until I met Jonathan. He has really helped me understand just how much damage she has done to me. If it were up to him, I wouldn't be here now. But despite the hurt and the anger and the resentment and the misery, I cannot not take care of her. She is like a baby bird. Unable to survive on her own. She will just wither away or work her way into a frenzy and do something stupid. I can't let her die. Now I am starting to get worried. She cannot have gone out. She never goes anywhere. And certainly not after dark. Where is she?

I turn to the right and open the door to the bedroom. The smell hits me like a hammer. A blend of industrial cleaner and shit and vomit. I turn the light on and wish I hadn't, because there she is. On her bed. All contorted, foaming at the corners of her mouth. My brain decides to shut down, and my legs give in. I slide down the door frame to the floor. My hands shake. I try to control my gagging. I sweat shock and fear. I don't how long I sit there stunned and numb, but after a while, my senses return. The smell is overwhelming, and I am grateful I cannot see her from here. I am overtaken by guilt. Maybe I did this. Maybe this is my fault. Maybe I killed her. Because I assume she is dead. But what if she isn't? I should check on her. I have to.

I crawl across the floor on my hands and knees since I deem myself unable to stand up, but as I reach her bedside, I see that is a mistake because that brings me eye-level with her face. It is frozen—her eyes full of pain and her lips all blue. I straighten out my back, still on my knees, and try to keep my balance as I grab her right arm that is limp across her body.

She is cold to the touch, and I cannot find any pulse, but I am not exactly sure what I am looking for. She is not breathing. She is dead; I already knew that. I know that in my head, but I cannot feel it yet. I let her wrist go and avert my eyes back to the floor because I can't bear to look at her. That is when I see the Drano bottle.

"Oh, you stupid cow!" I say out loud. "What have you done?"

Anger rises in me, and I can't stop it. All this to get back at me. This is too much.

"Why do you have to be so needy?" I yell at her.

"Why can't you just be a normal mom? No one feels sorry for you because you brought this on yourself! You have a miserable life because you don't change it! You just sit back and wait for someone else to come save you. Well, guess what? No one wants to save you! No one wants to be with someone who never does anything but sigh and wring their hands. It is all your fault!"

But she is dead so she can't hear me. Now she can't ever get it right. Never. I am sure it must have been an accident. I am sure she did not mean to kill herself. I am sure she only wanted to scare me a bit, so I would come back. For once, her actions had consequences. For once, she did something that worked. For once, she proved her point. Poor mom. Poor me. Poor us. My anger blends with sadness.

"Why couldn't you just be a normal mom?" I cry. "Why did you leave me? Why did you have to leave me all alone? You weren't a mother. You were just a blob in the kitchen that I had to take care of. No one should have to do that! No one should have to grow up without a mother. You can't just leave your child like that."

I won't miss her. That is the saddest thought I have ever had. I won't miss her. My shoulders shake with my sobs. I won't miss her because she was never there. I grieve because something inside me now dies, too. A faint hope that I didn't even know I had. A hope that the baby could have turned her around. That it could wake her up. That it could bring her out.

Once again, she has let me down. She has quelled my dreams. She has pushed me away.

"I'm not gonna take the blame, Mom," I say a little quieter. "This one will have to be on you. I opened the door, but you didn't want to walk through it. You chose this, not me."

I can hear her say,

"I didn't know how, Livvy, dear."

Meek as ever. As passive in death as she was in life. She made it like that.

Moment 12

Fresno, CA
Sunday, December 5th, 1965, 10:40 AM
I am 21 years old

"You are beautiful," Jonathan says.

It is a lazy Sunday morning, and we are lounging in the bed after making love. He has his hand on my baby bump.

"You are Mother Earth; you are Gaia."

I am meant to be here right now. We are meant to be together. This is meant to be. When we are together like this, there is light and warmth, and nothing can get to me. Maybe some people have to go away so we can appreciate who is left.

This is my first birthday alone, but I am not alone. The last bit of my family went away a month ago, but I am here with the family I am starting: Jonathan and I and the baby. I am in love with him. He is in love with me, and the proof of that is growing inside me.

I stopped feeling queasy all the time. It could have been bad energy because it went away right after mom died. She took it with her. She is gone without a trace. There is nothing left in this world that shows she was ever here—only me. I am the only sign she was here.

When I cleaned out the apartment, I found the envelopes from my dad. There was nothing in them; the money, of course, all gone and no return address on them. The envelopes must have been all she had. I thought about telling him mom died, but he doesn't want to be found. He wants to be gone too, and I will abide by that wish.

Because I am starting a new life. Literally. All the ties to my childhood have been cut, and I am starting another childhood. One that will be full of love and tenderness. Just like this moment.

"I love you," I say to Jonathan.

"You are love, Gaia," he says and caresses the bump. "And your child is love too."

I bask in his attention. I let myself be absorbed by it. I let go of all reservations and safeguards and flow away on the thick river of openness and possibility. A beginning begins.

Until this instant, I was unaware of how much I have held myself back. How much I have been on the outskirts of my life, looking in as if it didn't happen to me but to some other me that couldn't really feel pain or love. How much hesitation and uncertainty I have harbored. Now I am ready to step into me. Be at the center of me. Fill out all of me. Cast the doubts away and set sail for the future.

I need to pee, so I get myself upright and go to the bathroom. When I come back, Jonathan has fallen asleep again. He is on his left side in the bed with his arm still stretched out to where my belly was. His mouth is a little open, which softens his otherwise chiseled face. His neck makes a perfect bow from his jaw to his shoulder, only broken by a mark the size of a quarter.

I don't remember having done that. Our lovemaking was slow and deep. But I must have, no? The suspicions are lining up outside my head, waiting to get in. They knock on my temples to get me to open up. But I refuse. I don't need to know where he was last night. I don't need to know that I am the only one since I am one. I don't need to know who he loves because he loves me. That is what I tell myself as the baby flutters in my womb for the first time.

Moment 13

Fresno, CA
Tuesday, July 26th, 1966, 10:15 AM
I am 21 years old

I walk down the quiet street. It is already hot in the sun, but the street is lined with big trees. I like the cool shade. Still, I feel the sweat soak through my t-shirt and run down the back of my legs, so my long skirt clings to them. It has been almost four months since I gave birth, but I am as big as a house. Lily is a great eater, so the pounds should roll off me, but they don't. Right now, she sleeps in a sling around my chest. I am a slow wide boat sailing to foreign shores.

I reach the small cottage as I have done before. It is a dusty blue with white trimming. It has a picket fence. The door is lined with climbing red roses. Twice I have lost my nerve at the gate and walked on. Twice I have chickened out and told myself it doesn't matter. More than twice, it has haunted me, and now I need to do something about it. Today is the day. I open the gate and walk up to the front door. I pause to gather my courage.

This is the house I always wanted. Neat and quaint and just for me. I always imagined I would live in it by myself, but now my dream house has a nursery and a bed made for two. This is what I have come for. I ring the doorbell.

The woman answers immediately. I expected her to be frumpy and bitter, but she is nothing like that. She is tall and tanned and has short jet black hair and eyes. She has stunning red lips and teeth whiter than white. They match her silk blouse that is tucked into her turquoise pencil skirt. Where the skirt ends, her toned legs begin leading down into a pair of black high heels.

"Oh, hi!" she says as if she was waiting for me. "What can I do for you?"

The greeting throws me off. I came prepared to explain.

"Hey," I say, "I was wondering if I could talk to you for a moment?"

"Sure," she says. "But I haven't got long. I'm due at the store before noon."

She steps aside to let me edge through her small hallway and into a light and airy living room. There are a low beige sofa and a couple of armchairs around a glass coffee table. On top, there is a glossy book on French Haute Couture.

I won't be able to sit down or get up from the couch, so I choose one of the chairs. I have to squeeze myself into it. I end up sitting with my legs tight together in a 90-degree angle. My arms rest awkwardly on the chair since I don't want to squash or wake Lily, who is fast asleep. I feel like a whale wearing the chair.

"What can I do for you?" the woman asks again. She sits down on the sofa without effort and crosses her legs like she is posing for a magazine.

"You are Jessica Higgins, right?" I ask.

"Yes," she replies. "And I know who you are. Is it Olivia?"

"Yes," I say while I try to hide my surprise. How does she know?

"Jonathan has told me about you," Jessica answers from reading my mind.

I get an uneasy feeling in my stomach and not only from being crammed in the chair. It is from the fact that Jonathan talks to this woman. When was this? What has he said about me? But I won't let my head go there. I have to stick to the script.

"This is Lily," I say and look down at my sweet baby girl. Her small face with the chubby cheeks rests on top of my breasts. Her mouth is a little open, and her lips are pursed. She has a few fine strands of blonde hair on top of her head. The rest has rubbed off. My heart wells with love for her. My body responds by letting down milk, and I have to focus on Jessica.

"She is mine and Jonathan's," I say.

"I know," Jessica says with patience.

Again with the knowing. Where does it come from? Is there something I'm missing? I leap into it.

"Yes, so, I was thinking—we were thinking," I stammer, "now that we have Lily, it would be better if we could be a real family."

I search her face for resonance.

"I'm not sure I understand what that has to do with me?" Jessica says now a little terser.

"But you are still married to Jonathan!" I blurt out, afraid that the words will become even truer when said.

Jessica looks at me, clearly trying to put together a negative but polite response. Slowly and with deliberation, she says,

"If Jonathan wants to change our arrangement, it is certainly his right, but he has shown no desire to do so. He speaks of you and Lily with love, and I don't see that going against my relationship with him. Jonathan and I have always had wide boundaries."

As the words sink in, every sentence pulls the rug further out from under me. Soon it is gone. The bile rises up in my throat. I sweat. The room spins around.

"I gotta go," I mumble.

I struggle to free myself from the grip of the chair. I stumble out of the living room into the small hallway and get the front door open before I throw up. I have the wherewithal to hold onto the door frame so I can lean over and not hit Lily. I look down at her. She is still asleep.

"Do you need some water?" Jessica asks. She has followed me to the door.

"No, no…" I say and make my way out the gate and down the street.

Thoughts whirl around my head. Feelings kick in left and right. Anger, disappointment, hurt, heartbreak. I am stunned. I did not see this coming. Or what?

Did I know already? Did I know that he was such a coward? That he would rather hide behind his wife than commit? Maybe I knew. Maybe I chose not to see it. Because where would that leave me? A baby and nowhere to go. I can't make it on my own. And it's not as if he is mean to me. It's a roof over Lily's head. And a family. Maybe I am just a prude. Maybe this is all I get. Maybe this is all I deserve.

Moment 14

Fresno, CA
Thursday, November 16th, 1967, 11:25 PM
I am 22 years old

I sit by Lily's bed and wait for Jonathan to come home. I am so tired my thoughts run in circles. In and out of dreams and nightmares, and everything is real at the same time. It seems that is all I ever do. Wait for him. That bothers me. It makes me feel even more trapped. It is a power-trick. He has control over me because I can do nothing but wait for him. I have lost myself. I don't know where I went, and I don't trust myself to find me. So I wait for him instead. These days, I need him to tell me where I am. Who I am. I don't trust him either, but he has all the power, so what he says is real. What I say is wrong. Because I have all the faults. He has all the power. That is how it is. That is how it has become.

I also have all the babies. Lily sleeps next to me. The baby sleeps inside of me. That is why I wait for him. I have to tell him when he comes home. Somehow I hope telling him will save me. I'm optimistic based on nothing.

But it is time for me. That is why I wait. I am about to fall apart from tiredness. It goes with my condition. I do not like that word. Being pregnant is not an illness. That is what I am. Pregnant. And I have decided to tell Jonathan today.

I have known for a couple of weeks. I spent some time pretending it was not so, but then the morning sickness got too much for me to ignore. If it is anything like with Lily, I will start to show pretty soon. And if Jonathan figures it out on his own, there will be hell to pay. There probably will be anyway. That is why it has taken me some time to build the courage to tell him.

I could go to bed. Wait until tomorrow. That is a slippery slope. Tomorrow might not work either. Or the day after that. Maybe I should just not tell him at all and see when he notices. My thoughts run wild with this but always end up in the same place. He will not be pleased. My master will not be pleased.

But there is nothing I can do about that. I have to keep it. I cannot have another abortion. That would kill me. And it is not like I got pregnant on my own. He put it in me. It's his doing. I was not part of that. I rarely am anymore. He takes what he wants when he wants it, and that's that. That's how it is.

It is fine. Lily is my love. My love, my love, all of my love. I love her so much I am afraid it will break her. Having a sibling is a good thing. I wish I had that. Someone older to take care of me. A friend to talk to. Someone who cannot leave you just because life gets difficult. So this is my gift to Lily. Family. She deserves that.

That is the mother I am. That is the only thing I am. My father stopped me from being a child. My mother stopped me from being a daughter. Jonathan stopped me from being a lover. He punishes my love. It is always too much and never enough. So this is what I have left. Motherhood. Two babies. I am afraid of what he will say. I am afraid of what he will do. I am afraid.

I must have dozed off, but I am jolted awake when Jonathan stumbles in through the door. The small hallway is dark, but the moonlight shines through the bedroom window and makes a triangle on the floor like a spotlight. That is where Jonathan steadies himself on the doorframe. Always in the spotlight. He wears a thin beige windbreaker over a striped polo shirt, which is too cold for this time of year, but from the smell of cigarettes and booze, I can tell he is beyond caring.

I hate when he is like this. I hate myself for being with him when he is like this. Mostly I hate that I'm afraid of such a miserable and pathetic man. That I'm powerless against him. That I have locked myself in the cage with the dragon and thrown the key away. Another baby. I should not have let that happen.

"Hey, Babe..." he slurs. "Do you...come here...often?"

He giggles at his own comedic genius.

"You..." he loses the thread and has to start over.

"You shouldn't have...but I undersand...undersand you did."

I have to build up to what I have to say, too. I can't just blurt it out. He wouldn't understand. And I need him to understand. Understand what he has done. Understand that he needs to take care of us. Understand that being the god that reigns over our lives comes with responsibilities. Duties. But he is not that kind of god. He only believes in himself.

But I have to tell him. I still have to tell him. No matter how drunk he is. No matter how high he is. No matter how mean he is. That goes together—drunk, high, and mean. It gives him superpowers. He turns into a villain. An evil magician though he doesn't look like it right now. Hanging on the doorframe. Trying to say something. But I have been fooled too many times to think it will be easy.

I get up from the bed with the sleeping Lily and step forward into the moonlight. I stand between him and Lily so I can protect her just in case. I take a deep breath and say,

"I have to tell you something."

He tries to focus on me.

"You...you can tell me...tell me...anything!"

He spits out the last word for emphasis. He thinks he is so charming. So charismatic. So brilliant. And he can be. Just not right now. We have reached a point where he does not pull himself together for me anymore. He doesn't care at all what I think about him. Mostly because deep down, he knows that it's not good. And he knows I have to stay. So he can do whatever he wants.

Since Lily was born, he binges a lot more. Disappears for days. Comes home like this or worse and sleeps it out like a corpse. Then he gets up and goes to work for a few hours or hits up his parents for money, and then it starts all over again. I am not invited anymore, so I don't know for sure, but I have a feeling that there are more drinking and drugging and fewer women than before. I am the only sucker left. And then Jessica, of course, but she is not a sucker. She has the upper hand in this. He respects her.

I had hoped that Lily would change him for the better. That we could have a normal family. That he just had to get used to having her around. That's not how it has turned out. But now we have another chance. Another baby. Maybe.

"I am pregnant," I say.

There I have said it. I can see he takes in the meaning of that. That the words register, albeit slowly. Then he raises his back and lowers his head like a mountain lion preparing for the attack.

"What did you say?" he snarls suddenly sober.

I try to stand up taller and not be afraid.

"I am pregnant," I repeat.

His raging battle cry shocks me like an earthquake. Him, too, I think. It is all he can do to hold himself back by the doorframe and not come at me.

"Are you just out to get me or what?"

His voice builds from a whisper to a yell.

"Stupid bitch!" He screams at me.

Lily is now awake and crying. I turn around to pick her up. Hold her small body close to mine. It is just instinct; I cannot help it. But as I stand there at her bed, I feel so exposed. He could strike me. But he doesn't. Instead, I hear the door slam.

Moment 15

Fresno, CA
Tuesday, April 30th, 1968 2:15 PM
I am 23 years old

I walk in the door after having taken Lily for a walk in the stroller and find Jonathan sitting on the couch with his head in his hands.

"What are you doing home?" I ask. "Aren't you supposed to be at work?"

Jonathan now works at a bank. His dad wouldn't let him slack off at the dealership anymore. He has shaped up quite a bit. He is one of their best people. That makes me feel sorry for the bank, but I'm not surprised. He could sell sand in the desert. He sold me a fairytale, and here I am with nothing to my name and pregnant again.

"You have to be their dream," he always says.

And he is. He is the successful son of every man who walks up to the counter to get a car loan. He is the prince of every woman who needs help with the household budget. He is the savior of every newlywed couple who wants to buy their first home. Only it's a sham. He has never paid for a car, let alone having to borrow money to make ends meet. He has no clue what it means to have to plan to be able to eat. To not just have money show up when you need them. Not even now after his dad cut him off.

Jonathan looks up from his hands, and I see his eyes are red.

"My dad died," he says, his face contorted with emotion.

I don't know what to say. I cannot read what he wants me to do, but I do know that a wrong move can be fatal. I just stand there by the door, ready to go out again if necessary.

"Oh, no," I say, trying to make it sound like anything he might need from me.

"Mother called the bank," he says through tears. "Dad had a heart attack this morning."

"Oh, no," I say again.

Lily smacks her lips in her sleep as if to remind us she's still here. Maybe I should get some food for her in case we have to go to his parents' house.

"How could he do that?" Jonathan asks.

I am confused. Is he still talking about his father?

"How could he not let me say goodbye?" he says. "I would've made him come around!"

"Oh honey, I'm sure he didn't mean to have a heart attack," the words just fall out of my mouth in disbelief.

About two months ago, Jonathan's father called him over for a talk in his office. He said he had had it with Jonathan wasting his money with nothing to show for it. He had spoken to his attorney and had Jonathan removed from his will. Until Jonathan proved he was business savvy and cost-conscious, he would not be reinstated as an heir. Jonathan played it down. Said that it was just one of his dad's moods, and a little time would change his mind. The bank job is just for show. And it was not like his source dried up. His mother is always giving him money and taking his side.

"Don't honey me, you stupid bitch!" Jonathan snaps and sobs into his hands again.

Wow. He has called me names before but only when really drunk or strung out. It occurs to me that he could be that now, too. With Jonathan, I never know.

"Now James is gonna get all of it," he yells at the Universe.

"But you're probably okay with that, no?" he sneers at me. "Why don't you go throw yourself at him then? Tell him it's his brats. Could be true for all I know."

I try to tell myself he is in shock and hurting, but the words sting. Lily stirs in the stroller and then frowns her little face and starts to cry. I lift her out, and it hurts my lower back. I am going to have to stop carrying her around soon. She snuggles up to me and pops her thumb in her mouth. I try to rock her back to sleep with my body.

"I could've have made him come around!" Jonathan howls.

Lily opens her eyes and looks at him. She stretches out her arms and leans towards him.

"Get her away from me!" Jonathan snarls at me.

He gets up from the couch and pulls out a yellow pill envelope from his inner pocket, shakes out two tablets, throws them in his mouth, and swallows. He then leaves with nothing but a scowl at me.

Moment 16

Fresno, CA
Monday, February 10th, 1969, 9:35 AM
I am 24 years old

I am breastfeeding Maya while Lily plays on the floor of the living room. I didn't think that babies could be that different. Maya is just seven months old, but she already sets another agenda than Lily at the same age.

Lily and I are in each other at all times. The lines of communication are wide open, both when she was in me and since she was born. I know what she's thinking. I know how she feels, sometimes even before she feels it herself. And she can read me like no other. She adjusts to my moods, my emotional rollercoaster.

Maya does her own thing. She is a closed book. Not in a bad way, just not open to me. I have to figure out what she wants because she's not telling me. She will eat when offered. She will sleep when being snuggled, but she and I are not tuned to the same frequency.

This week, I have been glad we are not in sync. I have felt sick and queasy, but neither Maya nor Lily seem to have been bothered in any way. As I sit here with Maya at my breast and look at Lily taking a toy bus apart and put it back together, I feel a twinge in my uterus. It sparks a thought in my brain. I am pregnant again.

I do not need to take a test or see a doctor to know. As soon as I have the thought, I know that's how it is. I sit with that for a bit. Then I ask myself: how does that make me feel? I feel happy and content. I love my children.

They give me hope and purpose. I feel loved having children. I get as much love as I give to them and feel that it is what I am meant to do.

I also feel like a chicken, a coward, because there is no way that I am going to leave Jonathan if I'm pregnant. So I have just bought myself some time.

I feel selfish because I splurged on time. It is not fair to keep my kids here, but what can I do? I have nowhere to go with a toddler and a baby. I have less than nowhere to go.

I feel stupid. How could I let this happen again? I know I get pregnant in a blink of an eye. I know Jonathan is no good for me. I know I should know better. I know. I know. But babies are wonderful. They are life. They are purpose. They are what is meant to be. They make every wrong right. They make me right. And then I am back to the selfish part.

I am not going to tell Jonathan. I don't think he would listen anyway. These days he is out of my reach. He has been in a daze since his dad died. Drinking and drugging himself into a stupor. Either not speaking to me at all or going on endless rants about how his dad died to spite him, how the world is against him, and afraid of his genius and not ready for him at all.

He acts like he has nothing to do with the girls at all. Like they are mine alone. Something I brought home against his will. When Lily wants to get up to him, he gets stiff as a board and holds her like she has an incurable disease that he is at risk of catching. He has never held Maya. A neighbor down the street is a midwife and helped me when both Lily and Maya were born, but beyond knocking on her door to tell her it was time to come by, Jonathan didn't take part in either birth.

We rarely sleep in the same room anymore. I sleep in the girls' room because that is where I belong and feel safe. Jonathan takes what he wants when he feels like it, which is not that often anymore. Even that he is not present for, except one time right after his father's passing when he started crying and clung onto me like I was a life raft at high sea. He must have been so embarrassed that he has forgotten about it because it only happened that once. After that, he drifted away from me on his own tangent. I can barely believe he got me pregnant again. If there was any other possibility, I would say it wasn't his. But I am not a believer, and there has been no holy ghost or a virgin: just me and my babies.

Moment 17

Fresno, CA
Monday, May 11th, 1970, 8:40 PM
I am 25 years old

"You used to be fun!" Jonathan says.

So did you, I think, but I don't say anything. There is no point. He just needs to feel superior to me, and when his needs are satisfied, he will lose interest in me.

I am so tired I could die. The baby is killing me. He and Maya are far too close together but not close enough to be on the same schedule. It has been months since I last slept. But at least he has almost weaned himself off the breast. I guess there is more oomph in the formula, and he eats whatever he can get his hands on. He is always, always, hungry. I try to wait until the crying and screaming become unbearable before I feed him because otherwise, it would be an endless process. I think he is on to me, so he makes a fuss faster now. He has also noticed that Lily loses her patience before I do, and she will get him crackers and cheerios and maybe play with him. He loves his sister.

Right now, all of them are asleep—the girls in their room and the baby in his crib here in the living room. Ben Ben is passed out on top of a board with cut-out holes in different shapes. It is a toy that came in the mail from Jonathan's mom. Even if she lives only two miles away, she would never set foot in this dump, so Jonathan visits her when he needs money. Sometimes he brings the girls since they pay more than just him alone. It is a 'grandchildren for cash' scheme he has going.

Jonathan stands in the doorway as if he is either going or coming. I haven't seen him all day, but that doesn't mean he hasn't been here. Or I can't remember. From where I sit on the makeshift couch, it looks like he is so repelled by Ben's crib that he is unable to enter the room. I still have no idea where he is when he is not here. Doing drugs somewhere else, I assume. He doesn't have a job anymore. We live off his mother's kindness. I have to fight for money, for food, for the kids, and me. Jonathan doesn't seem to eat.

"You used to be up for stuff," he says from his doorway.

I can feel his disappointment and disapproval all the way over here. What am I supposed to do? I have three kids under five, and I never sleep.

"I am just so tired..." I say, by way of an explanation.

He looks at me like I am an alien. Like I am some strange being that exists under conditions that are completely foreign to him. Like these are not his children. Like he has no part in any of this, which is not far off. He does not take part in any of this.

Since he doesn't understand the issue, he changes his tactic.

"I can fix that, you know?" he says.

I'm in no mood to have sex. I'm in no mood to tend to anyone else's needs. I'm in no mood. So I play dumb to stall him, to discourage him. He hates that.

"What do you mean?" I ask and send him a blank stare.

He must be really horny because he is not dissuaded. He hears it as a '*Go on.*'

"I got this really dreamy stuff. Not acid but almost as good. And you can snort it for a fast kick. Or smoke it. Only the losers shoot it."

His voice is eager and boyish, like he is telling me about his brand new toy. I am speechless. I really don't know what to say. I can't believe him. Is he asking me to do drugs with him again? He mistakes my silence for another *'Go on.'*

"Come on, babe," he says, "it'll make you feel so much better!"

He hasn't looked at me like that in a long time. I don't understand why he does so now. My body is flappy and saggy. It doesn't look the way it did three children ago. It doesn't feel the way it did three children ago. It is drained of everything. I can barely drag it around. His faith in the drugs must be monumental if he thinks that a fix can change that. Most likely, I will pass out and sleep. I have maybe four hours or so before the baby wakes up for his bottle.

I was going to get a glass of wine or two to help me get some peace and quiet, but it doesn't really work. I just wake up even more tired and with a headache. Even if it has been a while, I remember Jonathan's drugs being like a black hole of forgetting. That doesn't sound so bad. That might not be so bad.

And if I pass out, he can just do with me what he wants. Then I won't have to be there for that. It could work for both of us. It wouldn't be the first time.

I can't be thinking about this. Where is my head at? I must have lost it. It is probably somewhere in the diaper pail or underneath Ben Ben in his crib. What I would give to get some sleep. I am so weak and exhausted and numb. I let go of my right mind, my reason, my resistance.

"How long is the trip?" I ask.

Jonathan smiles from ear to ear. I can't pretend it doesn't feel good when he does that. I can't pretend anything right now. Like in the old days, which were not so long ago. Only three children ago.

Moment 18

Fresno, CA
Thursday, March 18th, 1971, 10:45 AM
I am 26 years old

I ride a candy floss man slowly and deeply. He takes me through the clouds in flowing motions. Through meadows of green and blue and orange. The stars embrace us with their purple velvety points. Caress us and our love. Love the love so soft and cushioning. A blanket in the sky. A blanket sea of waves of joy. Every thrust lasts one forever. Every ebb tickles my spine with a peacock feather. Dandelion seeds glitter in the air and settle on us like a glaze. Another cub is born. He makes his room in the nest. So handsome, so strong. My air made something solid. The Candy Man can. Soon he will teach the cub to hunt down horses and deer. Baby takes a jackhammer to the hooves. I can't hear what he says behind the mask. Crystallized sugar flies in all directions. I bleed a girl on a pillow of ball gowns. Baby is mad. Floss is going fast. I am slow. My doll arms flop up and down. I cannot hold on. Diamond meteors stick to my eyelids. Rabbit's feet pound the pavement with a horrible noise. I cannot hold on. I can't get off. My legs are candy cane. I need to stop him. I press a thunder cloud against his face. He bargains with his angry eyes. I have to do this. It is better for him. He loves to ride on the milky stream. He will be gone soon. It is better. He will be with the deer mother. She is nice. Better than me. Pounding, pounding. I can't hear from the rain. His eyes must have closed. I feel the diamonds. They pop the bubble. The siren is here to get him. I hear her screams. She is better than me. He sucks on my sugar tits. It hurts. If he was gone, I would not need him. Not fair to crave a sugar baby. A million bullets rain down on me. Mercury washes into my bloodstream. I am drained heavy. There is nothing left but their hearts. Tiny ruby baby hearts. I keep souvenirs. They won't work for me. We all have holes for hearts. I ripped them out. No good, no good. I can't get up to save them.

…

I slowly come to. An elephant sits on me. My eyes take a moment to adjust to the light of the room. They are still faster than my mind. I carry the sensations from my trip with me. I am overwhelmed by the loss of them. Waking up to reality is painful.

I roll over on my right side and curl my legs up. I imagine myself being absorbed by the orange and purple pillows I lie on. The baby notices me moving and stops sobbing to see what I'm up to. His beautiful curly blond hair is matted with snot. His sweet chubby face is grimed with tears that run down on his too tight and short t-shirt. I can smell he is due for a diaper change. I can see it too. He stands up a little taller and holds on tighter to the bars of the pen. He is ready to be taken up.

But I am not ready. I must have fallen backward after I pulled the needle out from between my toes. I hope I pulled it out, but I can't remember. I see it on the upside-down crate next to me together with the spoon and the lighter. The high from shooting heroin is so much faster than snorting it, so I have to make sure I don't get hurt in the rush.

I hear Lily rummage around in the kitchen. She moves her little step stool around so she can reach the counter. Lily knows how to wash the dishes herself. She uses a ton of soap, but that is okay. Lily is an elfin. It is amazing how strong she is. She has my brown curls and hazel eyes, and Jonathan's defined cheekbones.

She must have gotten hungry. She is probably getting something for her and her siblings. I can't remember if I fed the baby this morning. He is always hungry, so maybe it doesn't matter. He will eat whatever Lily puts together. If the girls really got hungry, they could eat him. He would last a week or more. What a horrible thought. I love my baby. I love my children.

Lily Pad is serious and responsible and knows far too much for her age. Maya Bean is creative and independent and does her own thing. Ben Ben is really too old to be called a baby, but that is what he will always be. Round and lovable. And they are good together. Lily takes care of the younger ones, and they make sure she is still a child.

I am sick with guilt. I am the worst mother in the world. Even worse than my own mother. She stopped after having me. I am so selfish to have three. I could have stopped. I could have left Jonathan. I could have stepped up to the plate with Lily before having another one. But I didn't. I just went with the flow. I gave in. I gave up.

I look around. There are unopened mail and papers on every surface. Dirty plates and glasses on the table. Overflowing ashtrays, empty bottles. Unmatched curtains and bedsheets covering the windows to the back yard. Not that there's anything to see. There's nothing to see anymore.

Where did it all go? He was supposed to be this hotshot banker. He could sell anything to anyone. And especially credit. Here, have some. It'll be good for you. Don't worry, it will be fine.

He is a con artist. He conned me. He was supposed to love me. And if not me, he was supposed to love the kids. But he doesn't love anybody. Everything is an escape: all the parties, all the women, all the drugs—anything to get away. And now there's nothing left. The bank shut him down and out long ago. James won't have anything to do with him. His mom won't have anything to do with me. His friends are not friends, just junkies looking to score. I don't even know if he's here. He could be in the bedroom, tripping out. He could be dead.

I hear a crash from the kitchen, and Lily starts to cry. I get up and stumble out there. Lily sits on the floor among a pile of broken plates and glass.

"I couldn't do it, Mommy," she sobs. "I'm sorry I couldn't do it. I'll be better, Mommy."

Her words kill me. Her apologies stab me to death. Her tears drown me. She is not supposed to be sorry. I should be sorry. I should be punished.

I sit down on the floor and put my arms around her. She nestles her head into my chest, and we cry together. I know how it came to this. I have explanations but no excuses. I had hopes that didn't pan out. I thought I could outrun responsibility, but now, it has caught up. I will let myself cry for a little bit, but it has to stop soon. It has to stop now.

"Hey, Lily Pad, what do you say we go on a trip?" I say while I rest my chin on the top of her head.

"A trip where?" she sniffles from my heart.

"We will figure that out. You and I and Maya Bean and Ben Ben, we will decide that together," I convince myself.

"Will we have frozen custard?" Lily asks, now sitting up taller and looking me straight in the eyes. Beautiful, earnest Lily.

"Yes, of course," I say and hope that I'm right.

Moment 19

Fresno, CA
Friday, March 19th, 1971, 9:45 PM
I am 26 years old

I am a hundred years older than yesterday morning. My body is coming apart. It is hard to hold onto my spirit, but for once, I try. I am on the floor in James' bathroom. When I am not puking my guts out, I curl up shaking with cold, or I burn up from flames inside. My mouth is dry and bitter and sour like the sole of a sturdy leather shoe. I am so thirsty, but anything that goes in comes up right away. Hallucinations and nightmares about spiders and scorpions and blood and pain and pus squeeze me in their fists.

This is my punishment, and I'm going to take it. This is for not caring for my babies. This is for letting myself go. This is for letting myself be snake-charmed. This is the venom reluctantly leaving my system.

I knew I could count on James. I didn't have to explain, and he didn't ask. He came and picked us up half an hour after I called. Ben and I sat in the front of the truck with James. Lily and Maya and their stuffed animals were in the back. Our three small suitcases were on the truck bed where James' shop spare parts usually go. The kids thought that was funny. James has promised we can stay here until I get better. He checks in on me from time to time, but mostly, he takes care of the kids. They adore him. His house is a bachelor pad, but it is way nicer than the dump we left. He likes to keep things in order and get them done right away. And he cannot help but help. I think he enjoys having the kids around, too. It gives him purpose.

Another wave of nausea washes over me. I sit up on my knees and dry heave into the toilet. Nothing comes up, there is nothing left, and it hurts like hell and makes me sweat. I rest my forehead on the cool rim of the bowl, waiting to see if there is another wave coming. I could die right now. It would be a blessing. The kids could stay with James, and it would be okay.

Jonathan won't look for us here. Maybe he won't look for us at all. He wasn't home when we left, and I don't know where he was. I am close to not caring. He might have more families like us, who knows? Except we are not his family anymore. As of yesterday morning, we are on our own—just the four of us.

I want to hurt him. I want to get back at him. I want to punch him until he is sorry for what he has done to me. I want him to admit that it is unfair and cruel. That he is unfair and cruel. I know that will never happen, but right now, I need to push the pain out of myself and onto someone else. And he is the cause. He was always the cause.

My legs start to kick out of control. I am so cold and at the mercy of my flailing limbs. I strap myself to the mast of this captain-less ship and let the storm have its way with me. It will wash away the shame, blow away my guilt and, hopefully, spit me out on a quiet shore somewhere. Anywhere. Anywhere where we can start over.

I am ready for that. That is my anchor. The chance to start over. Find a new way. A better way. A way where I am the mother and the kids are kids. But first, I have to prove myself worthy. I have to survive hell. The bonfire of bile and broken dreams. The overwhelming stench of burned flesh and rotten soul.

Moment 20

Fresno, CA
Saturday, March 27th, 1971, 1:35 AM
I am 26 years old

I am an empty shell from the detox but well enough to realize that I have to fill up with something new to keep the past from catching up to me. It has to be gentle and with thought because I can't afford another mistake. I can't afford to let them down again. I can't afford to let me down again. It has to be light and strong at the same time. Like a bird's nest. I have to build a nest for my babies high in a treetop where nothing bad can get to them. I have to protect them at all costs.

They are sleeping. I can see some of the outlines of Lily and Maya in their makeshift bed of the couch, pillows on the floor on the other side of the coffee table. Lily snores. She always did. I remember when she was a baby, and it was just her and me. Her loud breath on my chest reassured me that she was alive. She was a tiny force of love, so soft and so powerful. Without her, there wouldn't be a me. I would have crumbled to dust under Jonathan's weight. There would have been no room for me to breathe. He would have taken up all the air. He would have killed me. He still could. But I cannot think about that. I have to keep moving to stay alive.

The children keep me moving. They are love batteries humming their power in the dark. Maya is a wildflower. She blooms everywhere. She stretches her petals towards the sun outside my shade. I have to not stand in her way, to not choke her with my concern, not poison her water with my inadequacy. I have to let her be.

Ben Ben is different. He needs a mother. More than anything, he needs a mother. And he would take anyone, but that is my job. He needs to be held and nursed and sung to and smiled at and kept warm and cleaned and kissed just to survive. He is the baby bird in my nest, much larger than I and calling for me at all times. I have to grow for him to grow. I have to hope for him to hope. I have to love for him to love. I have to. I do my best, but it's not enough. He clings on to me with his chubby toddler hands like I am a lifesaver, but I never knew about life, let alone saving it. I still have to learn. Who can teach me? Who would be willing to teach me?

I force myself to think about the future. Where to go from here. Because I—we—will have to move on. Maybe not tomorrow, but soon we will have outstayed our welcome here at James'. We mess up his day, his house, his life, and even if he doesn't seem to mind now, that time will come. I can't make it up to him. I can't make it worth his while. I have no means of payment other than myself. And I rather doubt that he would take me after how I have treated him. But maybe that is what I have to do. Maybe that is how I right my wrongs. Maybe that is how I atone.

I free myself from Ben's grip and wait until I am sure he doesn't wake up. I then swing my legs off the couch and tiptoe across the living room floor. I am in my worn-out underwear that matches my worn-out body. I try to conjure up something attractive, some sass, as I press down the door handle to the hallway, ever so slowly and quietly.

I close the door behind me again and stand in the no-mans-land of the hallway. It is cool and quiet, and there is a strip of moonlight slicing across the floor from the kitchen on the left. James' heavy boots are placed on an extra tile of carpet just inside the front door. They smell of gasoline and grease from the garage. The bathroom door right in front of me has a little brass sign of a kid sitting on a toilet on it, and I wonder if James is alone by choice. I grasp every straw to stall my errand. The bedroom is to the right, and I can reach it in one step, which is way too fast for what I am doing. I can still change my mind and go to the kitchen for a glass of water and consider my options.

But I have been considering all night, and now it is time for action. That is the least I can do. At the thought or maybe from the chill in the air I get goosebumps on my arms and legs.

Okay, here it goes, I think, and open the door to James' bedroom. It takes me a moment to make anything out because the room is in the moon shade, but it is hard to miss the outline of the bed as it takes up almost the whole room. James sleeps on the left side of the bed facing the middle. That is a sign, I guess, of his longings that he leaves room for another person in there. Or it could just be a coincidence. I scoot my way sideways past a dresser to the right side of the bed, and the window curtain caresses my back as I bend down to loosen the bedsheet on that side.

I am cold now and have nothing to lose, so I get into bed and pull the sheet over my left shoulder with my right hand. James' back in a white t-shirt is in front of my face, and my arms are pressed down my front in an awkward position. I don't know what to do now. I want to wake him up but not startle him with my cold hands. I squeeze them between my thighs for a second to warm them up. I can feel the bones in my legs and my skin sagging like a hide on top. That is the price of my life back. I put my left arm around James' back.

"What?" he almost jumps out of bed.

I guess my hands weren't that warm, after all. He is now on his back, propped up on his elbows, looking confused.

"It's just me," I say and try to snuggle closer to him.

"What are you doing?" he asks, half concerned, half interrogating.

"I just thought I would show you a little gratitude," I say, hearing how cheap it sounds but still sliding my left hand further down his body.

"Livvy, no!" he says with force and pushes my hand away.

I don't understand? What did I do wrong? Did I misread him? My face starts to burn and blood swooshes in my ears. How embarrassing. Time to go. Now. I swing my legs out of bed, but James grabs my hand.

"I am sorry," he says. "I didn't mean it like that."

We hold hands for a bit as I try to clear the tears from my voice.

"I understand," I say even if I don't. "You don't want me. No one wants me."

The tears keep coming as I realize that is true.

"Livvy," he whispers with tenderness, "it's not like that, and you know it!"

I wait for him to go on.

"It wouldn't be right!" he continues. "I love you. I don't want to take advantage of you. I'm not my brother."

I am at a loss and relieved at the same time. I have never offered my body to anyone and not have him take it. What if I lost it in detox? How am I going to get by then? On the other hand, this is James. The man I mistreated and mistook for a peasant for so many years but who has behaved like a prince for the past week. The man I hoped was *my* prince tonight. He is more than that. He is a friend. He is family. He is no strings attached.

I don't know how to be with that.

Moment 21

Fresno, CA
Monday, March 29th, 1971, 3:30 PM
I am 26 years old

"One of my mates' sister, Arlene, is looking for someone to help take care of her mother-in-law. It is an around-the-clock thing. I thought of you." James says and studies my face.

We are outside on the stoop, drinking tea and watching the girls walk Ben Ben around in the driveway. He beams at his sisters as he tries to keep up on his stubby legs and squeals when they go so fast he is off the ground.

"Are you kicking me out?" I say, more serious than not. I knew this moment would come and cannot help but think my late-night drop-in on James sped up the process.

"No, no," James apologizes. "But it might be good for you to get away from here. I heard from Mom that Jonathan is looking for you and the kiddos."

I should have figured that would happen too. I have been minute to minute, hour to hour, day to day, for the past two weeks—well, for years—and have fallen out of the habit of thinking about the past or the future. Panic tingles my spine when I do.

"Typical Jon to send Mom to do his bidding," James adds. "Such a wuss!"

That makes me feel a little safer. James will not give us up. James will protect us.

"What did your Mom say?" I ask.

"Just that you had no right to leave Jonathan, who has shown you nothing but kindness and compassion by taking you in," James says with a smile. "I think she is mostly upset that you took her grandchildren away. That is why I think you should go. She is way smarter and more alert than Jon, so it won't be long before she comes to visit here."

Jonathan and James' mother never was a fan of mine. She thinks I'm simple and dumb and not worth a second look. It wasn't until Lily was born, she showed the slightest interest in me. And after that, only because I was the kids' mother and she couldn't just snatch them away from me. She wanted to. She is a user like Jonathan. Takes what she wants and doesn't care about the rest.

In the beginning, when his father was still alive, we were invited over for dinner a couple of times, but then she decided I was below her favorite son's standards, and the invitations didn't include me anymore. Common courtesy did not apply to someone like me.

Jonathan's dad looked me the same way he would look a decent piece of prey when hunting. Not overly impressed but not about to pass it up if it walked in his line of sight. Those were uncomfortable times.

But when we had the kids, things changed. Jonathan can do no wrong in his mother's eyes, and any misstep of his is because the world is jealous of him and, therefore, out to get him. It was Jessica's own fault Jonathan left her because she was way too independent and couldn't have kids. Never mind, he never left her. It was my fault he got into drugs because I wasn't taking well enough care of him when his dad died. Never mind, he experimented way before I met him. Everything was spun into the story his mother preferred.

Lily, Maya, and Ben were all praised as gifts from above. They were proof of how wonderful Jonathan really is, how much he can really do, and that in spite of the circumstances as I am called. Jonathan's mother would have attended their births and taken them right then and there if Jonathan had been interested and present. But he wasn't. He was out boozing, drugging, and whoring somewhere, and couldn't be bothered on either occasion. He used the kids as tokens for his mother. He wanted to stay the chosen one so she would continue to support his habits and our children were good for that. If only, they came without me attached.

And now I have stolen them away. James is right. I need to get out.

"Where is your friend's sister?" I ask.

"I don't know for sure," James says. "Somewhere down by Los Angeles, I think. The deal is that the mother-in-law really needs someone to be there all the time, and Arlene could use some help with that. Chuck says they have a little guest house where you and the kids can stay. And they will pay you a bit to get you on your feet."

Sweet, sweet James, he set this up for me. He is not kicking me out; he is making sure I move on in the best possible way. All I have to do is take it. All I have to do is stand up for myself and my children and start anew. All I have to do is agree to let my life change. And since it hasn't been much of a life so far, why wouldn't I?

"Okay," I say.

Moment 22

South Pasadena, CA
Friday, July 30th, 1971, 6:35 AM
I am 26 years old

"Rise and shine, Ms. Betty!" I say in a low voice as I enter her room and turn on the lights.

Ms. Betty's small room is on the ground floor, just off the kitchen. I guess it used to be for the help, but now there is just the housekeeper Carol who lives with her family a few blocks away and then us, and we are in the guest-house out back.

"Already shining, Ms. Livvy!" Betty says. "But I'm gonna need some help on the rising. I am not a spring chicken anymore."

Same greeting every day. We both like the ritual. I walk around the bed to the nightstand on the other side and hands Betty her glasses. She looks so tiny in the bed, even if it is just a twin size. A female Mr. Magoo or an ancient turtle caught on its back. A bigger bed would have made it impossible to help Betty up.

"What do you say to a bath today?" I ask. From the smell, I suspect the diaper might not have kept her entirely dry through the night, but I don't want to embarrass her by saying that. I get the back pillows ready next to the bed, sit down on the edge, put my right arm tightly around Betty and lift her up while I arrange the pillows behind her with my left hand.

"Is it already Saturday?" She says on a light note into my neck as I hold her. "Then I better get fixed up and put on my dancing shoes!"

"No, no. Just Friday, but I'll take you dancing any day of the week."

I release her gently back into the pillows and give her the hand mirror she keeps next to the bed.

"Okay, you do your hair while I take care of the other end!" I say.

This is the least pleasant part of the morning, but it has to be done. I put aside the bedsheet covering Betty's frail body. I was right; Betty's diaper has leaked onto the bottom sheet.

"Let me get you dressed up," I say with a smile to not give anything away. "Hold on!"

I go grab a towel from the closet that has been crammed in between the bed and door on the back wall. Since Betty doesn't get out of bed anymore, she doesn't keep many clothes in there, and it is filled up with bedsheets and towels instead. I also take the tub of Ben's diaper cream that I have snuck in from the guest house.

Back at the bed, I take off the diaper, put the towel under Betty's skinny bum, and wash her off a bit with the wet sponge I keep in a tray under the bed. I apply the cream, take a clean diaper from the pile, and put it on. All of this is one fluent motion that I have rehearsed many times, first on the kids, and now on Betty. No one likes a diaper change to drag out. I pull the sheet back over her legs.

"There you go. What would you like for breakfast? An egg, toast, or maybe oatmeal?" Betty doesn't eat anything. Her medication takes away her appetite, and she is nauseous most of the time. It is a daily challenge to get her to take just a little bit of regular food. She does have a sweet tooth, so sometimes, I get ice cream with the kids in the afternoon and bring her back a milkshake or some frozen custard. Arlene doesn't like that and says it is not real food, but I figure it is better than nothing. That is one of our little secrets.

Betty and I have a few secrets. Not any bad ones, just small things that we don't tell Arlene about. Like how I read Lady Chatterley's Lover to Betty at night when she can't sleep. Like how we spritz Betty's favorite perfume on her pillow so she can have sweet dreams. Like how we discuss if there is a god and why He put us in this situation. Arlene is strict, and a devout Christian, and so is her husband, Edgar. Rules are rules, and they have to be followed. Anything fun is a sin. And we shouldn't question God and his will.

Arlene and Edgar don't know too much about why I am here. All James told Arlene's brother was that I had to move because of Jonathan. They interpreted that to mean Jonathan beat me, and I have not corrected that. Arlene has never mentioned anything about it, except I'm not allowed to have male visitors in the guesthouse. I never talk to Edgar. Only his mother.

Betty is a firecracker. She must have been something in her day. She is something now. Her body does not work anymore, but I forget that when we talk.

"I was an only child but still second." she often half-jokes.

"My father wanted a proper son to take over the business, so I had to marry young. I wasn't keen on that. I wanted to have some fun if you know what I mean." she winks at me.

"So I married Poor George," she says. "He was poor at everything; in the sack, money, hell–life itself! Got himself killed, didn't he? But Papa liked him. Maybe he should have bloody married him!"

Poor George died in a car accident when Edgar was just two, so Betty had to raise him by herself while also running the business.

"I had to, didn't I?" she says. "Papa was gone too, and Mama was no bloody good at anything but gin rummy."

Betty never remarried.

"Men just wanted the business," Betty says. "I promised myself I wouldn't be a stepping stone. But that doesn't mean I didn't have a party. I have no regrets!"

If I get to be Betty's age, I want to be able to say that. I want to be able to say that now, but I am not that lucky. Betty makes it better. She asks and probes and interrogates, but in a nice way. Like she is interested. I told her some of what happened. What I can put words to.

"If you get me some toast, I can break it apart and pretend to eat it," she answers. "And if I could get it with a side of Ben and the girls, that would be lovely!"

I smile at her. She loves the kids. The kids love her. Arlene and Edgar's children are sullen pale teenagers on a short leash. They are only allowed to talk to Betty under their mother's hawkish supervision.

"Arlene is afraid I'll teach them to sin," Betty says. "She is probably right. Sin is fun! That's what I used to tell Edgar; As long as you do no harm, there is no harm in living life. Then Edgar met Droopy Arlene and went all Christian on me."

I guess my children are beyond redemption. I walk into the kitchen, where Carol is making breakfast for everyone. The children sit in the breakfast nook. Ben is in a high chair at the end of the table, the girls on one side, the teenagers on the other. My babies eat like they have not been fed for days. Ben is probably on his third serving. Lily will have fed him a nice bowl of oatmeal, and then he usually dives into bread and jam like a professional. Rebecca—the girl teenager— is pushing a piece of bread around her plate while trying to avoid looking at Ben Ben and his happy munch. Daniel—the boy teenager— is busy wiping oatmeal from the book he is reading.

"Can I get some breakfast for Betty?" I ask Carol.

"Yes, sure. Help yourself," she says.

Carol is nice enough but very clear on not working for me. She is still checking me out, I guess. From what I hear, there has been quite a stream of caretakers for Betty, none of them lasting more than three months.

"It's because Arlene is droopy and stingy," Betty says with a grin.

They didn't have anyone willing to work for next to nothing until I came along. I can't complain. I get free room and board for me and the kids, and the day off every other Wednesday plus a little allowance. It is far better than having to steal from Jonathan's pockets when he was passed out.

"He must've been one hell of a hunk," Betty said when I told her.

He was. He was elegant. He was charming. He knew what to say to make me feel special. He made me feel like a princess because he chose me. He played tricks on my mind and my body. He told me that without him, I would be nothing, and I believed him. I believed him until I was nothing with him. Until I was less than nothing with him.

"Well, that's men for you," Betty says. "They can't handle a woman with a free will."

He came looking for me at James' after we left. James told me on our call. I call him on my days off from the train station in Pasadena, where there is a payphone. We talk. His mother must have gotten wind of us being at his house because Jonathan would never have come to see James on his own. James did not tell me everything but said that Jonathan was in a bad state and was looking more for quick cash than us. James stands up to Jonathan. He is the only one who does. He is the only one who sees through him. Sees the snake in the charm.

I find a plate and toast two slices of bread at the counter. I butter them a lot and put a dollop of jam and a teaspoon on the side of the plate.

"Lily Pad, do you want to come to sit with Grandma while she eats breakfast?" I ask in the direction of the nook. Lily is done with her own food—eats fast to be ready to feed others. Maya almost has her face on her plate, trying to see the lower part of Daniel's book that he has stood up in front of him to shield himself from the world. Maya is attracted by the teenagers' standoffishness. The more they ignore her, the more interested she gets. I am going to have to make sure she does not get hurt. Ben is still stuffing his face. He has jelly up to his ears. Maybe I will just take Lily today.

"Mom, can I do the toast?" Lily asks and jumps down from the bench. She comes over and carefully carries it into Betty's room.

"Well, I'll be…stumped!" Betty catches the curse word in time.

"Who do we have here? Is it Queen Elizabeth of England?" she asks.

"No, it's me, Lily." Lily giggles. "I have your bread, Grandma. And there's jelly too."

"Oh, that sounds like my order!" Betty says, "Why don't you climb up here and give it to me?"

I help Lily up on the side of the bed and stand back to let them do their thing. Lily breaks off small pieces of toast and puts a little jelly on them and feeds it to Betty like she would with her doll. Or her siblings. Their conversation is for a tea party.

"Lady Lily, how are you today?" Betty asks in an affected tone.

"Very fine, Lady Grandma!" Lily replies, trying to sound posh too.

"Pray tell me, Lady Lily," Betty continues with her mouth full of toast, "do you have any plans for the Royal Ascot next year?"

"Why yes, Lady Grandma," Lily says, "I am having the most amazing hat made out of my beautiful pillowcase!"

"Oh, that sounds marvelous, Lady Lily," says Betty. "I ordered one myself made from the bathroom rug."

Lily snorts a giggle, and Betty coughs from eating and laughing at the same time.

No one has ever talked to Lily like that before. Like a person. Like an equal. With respect. This is the first time someone besides me has loved her for her, not seen her as a nuisance, a chore, a thing to be bargained with, negotiated with, dealt with. She sits a little taller. She grows into herself. Both of them do.

I still love her too much. I cling on to her like a raft in a storm. It is too heavy a burden on her. Too heavy on her small shoulders. I love Maya Bean and Ben Ben, too, but I do not rely on them to save me in return. Lily is my purpose for still being, and the responsibility weighs on her. I will have to stop doing that to her. I cannot break her like I was broken.

But I never had someone. I never knew my grandparents. I hardly knew my parents. I do not want the kids to end up like that. And I feel a flicker of hope that they won't.

Moment 23

South Pasadena, CA
Saturday, April 8th, 1972, 11:30 AM
I am 27 years old.

Ben gets scared and cries when the organ starts to play. I expect to see Arlene turn around and shoot me a cold look, but she must not have heard him all the way up there in the front of the church where the family sits.

Betty died on Sunday. While Arlene and Edgar and the teenagers were at the Easter service in this same place. That was when she chose to let go of life and slip into something more comfortable. For her, it was a day like any other—a little bit to eat in the morning, then her pills, then a morning nap. Only she did not wake up from her nap. She decided that it was her final shut-eye. No drama, no fuss, no wringing her hands. With Betty, there was no distance between intention and action. Once she made her mind up, it was done.

"Can't wait for the cows to come home, can I?" she said. "I will have lost my good looks by then."

Arlene has been angry with me ever since. Angry, because I did not come to get them at church. Angry, because Betty cheated her out of an opportunity to show off. Angry, because Betty loved the kids and me. But most of all, angry because Betty put me in her will.

I didn't ask for that. It never even crossed my mind that she would do a thing like that. But back in January, Betty said,

"Can you have Arlene ask Hanson to come to see me? I want to change my will."

When I did so, Arlene looked like I had commandeered her to go slaughter the family dog so I could feed it to the kids.

"How?" she asked. "Did you put her up to this?"

"What? No!"

I couldn't believe Arlene would think that. She then marched into Betty's room in her sensible sturdy shoes and closed the door behind her so I couldn't hear what they were saying, but from the look on her face the rest of the day, I knew that Betty had not budged on her demand. After that, Arlene started finding fault with everything I did.

"You shouldn't use so many bed sheets for Betty," she said one day.

I didn't dare tell her that Betty's bedwetting was getting worse, and on some days, she needed several changes.

"You use too much ointment on the bedsores," she said another time. "She does not have to swim in it."

Yes, she does! I almost said. Betty kept getting thinner and bonier, and the cheap mattress on her bed was making the sores worse. But I had pointed out the poor mattress before and had just gotten the brush-off. Apparently, a new and softer mattress would be a waste of money for such a short time.

"Please don't agitate her so much," Arlene said one day when Betty and I had been laughing out loud at one of her dirty jokes. It seemed to me that Betty was a lot happier than when I first came, despite her health going down the drain.

"Livvy, you make it worth sticking around again!" she said. "You are a much better reason than just trying to piss off Mrs. Droopy."

I couldn't help but smile when she said stuff like that. It made me happy to make Betty happy. Now she is gone.

She looked so peaceful and content when I found her. No pain imposed on her anymore. I sat on the side of the bed and held her hand for a while. The kids played just outside the window, and I could hear Ben squealing and Maya singing a song she made up. I can't think of better sounds to be the last to hear. And even if Betty didn't believe in God and often made fun of Arlene and her mission, she did say that Sunday was the day to work out the big questions of life and death.

"Like what I am going to wear to the Oscars," she joked. She was obsessed with Hollywood movies and knew a lot of people in the industry from back in the day when she was a business power lady. She showed me photos of her on the red carpet with celebrities.

"Make a wave in this town, and people will line up to kiss your ass and take a picture of it," she said. She was beautiful. I miss her.

"We are gathered here today to bid our last farewell to Betty Williams," the priest says. "She leaves a substantial void in our hearts and our community."

More like your wallet, I think. I look around the church and see no one I know except the family. Not a single one of these people called or wrote a letter or came to visit in the year we have been here.

"That's getting old for you," Betty said. "Your so-called friends lose their minds, get sick, and die. What a pity party!"

She hated pity.

"It is so useless!" She said. "It makes you go numb and limb."

She was right about that. That was my mother. Numb and limb from feeling sorry for herself. And Jonathan too, paralyzed by pity and guilt and shame.

Now I am here on the spot again. I am on borrowed time because Arlene will kick us out at first chance. Tuesday we are going to attorney Hanson to have Betty's will read, and if Arlene has her way, we will have to leave right after.

"Don't worry," Betty said. "I will take care of you and the kids."

I trust her. I have to. I can't think that I will be out on the street with the kids. In a strange way, that tells me it won't happen because I can't wrap my head around it.

Betty made my life, my world, so much better, and it can't be that it's all gone now. Her spirit was so strong that it couldn't have vanished just because her body left this life. She must still be out there. She looks down at us now and has a good laugh. I can hear her voice.

"Oh, everybody dressed up for me!" she says. "So, that's what it takes to get them to come to your party!"

"Betty Williams lived a full life with family and purpose and fortune." the priest continues.

"Damn straight, I did!" Betty says. "But God had nothing to do with it. I made my own luck and fortune, you pompous ass."

"Though she met hardships in her life, she was also blessed with a wonderful son and daughter-in-law and grandchildren." the priest says.

"Pthpppthppth!" Betty blows a spirited raspberry. "What a load of glorified dung! I worked for them all my life, took all the hits on my own body, and when the time came, and I needed their help, they just gave me the scraps from their table and cursed me for having had a good time."

"She will be sorely missed!" the priest concludes his speech.

"Now, you are right there, Mister God-man," Betty says with thought. "You are right there."

Lily and Maya were shocked to hear that Betty was dead. Lily has cried herself to sleep every night this week. For her, it is doubly sad because it was her birthday. Maya keeps looking to the sky because Arlene told her that Betty rests with God in heaven. Ben asks,

"Where Gama? Where Gama?"

He was so drawn to her. He would snuggle up to her in her bed, and they would look like birds—her a tiny, strong mother bird cradling her enormous fuzzy baby bird under her wing. Now he sits under my wing and sniffles. He knows things are not right. He needs me to do something about it. And I will.

Moment 24

South Pasadena, CA
Tuesday, April 11th, 1972, 10:00 AM
I am 27 years old

I have to be a grownup today. I sit next to Edgar and Arlene in front of Attorney Hanson's big polished desk. I wear the same dress as I did at the funeral because I only have the one. It is hot, and I feel sweat trickling down my sides from my armpits.

Edgar sits in the middle, looking at his hands in his lap. He has imploded since his mother died. Not that he was loud before. Or I don't know that. He is never home. I like him. I figure any son of Betty must have something good and decent inside. And he forms a barrier to Arlene.

She stares into space, or maybe she tries to make out the book titles on the shelves behind the desk. The whole wall is covered by them, and there is a ladder to the right attached to a brass railing running across up high, so I guess the books are all real and not just for show.

It would be funny if Attorney Hanson were, in fact, a secret spy or superhero, and he could get into his hidden lair behind the bookcase by pressing the spine of *The Meditations* by Marcus Aurelius, which I spot on the fourth shelf from the bottom to the left of me. Maybe Betty was his master or what that is called—the one who told him which cases to take, which people to save.

Carol watches the children while we are here. I could see she wasn't keen on it, but the order came from Arlene, so she didn't dare complain.

Arlene is still mad at me, but she is hedging her bets, just in case, Betty has left it all to me.

The door flies open, and Attorney Hanson swirls in. He is a big bumblebee, light on his feet despite his girth. Imagining him in tight spandex and a cape puts a smile on my face. He meets my eyes with a confused look. Me grinning from ear to ear was not what he expected on this somber occasion. He must think there is something wrong with me.

"Good morning," he says in a loud and enunciated manner as he reaches out his hand to me.

He definitely thinks I'm slow. He shakes hands with Edgar and Arlene, too, but without shouting into their faces. Then he sits down and rings a little bell on his desk. A lady in a tight skirt and high heels opens the door and steps in with a leather-bound folder. She hands it to Attorney Hanson. She must have stood right outside the door, waiting for the bell.

"Thank you, Julie." Attorney Hanson says in his booming voice, and on that signal, Julie leaves the office again.

Attorney Hanson puts his hands flat on top of the folder and looks up at us.

"Before I read Betty's will to you, I just want to extend my deepest condolences once more. Betty was a wonderful being, and the world will lose some sparkle, now that she is no longer with us." He says.

"Thank you!" Edgar mumbles to the edge of the desk in front of him.

"Shall we get started?" Attorney Hanson asks as if to cheer Edgar up. He brings out a pair of reading glasses from his jacket pocket and opens the folder.

Taking our silence as agreement, he begins,

"I, Betty Anne Margaret Williams of 1715 Marengo Avenue, South Pasadena, California, declare that this is my last will and testament. I revoke all prior wills and codicils. I have one living child, Edgar Horace Williams. All references in this will to "child" "son" or "issue" include the above child."

Attorney Hanson takes a break and looks at us. Arlene moves a little further out on the edge of her chair, urging him to go on with her entire body.

"Here we go," he continues. "I give my entire interest in the real property, which was my residence at the time of my death together with any insurance on said real property, but subject to any encumbrances on said property to my son Edgar Horace Williams."

Arlene's exhalation almost interrupts Hanson.

"Okay, next one," Attorney Hanson says, and Arlene sucks in air and holds her breath again.

"I give and bequest my entire interest in the real property located on 924 Palm Avenue, South Pasadena, California, and all its current furnishings subject to any encumbrances to Ms. Olivia Martin, my caretaker since May 1971."

It takes a minute for the words to sink in. Betty left me a house. Me. I just got a house.

"Hold on, Ms. Martin." the attorney says. "There is a bit more here."

Arlene turns to stare me down, asking me to stop this nonsense.

"I also give and bequest all my jewelry to Ms. Olivia Martin as she will appreciate it and put it to good use."

Arlene gasps at the insult.

"In addition, a fund of $60000 shall be set up within 30 days of my death, of which Ms. Olivia Martin shall receive $200 per month until the fund runs out. The fund should be administered by my financial adviser Mr. Thomas Bradford of John Hancock, or any appointee of his, and he shall ensure it earns an annual return of at least the average market return."

I don't really understand the last part except that I will get $200 every month for years to come. I have never even seen that much money. And Betty's jewelry. Betty's beautiful jewelry.

"I devise and bequeath all of the residue and remainder of my estate after payment of all my just debts, expenses, taxes, and specific bequests, if any, to my son Edgar Horace Williams. If he fails to survive me by twenty years, I direct that his share shall pass to his surviving children."

"That was the main part of it," Attorney Hanson says. "I have had a copy prepared for both you, Edgar and Arlene, and you, Ms. Martin. You can see the general provisions and signatures there for yourself. Betty signed the will on January 25th this year, and she was of sound mind then, according to her doctor."

I am dizzy with the details. A house and money and jewelry. What am I going to do with all of that? I'll have to take the children to see the house this afternoon. Maybe we can move in today?

"Oh, Ms. Martin, before I forget…" the attorney says. "I have a new set of keys for the Palm Avenue house for you. Betty had the locks on the house changed at the same time as her will. You can pick them up at the front desk with your copy."

He must have read my mind.

Moment 25

South Pasadena, CA
Wednesday, May 10th, 1972, 9:05 AM
I am 27 years old

"Have you ever worked with filing before, Ms. Martin?" Mrs. Tillerson asks me.

She is around 50, wears her dark brown hair with gray streaks in a tight bun on top of her head, and has big cat eyeglasses in a pearl necklace resting on her considerable bust. I sit in an uncomfortable wooden chair across from her in her office at Hanson & Hanson Attorneys At Law.

It has been a month since Betty died. The kids and I have settled into our house on Palm Avenue, but the monthly allowance is not enough, and we cannot eat bricks, so I got to get myself another job. There is, of course, Betty's jewelry, but I can't bring myself to sell out of Betty, and besides, I need something to do with my day.

When I was here at the law office for the reading of Betty's will, I saw they were advertising for help with filing, and it is a place to start. That is if I can get the job.

"No, I can't say that I have," I admit. "But I am neat and organized and a fast learner."

I suppress the memory of me lying on the floor with a needle between my toes in the middle of a chaotic filthy mess and crying children. Mrs. Tillerson puts on her glasses to take a closer look at me. I have bought a new yellow summer dress and flat shoes to look presentable, yet ready to go to work.

"Well, I will be the judge of that." She says a little brusquely. "But since we haven't had any other applicants for the position, I guess we could give it a try."

"The hours are Tuesday and Wednesday from nine to five and Friday from nine to one." She continues looking down at her papers in front of her. "The hourly wage is three dollars. You can start on Tuesday."

She closes her folder and looks at me to signal that the interview is over. I get up from the chair, reach out my hand to shake hers, and say, "Thank you so much."

"You are welcome," she says, ignoring my hand, and gets up to open the door. "We will see how it goes."

Moment 26

South Pasadena, CA
Thursday, September 7th, 1972, 4:55 PM
I am 27 years old

I pass Attorney Hanson's office with some files and notice his door is open, and he is in there. Before I can change my mind, I knock on it to make my presence known.

"Ah, Ms. Martin," he says and waves his hand. "Come in, come in."

I step into his office and stand next to his desk, clutching my files to my chest.

"Sit down, sit down," he says. "How are you? How do you like working here?"

I sit down in the same chair as that day back in April and feel a pang of loss and gratitude toward Betty. How randomness and coincidence have impacted my life. It is all about the time and the place.

"I like it a lot," I tell him. "Thank you so much for having me!"

"I hear from Abigail the pleasure is all on our side. She tells me you are the best filing assistant we've ever had. That is, except for her, of course."

He smiles and winks at me. I am confused about who Abigail is, but then I remember Mrs. Tillerson's first initial is A. I have really grown to like her. She can be short and to the point, and she has high standards for the work done at the office, but she will be more than fair to you if you meet those standards.

"Thank you." I smile back. "Mrs. Tillerson said to come to ask you if I had any questions?"

I want to put my being here into context, so he doesn't think I was just dropping by his office to take advantage of us knowing each other already. The thing is, I have realized that I can't just do the filing and not care about the documents and the cases. Then it is the most mind-numbing job in the world. So I started taking a peek in the folders and built up the courage to ask Mrs. Tillerson about the things I didn't understand.

"Ms. Martin, you are not supposed to do that," she said in her stern voice the first time. "A lot of this is confidential information about our clients."

I thought I had gotten in major trouble and waited to be called into one of the attorney's offices, but a few days later Mrs. Tillerson brought me a non-disclosure agreement to sign and said, "If you want to know about the cases, you can, but it can't get in the way of the filing."

"Thank you," I said, "it won't!"

"Don't thank me," she replied. "I had to ask Attorney Hanson, and he wants you to come to see him if you have questions. I hope I can trust you not to waste his time."

That was an order, not a request. Mrs. Tillerson is the gatekeeper for the attorneys, and she guards them well. She is the one who keeps the law office running. She is in charge of hiring and firing, and nothing escapes her attention. That is why the office girls gossip about her. They are afraid of her, and with good reason, because if she finds out, justice will be swift.

"Sure," he says. "You can ask me anything you want. It's not often we get someone interested in the intricacies of estate law, so shoot away!"

My head is churning on how not to make my question sound too dumb.

"I understand that estates go to the probate court when there is no will," I begin, "but it can end up in probate court even with a will. Why is that? Wouldn't it be easier just to settle it here?"

"That is a very good question, Miss Martin," he says, just as someone passes the open door.

"And my son Robert would be excellent at answering it," he says louder to the person in the hallway.

A younger, much trimmer version of Attorney Hanson takes a couple of steps backward and pops his head into the office.

"Yes, Dad?" Robert asks.

"Robert, I am not sure you and Miss Martin have met yet," Attorney Hanson says and points to me. "She is our new brave filing assistant, and she is very smart."

He then turns to me.

"This is my son Robert, the other Attorney Hanson in our name. He knows everything worth knowing about probate court and at least enough for me to feel safe when the time comes to kick the bucket."

Robert steps towards me with his hand out, and I get up to take it so fast, my files fall down and spread all over the floor.

"I am sorry," I mumble as I try to pick them up again.

"No worries," says Hanson Sr. "Tell us your question again. I want to hear how Robert would answer it."

"Well," I say, looking up at Robert from the floor. "Why do cases end up in probate court even if there is a will?"

"That is a good question," Robert agrees. "Cases can end up there for all sorts of reasons, even with a will. A will might not be clear enough, or outdated, or the devisees might be unhappy about their share, or people not in the will might feel they should be and contest the will. These things can drag out for a long time, but that's good business for us. No matter which way the court's decision goes, we get paid."

He is taller than his father and has a cowlick in his shiny brown hair. He carries himself in a reserved and a little stuffy manner that he seems too young to have yet. I like that he didn't laugh my question off. He was more interested in the answer than me. I don't know why that makes a difference to me.

I try to stay out of the grapevine, but I do know he is married and has two boys. That might explain why he is not eyeing me up. Not all men are looking to sleep around—just the ones I get involved with.

"So nice to meet you, Miss Martin!" Robert says and sticks out his hand again but thinks better of it and waves awkwardly instead. "Feel free to ask again!"

He nods to his dad and leaves.

Moment 27

South Pasadena, CA
Wednesday, December 13th, 1972, 5:20 PM
I am 28 years old

"That's a lot of questions," Robert laughs. "Maybe you should study to find the answers."

There is this case Robert works on that is really interesting and that I have read through several times. There are so many things I want to find out about and to keep my head straight, I have written them down and handed them to Robert.

I don't think I have heard him laugh before. He laughs like Santa Claus. All the way from his belly. Much deeper than expected for his size. It is a rare laugh, something he saves for special occasions.

We are having one of our going-home sessions in his office. I have told the lady next door who watches the kids when I am at work that I might be a little later tonight. She has small kids too and stays at home with them, so she is there every day. I pay her some. Enough to cover meals for the kids and not make it a thankless chore to have my kids around. I am impressed that she doesn't go crazy, but she says she likes it. Her husband always works late, so it is just her and me and the children for dinner.

"I'm not joking," Robert says, now in a more serious tone. "I've been thinking that you might want to get certified as a paralegal. You'd be good at it."

Part of me agrees. I want to know more. Do more. I feel restrained on the sideline. I want to be part of the cases. And I would be good at it.

Another part of me says I am overstepping my role. That I am a fool to think I can ever be anywhere but on the outskirts of things looking in. That it is not for me to be in the front or even in the middle of things. That I should instead stay home with my kids because they need me. I argue with that part. I argue that they need me to be happy when I'm home more than they need me to be home all the time. I argue that I need to set an example for them, of how to provide for themselves, how to set goals and reach them, how to be whatever they want.

I would be even more of an outcast at the office. The other girls are already talking about me because I have these sessions with Robert and Hanson Sr. They make up stories because I'm not telling them anything but the truth. It's not juicy enough for them that it is out of strictly professional interest, so they fill in blanks that don't even exist.

The main gossip is that I'm having an affair with Robert, and it is with Hanson Sr.'s blessing because Robert's wife is not right in the head, and Hanson Sr. wants his son to divorce her. All of this is made up by some women that should put the same effort into their work as they do into pure imagination.

I do get special treatment. But that is not based on anything else than me being interested in what this place does. Anyone could get that. I think. And I have not asked for it. It would be so much easier if I didn't. But I cannot pass it up either. It is an opportunity for me. Something I have earned. It just doesn't make sense not to seize it.

"I know you have small kids at home," Robert continues.

How does he know that? Maybe his father told him. He would know from the Williams'. So no mystery there.

"But if you could find the time to study when you're not here, maybe you could take the exam in like two years," he says. "I heard they've started a program at Pasadena City College so you wouldn't have to go far for classes."

Two years is a long time—longer than I have ever planned for the future. To me, things happen at warp speed or not at all. I am not used to a steady pace. I must have become a normal person when I wasn't looking. A career woman. That sounds so glamorous. That is not how I had pictured myself, but then I don't know what I had expected from me. My expectations have been low and high at the same time. All I know is that I have to move in the direction of independence. I can't rely on others—men—to provide for me. And I'm not. I am already on the path, and this is just the next step.

"I think I could do that," I say out loud what I had meant it stay in my head.

"Well, that's settled then!" Robert smiles.

"Then maybe we can talk about more interesting things than estate distribution," he says and looks like that was meant to stay in his head.

Moment 28

South Pasadena, CA
Monday, July 16th, 1973, 1:35 PM
I am 28 years old

"I'm a princess!" I hear Lily say outside on the porch.

"I know! Just like your mother." a familiar voice answers.

My heart starts pounding, and I break into a cold sweat. What is he doing here? I open the screen door to the porch and step out.

"What are you doing here?" I ask Jonathan.

His clothes are hanging on him, and he looks 20 years older.

"Well, it's good to see you too!" he says with a nervous smile and leans towards me for a hug. I move backward until I hit the doorframe with my back.

"Wow," he says, with his hands up in defense.

Lily senses something isn't right and gets up from the picnic blanket that she had spread out to play with her dolls and comes over and takes my hand while she watches her dad. She often asks about him, but not in front of Maya and Ben. Why did he not come with us? Where is he now? If he's coming to her birthday.

I try to be fair to him in my replies. I do not want her to grow up not knowing about him. When she is old enough, I need her to understand my choices. Be on my side. I don't want to be the devil or the chicken.

So I tell her I could better take care of her and Maya and Ben if we were just by ourselves. I tell her if we had not left, we would never have known Grandma Betty or had this house. I tell her she wouldn't be going to school with her best friend Anna-Lisa down the street or play the piano on Tuesday afternoons at Mrs. Kellerman's.

I don't tell her that if we hadn't left, I might be dead now or that she and her siblings might have been taken away from me or that her father doesn't care enough about her to find her.

"What father waits more than two years to come looking for his kids?" I ask without disguising the anger in my voice.

His face breaks into a sly smile, and I realize he thinks it is a challenge, a game.

"What mother takes off from her home in the middle of the night to roam around like a gypsy from place to place constantly putting her children at risk?" he counters.

Lily frowns in confusion. She doesn't know the answer to that one. Then her face lights up, and she says, "I got one! What girl just turned seven years old and had a birthday party with cake and balloons?"

I squeeze her hand to let her know she did well and say,

"Lily Pad, can you go out back and make sure that Maya Bean doesn't let Ben Ben eat ants?"

"Sure!" She says and gives Jonathan a little wave before she runs through the house, yelling,

"Maaaaayyyyaaaaaa, Mom says Ben is eating aaaaaaants."

"She has grown so much," Jonathan says while watching her go.

I search his face to see if he is high, but nothing gives him away. He is wearing a long sleeve shirt on a hot summer day, but it is a stylish one that goes with his pants and loafers. I remember I never was able to tell.

"Why are you here?" I ask, but I don't want to know. I just want him to go away and not disturb the life we have now.

"I missed you!" he says and looks straight into my eyes.

Butterflies swarm in my belly, but my mind knows how false and flaky he is and screams for me to keep my distance.

"What? Did your wife and your other girlfriends dump you?" I need to remind myself out loud that he is a conman, a charlatan, a cheat, so I do not get sucked into his force field of shiny charms and perceived promises.

"Come on, baby!" he says. "That is unfair. You know I love you!"

And I know. That is the trouble. That is the truth but not the whole truth. He loves me as well as a lot of other women. He is sowing his seeds with pleasure, but that is it. There is nothing more. I thought other things would follow—responsibility, faithfulness, togetherness—but that is not part of his deal. You either take what he gives or not. Simple as that.

"What do you want?" I try again.

"I want to see you and the kids," he says. "It's been a long time."

"Yes," I say, "which makes me wonder, why now?"

I bet he is broke, evicted, without a job, or all of the above.

"Well, I have some free time on my hands right now, so I thought I would come down."

Bingo.

"How did you find me?" I ask.

I can't believe that James would ever tell him, so I am genuinely interested to know.

"That's not important. The important thing is that I'm here."

Good. He didn't find out from James because he would have rubbed my face in that.

"Aren't you gonna invite me in?" he asks.

I really don't want to, but on the other hand, it is getting a little embarrassing to have this conversation out on the porch where everyone can see us. I step aside, so he enters in front of me. That is a mistake because rather than stopping in the living room right inside, he walks through the house towards the door to the back yard. Every step is a violation of my being. Every step, he poisons my personal space. Every step, he soils my home.

"Are the kids back here?" He points to the back door.

"Yes, but..." He is already out.

I rush after him. I panic over what he will say to them. Maya and Ben won't know who he is, and I prefer it to stay that way.

"Hi, kids," I hear him say from the bottom of the stairs outside. "Do you know who I am?"

Maya and Ben look up dazed and confused from whatever they were digging up under the bushes in the back, but there is no way that Lily is going to sit a question like that out. And sure enough.

"I know!" she says, waving her finger in the air like in school. "You are my daddy!"

"Yep, that is right!" Jonathan says. I can hear him smile triumphantly. "And I am Maya and Ben's daddy, too!"

Maya and Ben perk up like two prairie dogs at the mention of their names. They smell the hot backyard air to figure out what it means. Lily sends me a smile of confidence. She is two for zero.

I want to throw myself in between Jonathan and the children in that slow-motion manner to save them from what is coming next. But I just stand up on the back porch and let the scene unfold, unable to move from the spot.

I see all I have done for myself the past two years come undone in a heartbeat. I realize how short a distance I have moved. How little it takes to put me right back where I was. How false my sense of security is.

Then something else shows up—anger from pride and accomplishment. A fury of having everything I earned walked all over. I got clean. I found a job. I am good at it. I take care of my children. I do what is best for them. I will not let him take that away.

And suddenly my legs work again. I go down the stairs and past Jonathan and gather the kids up in a huddle with my back to him. I look at their sweet, sweet faces and whisper,

"Can you go get some secret ice cream for dessert at Trader Joe's? Lily Pad knows where my purse is, and you can bring that along."

They all nod in solemn agreement. They know their mission and will carry it through.

"Okay, let's go!" I say and send them on their way.

They file past their father with their heads down to not give their errand away and into the house where I hear giggles and hushes. I grab the big shovel the kids were struggling with in the bushes, raise it to my shoulder and turn around to face Jonathan.

"I don't know why you are here, but if it's to get back with me, you can just leave because that won't happen," I say. "If you want to be a father to the kids, I am all for that, but you can't take them with you, or they won't visit you. You have to come here to see them. If you ever blow them off, let them down or hurt them, you don't get to see them ever again. Is that understood?"

For once, he doesn't know what to say. I am as stumped as he is. It must be that no one has ever talked to him like that before. Or maybe he is just gauging if I am serious.

"I'm dead serious!" I say. "And the longer you take to think about it, the less you want it. This is a one-time offer, and it won't stand forever. What's it going to be?"

"Okay, okay," he says, hands up again. "Fair deal. I'll be good."

I do not believe that for one second. But I have to set my boundaries to not get sucked in again. I have to state my terms to not be walked all over again. I have to be in control.

"Alright, so here's how it's gonna go," I continue, "you leave me an address and phone number where you can be reached. I will let you know when you can come. Don't show up without being invited. And then get out!"

I motion for him to turn around and start walking. He walks in front of me and into the kitchen. I put down the shovel at the door, thinking I can always grab a kitchen knife if necessary.

I find a notepad and a crayon and hand them to him. He bends down over the kitchen table and writes his mother's address in his boxy even handwriting that he used to leave me love notes in.

He puts the crayon down and turns to me with an apologetic smile.

"I don't really have a place right now, so it is probably easier," he says.

Bingo again.

Once more, he leans in for a hug, but I stand aside and point to the street.

"Well then," he says as he reaches the screen door. "I guess I'll see you when I see you?"

"Yep, that's right," I reply.

We step out on the porch and down on the street. He walks left and disappears around the corner at the same time as the kids run down the street to me from the right.

"Moooooommy," Lily screams at the top of her lungs while sprinting along. "Ben found the monkey at the store, and then he peed his pants!"

"Okay," I say as they reach me in front of the house. "Let's go get him cleaned up."

Moment 29

South Pasadena, CA
Friday, October 12th, 1973 7:15 PM
I am 28 years old

"Damn it!" Robert says.

We are working late in his office. He never makes outbursts like that. Not never but not often. It is getting late, and it is Friday, and I am sure he would rather go home to his family and spend the evening with them.

The kids are at the neighbor's house, as always. They are just as much part of that family as ours. Maybe even more. It is an extension I can't do without these days. Between work and school, there are not many hours left to be a single mom. I feel guilty for not being in a rush to get home to them. Friday night is tricky. Everyone is tired from the week, and there is a lot of blame and whining going around. I don't want to catch it. I would much rather be here and get some work done and then be the perfect mother tomorrow morning when they wake up.

This must be how husbands feel. This must be why they stay late at work. This must be why they don't cook dinner and bathe the kids and go grocery shopping. Because it is a pain. Because those hours of bored and cranky kids are mind-numbing and don't make the good times better at all.

I do miss some of it. I miss the small things. I am not the first one to know that Lily got an A on her math test or that Ben lost a tooth or that Maya and her friend Sunshine got into an argument and are not speaking at the moment. Donna, the neighbor, deals with that just as she deals with the victories and challenges of her own children.

But even if the small things add up, it is not enough for me. I can't live solely for them. I have to live for me, as well. Because otherwise, it doesn't work. If I didn't live for me, then one day, the scales would tip, and the tables turn. They would have to live for me instead because I would have forgotten how to.

That was my mother. All sacrifice and not only hers. She forgot how to live long before she died. I'm sure she didn't mean to. I'm sure that was all she could do. I'm sure it was a choice between her and me, and she drew the short end of the stick. She didn't know she had to live too. You cannot get water from a dry well. I'm not going to end up like that. I will not let myself waste away for my children. It's no use. I will not be a burden.

Therefore, I'm here on a Friday night working hard on a difficult case with a frustrated boss. It is not about the case. Robert is energized by challenges. That much I know. It's not about the case.

"I'm sorry," I say and mean it.

He looks up at me from the other side of his desk, almost surprised to see me. There is a conversation going on in his head.

"No, I'm sorry," he says. "It has nothing to do with you. It's just that..."

He changes his mind last second. Pulls himself together and steps back from the ledge.

"Never mind," he says. "Can you find the first divorce settlement? I want to go over it again to make sure there aren't any loopholes for them to jump through."

Relationships are complicated. I see that in cases all the time. That is why I like the job. It is about making sense of relationships. Make sure everyone gets their fair share when they are over. This one is a tricky one. Rich man meets poor girl and marries her. They have two children. After a decade, they divorce. She gets custody and substantial alimony. A few years later, he marries another woman who already has a son. He adopts the son, treats him like his own. And then they have a daughter together as well. Everything is bliss until it is not. They divorce. The man gives up on marriage and turns to a bachelor's life with all that entails—sex, drugs, and rock'n'roll. Unfortunately for him, that includes sudden death. The coroner calls it a heart attack but is vague on what it's caused by. There are two ex-wives, four grown kids, and no will. Everyone wants everything—especially the biological children of the first marriage. We represent the adoptive son of the second marriage.

He just wants what is fair, but what is that? Fairness depends on the circumstances—who said, what, and when. Fairness is constantly changed by actions and statements and the ebb and flow of entitlement. Fairness is in the eye of the beholder. Fairness is also sensitive to time; the longer it takes, the harder it is to obtain. Too many words bring it out of reach.

I am learning that, in the end, it comes down to the quality of your representation. A good lawyer will get you what you want. And Hanson & Hanson are excellent lawyers.

I dig out the case file from the divorce and hand it to Robert. He skims through it for a bit. I make a note to myself about summarizing the two divorce settlements for Robert before he goes to court.

"So many broken children," he says to himself. "All because grownups can't work it out."

There is a bitterness to his voice that I haven't heard before. He normally doesn't let cases get to him, but for some reason, this one affects him. I wonder if my children are broken. If it had been better that I stayed. There is no doubt they miss Jonathan. Or rather Lily misses Jonathan, and Maya and Ben miss a father. All three of them were excited after his visit. I have kept quiet about the prospect of him visiting again. Been vague about it every time they've asked. If it doesn't serve Jonathan, it won't happen, and why would it? We are liabilities. Burdens. Something he has to work for. And he won't win me back, so that might sour the deal. But they have written him letters. I have helped them with that. Lily can write to him herself. Maya and Ben draw instead. And we have taken the letters to the post office and put stamps on and send them off to Fresno. We have talked about that; it's like writing letters to Santa. That they can't expect an answer right away.

"Is it because Daddy has a lot of children to write to?" Maya asked.

I don't know. He might have. But it doesn't change his responsibility to my three babies. If he wants to be in, he has to be in—no lurking around the door and slipping out when he loses interest.

"No, Maya Bean," I said. "It's just that he isn't home a lot, so it might be a while before he gets the letters."

"Sometimes it can't be worked out," I say to Robert. "Sometimes, it's better for the kids to break up."

That's what I have to believe.

I must have sounded defensive because Robert looks at me and says, "Oh, I didn't mean to imply that you did anything wrong."

Like everyone else, he knows very little. Only that I have small children and the father is not around. And then whatever he can infer from my opinion about cases, I guess.

"And you are right. Sometimes it is better for everyone to part ways," he says. "But that doesn't mean the process isn't grueling."

His voice trails off. He's lost in thought again. It's not about the case.

"I'm getting divorced," he says and exhales. He must have held it in for a long time.

"I'm sorry," I say again, wondering if that is true. "I'm sure it hasn't been an easy decision."

Suddenly, we have shifted. Our balance is not the same anymore. He has ventured into my territory of loss and loneliness and regret. Now I have some expertise to bring to the table. I look at him as if for the first time. No longer the boss, the mentor, the all-knowing, the one above lowly concerns of love and relationships. He has joined my team. I have something to teach him. That makes me feel happy and grateful and embarrassed. He is human, after all.

"No, it wasn't," he says. "My wife isn't well. I'm looking to get full custody of the boys."

Is he leaving a sick woman and taking her children with him? That doesn't seem right. My face must give me away because then he says,

"That sounds like I'm a horrible person. That's not how it is."

"Well, then how is it?" I snap a little too terse.

"Not that I have to answer to you," he bites back, "but my wife is mentally ill and in an institution. She had a severe breakdown and doesn't know who we are, and there is little hope she will ever come home again. Her family will take over her care, and I'll take on raising our boys. The boys are too small to understand, and they're scared, so for now, we will spare everyone the agony of visiting. Maybe when they're older."

His face is hard and tired. Telling me takes effort. He isn't used to sharing personal stuff like this. It makes him uncomfortable. I can relate. It is not like I go around telling people what I have gone through.

"I'm sorry to put this on you," he says. "I would prefer if it stayed between us."

"Of course," I say. "And I didn't mean to snap at you."

It is safe with me. I don't gossip. And it is more important to keep his trust than to gain a moment's fame with the girls at the office. His trust means something to me. I will keep it. I will keep the softness this has created.

"Thank you," he says. "I think that's enough for tonight. I will bring home the settlements over the weekend if you can type up the notes first thing on Tuesday when you're back. That should make us ready for Wednesday."

And just like that, the moment is over, but the tenderness lingers.

Moment 30

South Pasadena, CA
Wednesday, April 10th, 1974, 4:55 PM
I am 29 years old

I look at my watch one more time. I have to be out of the office by 5 PM sharp, so I can get the last bit of cramming done tonight. I have final exams on Thursday and Friday. Then I will hopefully be a certified paralegal. Who would have thought?

"You look ready to go," Robert says as he passes my desk by the filing room.

"Yes!" I say, "tomorrow and Friday are the big days, you know."

He stops and looks back at me.

"You'll do perfectly!" he says with a reassuring smile. "You worked hard for it, and it will pay off. Don't worry."

He helped me study for the past two months. Every Friday afternoon, when there were no pressing cases, we went through the most difficult topics. That has been nice. He makes me feel safe. Like I am in good hands. Like I can do this.

In return, I let him talk. He doesn't need a lot, only five-ten minutes when we meet. He talks about his boys and about his soon to be ex-wife. His boys are five and seven, and very and not so different from Lily and Maya. Like their father, they seem to have trouble finding an outlet for their feelings. The little one has started wetting the bed again. The big one bites his classmates at school. His wife is getting worse. She suffers from severe catatonic depression and is paralyzed and speechless for long stretches of time. Her family is hesitant to take on power of attorney for her. That slows everything down and prolongs the proceedings.

Robert doesn't need me to say anything. Just listen. That is all that is required of me. I can do that. When he has said enough, he goes back on topic with a sad little smile.

I do feel bad for him. His perfect life is falling apart. He married a beautiful woman, and now she is gone. She doesn't acknowledge him anymore. She doesn't acknowledge the boys. She doesn't acknowledge anything. It might be better if she were dead. If her physical presence were gone too. Now she is a shadow forever hanging over him. He is caught in a no-man's-land. He is in limbo untethered, but not free.

And he's alone in this. He doesn't let anybody in. Only a little. He has this layer of manners and correctness all over that doesn't allow anything to get to him or the other way. He is like the tin man noticing something is wrong with him and then reading up on what to do about it. That is how he knows to talk to me. In theory. Following a diagram from a book.

I am okay with that. It makes the thing between us delicate—a tiny feather blown onto my skin by a slight breeze. And any sudden moves will make it disappear again. So I keep still and watch it. I let it be.

"Thank you for all your help," I say and mean it.

Without Robert, I would never have done this. I would never have thought I could do this. I would have settled in for filing papers for the rest of my days. My interest in the cases would have stayed just that—an interest, a hobby, something to carry me through. But not something I could be involved in. Because of him, I have stuck my neck out. Now I have to prove that I can do it, which is both worse and better. What if I fail? Then it will be one more defeat. One more thing I thought I could do but couldn't. How am I going to live with that?

I push it away. I can't think like that. That will make it come true. I have to think I can do it. I am prepared. Tonight is just double-checking that I know what I know. There is a certainty, a solid mass inside me that knows I know. That the exam can't take away because if it does, the exam is wrong. I have studied so hard. I have done everything by the book. That can't make me fail. I hope.

I'm lost inside my head when Robert takes a step toward me, leans over my desk, and kisses me on the cheek. Just a butterfly kiss, smelling of breath mints, and aftershave. I am nailed to the ground. Heat shoots up through my body, and blood swooshes in my ears.

I look up to meet his eyes, and they smile at me. Then he walks on down the hall and into his office.

Moment 31

South Pasadena, CA
Saturday, January 4th, 1975, 10:50 AM
I am 30 years old

"Are you Olivia Martin?" the lady voice in the receiver asks.

"Yes. Yes, I am." I stammer into the phone, not knowing what this is about but heart already throbbing in my throat.

"Good morning! I'm Wendy Miller, and I'm calling from Saint Agnes Hospital in Fresno," she says, "you are listed as the person to contact for Jonathan Burke, and we have a situation here."

I draw in air.

"Mr. Burke was brought in unconscious early this morning, and we've been unable to wake him up here at the hospital. He is very dehydrated and malnourished, which isn't helping him right now. We think he might have overdosed on something but need to find out what in order to counter it."

Damn it, Jonathan! Why do you have to crash into my life like that?

"I don't know," I say, "it's been a while since I saw him. A year and a half, I think."

And not a peep from him since. Arrogant bastard. So easy to see through, only I didn't. Not then, not ever. I always came running when he called. He always got to take what he wanted. Now is no different.

"And you have no idea what he might be into? Cocaine, meth, heroin?" the Miller lady asks. "We found track marks, but not fresh ones."

This is more information than I can process. Even when we were together, we never discussed his drug use. He was above that. He could handle it. He would not be questioned. It was just something that was part of being around him. And he was better at taking drugs than anybody else. Somehow, he tamed the drugs, never submitted to them so much that he gave himself up. He enhanced and empowered himself with them. He was never a slave, an addict. Until now.

"No, no, I don't know," is all I can say.

"Do you know anybody else who might know? Does Mr. Burke have any family?" Ms. Miller presses on and gets my brain into gear.

"He has a brother James," I say. "He lives in Fresno, too."

I have not talked to James in a while, either. Not since I started seeing Robert. Somehow, there isn't enough room for both of them at the same time. I can only handle so much reliability. I don't want to betray either of them and to get them mixed up seems like that. I have a new life now, and to be in it, I have to let the past go. James was a stepping stone into that life—a very important one that I am grateful for—but keeping him around reminds me of how bad I was, how miserable I was, how weak I was.

I am not like that anymore. I am strong. I built something for myself. I have a home and a job, and I am seeing someone nice and normal. Someone I can be normal with. Someone who does not put me down or uses me and then throws me away like yesterday's paper. I have moved on. But all it takes to bring me back is a phone call.

"Oh, I wonder why he didn't list him to call." Miller lady speculates to herself.

"He wouldn't do that," I say. "They're not on speaking terms."

I wonder why he listed me. He must have run out of lackeys and hang-arounds. But then why not his mother?

"And he only listed me?" I ask.

"Well, this time, he didn't list anybody because he hasn't been conscious since he came in. But you were the only one listed in his charts from previous visits. This is not the first time we've seen Mr. Burke." Miller lady says.

"Would you happen to have his brother's contact information?" she continues.

"Yes," I say and give her James' number.

"And if I can't get ahold him, can you come to see us here at the hospital to make decisions on Mr. Burke's further care?" Ms. Miller asks.

No. No, I cannot get involved in that. I can't go back to that. Jonathan is not my responsibility, just as he never considered me his.

"Yes," I say, "it will take me a little time, but I can come…"

Moment 32

Fresno, CA
Saturday, January 4th, 1975, 8:10 PM
I am 30 years old

I get a physical shock when I see him in the hospital bed. He looks like a corpse. He is bruised and beaten up. There is a nasty scratch on his chin. His high cheekbones that used to make him look so aristocratic are now so pronounced that his face is a skull with the eyes hidden and closed in dark sockets. He has an IV drip in his arm and a heart monitor on his finger, beeping away next to the bed. He is still unconscious.

I must have stopped because Robert bumps into me from behind and starts to apologize, but then sees Jonathan as well. Robert convinced me to come here. I didn't want to. I didn't want to get sucked into Jonathan's world again. I didn't want the drama. I wanted to stay safe.

"You know it's the right thing to do," Robert said. "He has nobody or else they wouldn't have called you. And he is the father of your kids."

Robert is turning out to be my conscience. There is no cutting corners or sneaking out with him. Everything has to be by the book. I have to be nice to other people. I have to have manners. And if he had his way, I would have to go to church on Sundays. That is where I draw the line. I have way too much guilt for that. He says it doesn't matter; the church has room for everyone. But not for me.

He does make me a better person. Sometimes I wonder if that's what I want to be. A better person. It comes with so much responsibility.

"Hi, Livvy," James says and gets up from the chair next to Jonathan's bed.

I hadn't noticed him at all. He has aged too. He is more solid than before. He lost his puppy look.

"Hi, James," I say as I slip into a hug of his.

He smells like gasoline and cigarettes and hard work. I feel his evening stubble on top of my head.

"This is Robert," I say after I'm out of his embrace again.

"Hello, Robert Hanson," says Robert and bends around me to shake James' hand.

"Robert is my…" I start to explain, but can't think of a word to use.

James nods in understanding. Enough said.

"So, I guess they did get a hold of you?" I say just to make conversation.

"Yes, yes." James says, "It was good of you to give them my number. I got here just after lunch."

"Oh, good," I say because I can't think of anything else.

Robert walks over to the wall and gets two chairs and puts them next to Jonathan's bed. We all sit down, me in between James and Robert. I take off my coat and fold it over my lap.

"So how is he doing?" I ask James.

"Not great," James says. "The police found him at a bus stop this morning. Someone called it in. They are afraid that the cold might have done some damage as well. But he needs to come to for them to say anything for sure."

"I spoke to a doctor late this afternoon," James continues. "He said he is stable, and there is nothing to do but wait for him to wake up. His vitals are getting better, so they hope it will happen sometime soon."

We all go quiet and look at Jonathan's hand on top of the blanket. It is blotchy and calloused. It is as if the weather has eaten away at him. He looks so small even if he is higher up than us. Like an open casket wake. That might be what is next. Even in his miserable state, he forces us to look up to him. Always him.

"I was surprised they called me," I say to break my stare.

"Well, there's really nobody else," James says. "Mama died last April, and as far as I know, he has been on a binge ever since. They told me this wasn't the first time he ended up here."

"Yes, that's what they said," I mumble.

"He would, of course, rather die than call me," James says. "That might still happen, I guess.

"There isn't a lot left. I sold Mama's house in May, and we split the money. But that wasn't much, and I think he had so much debt all over town that it couldn't have lasted long. I wouldn't be surprised if he's been living on the street."

James talks as if Jonathan is some poor stranger. And in a way, he is. There is nothing left of the charm, the magic, the danger that Jonathan was. He is just a miserable hobo. That makes me sad. Not only for him. It is like discovering the monster under my bed that I feared and revered for so long is just an old woolly sock covered in dust bunnies. What does that make me? A wannabe bride of a no-good rag. And at this moment, there is no way to justify me without glorifying him again, and that just can't be done. So I'm stuck with myself as I was. Gullible and stupid and naive.

I can't trust myself. I have to rely on others to get me out of trouble. I have to rely on these two men that I sit between to take care of me. And they are good men. Decent men. But I am still a disappointment.

That is how Jonathan made me feel. Worthless. I had to work hard to earn love. To deserve it. I was ashamed that I needed more than he was willing to give. Convinced there was something wrong with me for feeling that way. That I was too needy, not enlightened enough.

Sometimes I feel that way with Robert, but it is different. I am not madly in love with him. I like him a lot. I might even love him. But I'm not in love with him. It's not this all-consuming fire and ice it was with Jonathan. A colorful roller coaster ride when we were together, the darkest winter night when we were not. A hunger demanding to be satisfied so much so that I let myself be devoured over and over and craved it. With Robert, I sit patiently at the table and wait to be served. And if I don't feel like it, I can just skip a meal. I cook myself now. I am not at his mercy at all times.

My thoughts are interrupted by Jonathan tensing up and grabbing on to the mattress with his whole body. We all stand up and look at him, and he returns our stare with confusion.

"Hello?" he says in a raspy voice. "Why are you here? Where am I?"

"You had a blackout. The police found you and brought you here to the hospital." James explains.

Jonathan looks around and notices the IV drip and the heart monitor. A nurse comes into the room and makes us move away from the bed while she rolls a curtain all the way around it.

"Good evening, sir." we hear her say behind the curtain. "I just want to ask you a couple of questions before I call the doctor in here. Do you think you can answer them?"

"Sure, I would be delighted!" Jonathan says, and I can sense he smiles. Always the charmer.

"Do you know your name, sir?" The nurse asks him.

"My name is Jonathan William Burke," he answers, "but you can call me anything you want! What is your name? Oh, it says there on your uniform. Marie Thompson. That is a beautiful name. Can I call you, Nurse Marie?"

He just can't help it. However, he does sound weak and congested and more than a little drunk or high.

"You can call me Nurse Thompson or Mrs. Thompson, sir," she says in a terse voice. "Do you know where you are?"

"Well, looking at you, I would say I've gone to heaven, Nurse Thompson," Jonathan says, undeterred by her snub. "But they told me I'm in the hospital, so I guess you gave me another chance."

His answer trails off into a violent cough.

"I will need to take your temperature, sir." She says.

They are both quiet for a bit. The nurse must have stuck the thermometer in Jonathan's mouth. Then she says,

"102.9, sir. I guess we'll keep you then."

"I can't think of anything better than spending the night with you, Nurse Marie."

James, Robert, and I are still standing around uneasily, eavesdropping on the conversation but with nowhere to go since the nurse needs the space by the bed.

"I'm gonna see if I can find us a cup of coffee," Robert says and looks at James to see if he wants one too.

"No, I've already had enough," James says, and it seems to cover the whole situation.

We all leave the room, and Robert disappears down the hallway to find coffee while James and I sit down on a bench opposite the door.

"So how are you?" James asks, looking at his hands.

"I'm fine!" I say a little too fast. "You know, the same as always. How about you?"

I'm embarrassed. Embarrassed that I haven't talked to him in so long. After everything that he has done for me, the least I could do is stay in touch. Give him a call once in a while. But I haven't done that. And at this moment, I can't think of why not. I might have wanted to avoid telling him about Robert. But James would never wish me anything but good luck. He doesn't see me that way. He said so. And besides, he is the reason I met Robert in the first place. More likely, I might have wanted to put that part of my life behind me. Forget about it. Pretend I didn't make those mistakes. I thought I knew better. Better than my mom. Better than James. Better than everyone. I didn't. What I did do was end up on James' couch broken and broke. He helped me. He had patience with me. He didn't judge me. And the way I repaid him was by staying away and not call—shame on me.

"Okay, I guess." He says. "The shop's busy, but I'm trying to cut down. I hired a couple of guys and a foreman to take off some of the load."

"Mama's death was hard," he says. "She held on for as long as she could, but in the end, she had to give up. Jonathan wasn't gonna settle down. I think that's what killed her. She lost hope."

We sit in silence and take it all in. Now it's my turn to look at my hands—no wedding ring on any finger. Just a simple but beautiful emerald ring of Betty's, so I have her with me. I don't know if I have settled down. Betty would have told me not to settle, but I hope she would have liked that I'm together with Robert.

"I'm so sorry," I say and mean it with all my heart. "I should've been there."

"Nah," James says. "It wouldn't have mattered. All that mattered to her was that bastard."

His voice drips with anger and bitterness, and I can understand that, but that wasn't what I meant.

"No, I mean, I should've been there for you," I say.

"That's okay," James says, but it isn't.

Robert returns, balancing two hot plastic cups of vending machine coffee. He hands me one of them and offers the other one to James, who again refuses. I take a sip and burn my tongue.

"That's hot!" I lisp.

James gets up from the bench for whatever reason. He and Robert now stand around and face each other like two mates having a beer next to the barbeque. They could be friends, I think. They will be friends, I hope. They are very much alike.

"So what do you do, Robert?" James asks.

"I am a lawyer," says Robert. "I specialize in wills and trusts."

"Ah, so you are one of those who took my money when my mother died," James says as a joke.

"Yes, and what a nice set of golf clubs they went into!" Robert smiles back.

They go into a conversation about James' attorney, whom Robert knows from law school and other manly stuff. I tune out and watch the door to Jonathan's room. Nurse Thompson comes out and walks in the opposite direction of the coffee machine, and a few minutes later, she comes back with a doctor, and they go back in.

Robert and James take up a discussion about football and their favorite teams and the Super Bowl coming up. They agree the Pittsburgh Steelers have a good chance even if it is their first time. I lose interest.

The doctor comes out of Jonathan's room and over to us.

"Are you the family of Jonathan Burke?" he asks.

"Yes, I am his brother," says James.

"Hello, I'm Dr. Wollitz." the doctor says. "Maybe we can talk in private?"

"No, it's okay," James says and points to me. "Livvy is the contact person for my brother."

"Oh, alright!" says Dr. Wollitz and looks down at his chart. "There are some decisions to be made regarding Mr. Burke's care, and I'm just going to talk you through it.

"Mr. Burke needs immediate care for pneumonia. I would like to put him on intravenous antibiotics to start clearing that up. Under normal circumstances, it would take about a week, and we would be able to discharge him as soon as we saw the antibiotics working. There is, however, a snag here. If not already, then in a few hours, Mr. Burke will go into withdrawal from whatever drugs he's taken, and that'll complicate his recovery considerably. We can keep him here and see him through that, but I am obligated to tell you it can be costly, and we have to have consent from Mr. Burke. Right now, he denies any substance abuse, so you might need to talk to him. I can give you about 30 minutes to talk it over, but then I would like to get started."

"Excuse me, Dr. Wollitz, I'm Robert Hanson, a friend of the family," Robert says. "What is the alternative? What if he doesn't consent to the detox?"

"Well, if Mr. Burke wants to stay here and get treated for his pneumonia, he will go through withdrawal with or without consent because I can't prescribe any medication to get him high again." Dr. Wollitz says while looking Robert straight in the eyes. "What I can do is monitor and alleviate the symptoms of withdrawal for as long as it takes, as well as make sure the pneumonia doesn't exacerbate the detox and vice versa."

"Thank you, Dr. Wollitz," Robert says as if he has just concluded testimony in court.

Dr. Wollitz gives us a little wave and walks down the hallway. When he disappears into another room, James says,

"I vote that he stays here. I can tell him he has no other options. Unless you want to take him home?"

James looks at me. No, I don't want to take him home. I just want him to go away and never come back. It was hard enough to get myself out of that, and I really don't want to go through it again. More than that, I do not want Jonathan to be part of my life, not even if he gets off drugs. I feel bad about that. That is not being compassionate. But that's how I feel. I just want him gone. Robert also looks at me.

"I vote he stays here, too," I say. "I think that's the only way."

"Okay," says James. "Let's go talk to him then."

We all file back into the room. The nurse has rolled the curtain away again. Jonathan sits up in the bed and looks as if he is ready to go. James and

I take a stand next to each other at the end of the bed while Robert keeps in the background.

"We just talked to the doctor," James begins.

"Yes, me too," says Jonathan. "What a quack! Completely incompetent!"

He starts to cough so much his eyes water.

"Gotta stop with the fags," he says out of breath.

"We think you should stay here and get clean," James says. "There's nowhere else for you to go."

"Come on, Jimmy Boy!" Jonathan says with impatience. "It is just an itty-bitty cold. I'll be fine!"

He has another coughing fit and struggles for air as it rolls over him.

"No, it's not," says James. "It's pneumonia, and you'll die if you don't get it treated."

Jonathan looks at us to gauge how much he has to give to get us off his back.

"Okay, okay." he wheezes. "I'll take the antibiotics and come crash with you, Jimmy. I just have to go get my stuff, and then I'll meet you there. Does that make you happy?"

He starts to turn in the bed to get out, but can't get the bed rail down.

"Goddamn trapped in here." He mumbles.

"Jonathan, you have to stay here and get clean," I say. "Otherwise, you won't get to see the kids. I'll tell them what kind of person their father was, a druggie who couldn't be bothered to get to know them."

"Livvy, that is a low blow even for you," Jonathan fumes as best he can for the wheezing. "But okay, if that is what you, want I'll stay for the pneumonia."

"You have to get clean," I say. "Otherwise, no kids."

He leans back in the pillows and closes his eyes.

"You can go now," he says, still angry.

The three of us leave the room and head to the nurses' station, where nurse Thompson sits and fills out some papers.

"Nurse Thompson," James says, "my brother has agreed to be treated, so please let Dr. Wollitz know."

"That's good," she says. "I'll let the doctor know right away. You'll need to see the business office downstairs in the lobby to take care of the financials."

James looks at me and says,

"I'll handle that. You just go home. I'll keep you posted."

Once again, I am flushed with gratitude toward him. Gratitude and guilt. He comes through for me every single time, and I flake out on him. I don't know what I would have done if he had not been here tonight. Or Robert. Without them, I just wouldn't have gone. I would have let Jonathan do whatever he does. Not cared if he lived or died. What kind of person am I?

"Thank you, James!" I say and give him a hug. "I'll call you tomorrow to see how it's going."

"Well, you know how these things go," James says. "Tomorrow will just be the beginning."

I give a little nervous laugh. I haven't told Robert about my detox and would rather not have to here at the nurses' station. But Robert doesn't seem to have picked up on the comment, or if he did, he is gracious enough to keep quiet.

"Yeah, I know," I say. "Thank you again. For everything."

Robert and I walk out of the hospital and start on the drive home. As the landscape flies by in the night, I think about how lucky I am. How many near-misses I have been saved from. How much I have messed up and gotten away with almost scot-free. There must be a price. There must be a time when I have to pay it back. But that time was not today.

Moment 33

South Pasadena, CA
Monday, January 6th, 1975, 6:15 PM
I am 30 years old

"Jim's house, this is Sandra."

Her voice is confident, mature. It surprises me. Like touching an electric fence by accident. It smarts. There could be a thousand explanations for her being there other than her being with him.

"This is Livvy; I mean Olivia," I stammer. "Can I speak with James?"

"Oh, hi," she says as if she knows me. "Jim's not home yet. He said he'd stop by the hospital to see his brother on the way home. I hope he's here soon. I made meatloaf for dinner."

That is too much information for me. I don't need to know that much. She is free to tell me, but I wish she hadn't. It is not like I have any claim to him. He can see anyone he likes. It's not like I wanted him. At least not when I had the chance. So I have nowhere to put my jealousy. It has to go.

"Okay," I say.

"I'll tell him to call you!" Sandra says.

"Okay," I say again.

She must think I am slow. That bothers me.

"Bye," she says and hangs up.

"Bye..." I say to the receiver.

That hurt. That hurt much more than I expected. I don't know why I had settled on the thought that James would be alone forever. Maybe it was to flatter myself. Because if he can't have me, he shouldn't want anybody.

I can feel myself getting angry at this Sandra woman. I want to belittle her. Trash talk her. Because clearly, she can be no good. Her name is ugly. She must be fat. She hasn't known James for as long as I have. He hasn't gone out of his way to save her. And what is up with this Jim business? His name is James. I am back in high school. I am looking for clues that he likes me more than anybody else. He smiled at me in the diner. Our eyes locked for a second in the all-school assembly. Our star signs are only two months apart. It is meant to be. Why can't she see that? Why can't she abide by that?

I wrestle my teenage self to the ground. Yes, it stings, but that is not my feeling to have. I just got to get over that. Suck it up, buttercup! This is completely unreasonable, and I have to stop it. Now.

It is not like I am missing anything. I have everything and everyone I could possibly want. Robert is wonderful. He takes good care of me. Like James always has. And long before James turned me down, I turned down James. I can't start crying about that now. Where do I get off thinking such mighty thoughts about myself? I have no right.

And still, I rake my brain for excuses to justify my feelings. There must be a reason why James didn't tell me about her on Saturday. It is probably not going to last. He must be embarrassed by her. Or she is just like me. A me wannabe. He still has a crush on me. I am sure of it.

I make a great effort to forget I haven't called James in years. That I have never truly thanked him for all he has done for me. Still does for me. That I treated him like a nobody when I was with Jonathan. From the very first moment. That just two days ago, I had no other interest in him than getting him to take Jonathan off my hands. That I did not call him yesterday because I did not want to deal with this whole thing even if I am the one on the hook. That I was too embarrassed about him to tell Robert how we met. Or too embarrassed about myself.

And I should be embarrassed about myself. I should be ashamed. Because I am not a nice person. I don't act like a grownup. I don't appreciate what I have. I need to be beaten by a big stick like this to appreciate what I have. To appreciate what I have thrown away. I hear Joni Mitchell's words in my head:

"Don't it always seem to go

That you don't know what you've got

'Till it's gone."

Yes, it does always seem to go that way for me. I promise myself to do better. I should.

The phone rings.

"Hello?" I answer.

"Hi, it's me, James," James says. "You called me?"

I notice he does not say, 'Sandra said you called' or 'you spoke to my girlfriend' or 'she does not mean anything to me I still only want you' and curse myself for going right back there.

"Yes, sorry, I didn't call you yesterday," I say with more genuineness than I feel. "I just wanted to check how he's doing."

"That's okay," says James. "He is in the throes of it from what I hear, and they're just trying to get him through it in one piece."

I remember that. I remember wanting to die so badly. The withdrawal is the biggest deterrent for doing drugs ever again. But that is like saying that the pain of childbirth is the biggest deterrent for having sex. It does not matter in the moment.

I get a jolt of sympathy for Jonathan. He is going through unspeakable pain and agony. And even if he deserves it, I do not wish that for anybody, not even him. I wish it could have all been different. I wish I had known what was good for me back then. I wish I knew what the right thing to do now is. I wish I could make myself do the right thing.

"And what do they say about when it'll be over?" I ask to buy myself a little more time.

"Somewhere between a half and a whole week," James says. "A bit slower than you, I guess, because of the pneumonia and his miserable health."

"Yes, about that," I say. "Thank you for not mentioning it on Saturday. I appreciate it. I appreciate everything you're doing!"

There I go. That didn't kill me. And it felt good to say.

"Oh, you're welcome," James says suddenly, sounding a little shy. "I figured it's your own business."

"Yes, thank you!" I say and decide not to pry into his. "And thanks for calling me back. I'll let you get on then. Call me if there's anything I can do!"

"I will! Bye, Livvy," he says and hangs up.

Moment 34

South Pasadena, CA
Friday, March 17th, 1978, 2:50 PM
I am 33 years old

I turn the corner to our street. I am still getting used to driving here. If I'm not careful, I find myself in front of my house on Palm Avenue. That has happened more than once. But we don't live there anymore. Someone else soon will. Hopefully. The house is good, the rent reasonable; it is just about finding somebody worthy. I would prefer another single parent with smaller kids. It is a way to pay forward what I had. What the house meant to me. What it still means.

I can't bear the thought of parting with the house. It would be disrespectful to Betty. And I have a feeling she wants to stay there. Her spirit has not moved me at Robert's house. I have only heard her voice on my accidental arrivals on Palm Avenue.

"Oh, back so soon?" she asks with one eyebrow raised.

She reads me like a book. She knows why I'm there.

"Boring boyfriend not doing it for you anymore?"

I want to tell her that it's complicated but can already hear her say,

"Complicated, schmomplicated!"

So I don't even bother. I just let her talk roll over me. Eventually, she fills me up, and I get the energy to go to the new house. Robert's house. He still tries to convince me it is my house too. He has gone to great lengths to change it away from what it was. To air out the ghosts in the closets. To dim the memories. It got repainted. The bedrooms upstairs got switched around. His boys moved in together into the biggest of their old rooms. Less change for them is part of the deal. Ben and Maya share the master bedroom. Lily got the smaller of the boys' room. Robert and I are using the guest room as our bedroom. We got a new bed. Yes, Robert has been sensitive to my concerns, spoken or not. I couldn't ask for more. I won't ask for more. That would be unreasonable. That would be ungrateful. That would be pissing on everything he has done for me.

And I see how the whole thing has brought up old times for him, both good and bad. After all, this is the house where he lived with his wife, where she was pregnant with the boys, where she was waiting for him with dinner ready every night, where he went to sleep next to her every night, where she was brought after she had the breakdown a couple of blocks away, where the decision to part was made. Not because they fell out of love, but because she fell into a dark hole that she wasn't able to get out of.

Robert is determined to be practical. He will not let feelings trump a low mortgage payment and room enough for all of us. And his wife is fine with it. That is what she said when he asked her. She is the third person in our relationship. She has been from the beginning. I'm used to it. I'm actually quite okay with it. It takes the pressure off me to be what she was. I don't have to fill her shoes since she is still wearing them. I don't have to go all-in because there is no room for me. I can keep the back door open just a little bit. Just in case.

I know I'm tainted too. I have lost the capacity to give all of myself to another person. I have a piece of me that needs to stick with me. Always. Over time, my core has become encapsulated. It can't be touched by anyone. Only I can go there. When necessary, I can retreat into that oasis, that patch of green underneath a big tree, where the sun sends down its rays in the late afternoon and where I can watch the clouds go by when I look up through the big branches. It is a diorama in a glass box deep inside of me that I have to protect and can't share with anybody. Not even those I love.

I do love Robert. He is kind and warm and wants the best for me. And he wants a family. That is important to him. To sit down to dinner with the kids and me at night. To play basketball with the boys in the driveway. It is a little bit harder with the girls because, well, because they are girls and much more difficult to strike up a conversation with. Lily in particular. She is not a fan of Robert. Not by a mile. I will have to figure that out. It can't be a competition. I hope she will come around. So we can be that family. I never had that. I want to have it now. I want my children to have that.

I see the driveway now. Robert's car is parked there. That is odd. He is not supposed to be home at 3 PM on a Friday. He had meetings all afternoon. Maybe somebody canceled, and he thought he would come home early. He has been talking about getting the boys acquainted with his woodshop behind the garage. Maybe today is the day.

But that's not what my gut is telling me. I get a chill down my spine. In my life, men being home early means something dreadful happened. Just like late-night phone calls. Or packed suitcases.

I park behind Robert's car and collect the groceries and my bag and wiggle out the car, trying to avoid hitting the horn in the process. I walk around the house to the back door and through the laundry room to the kitchen, where I put down the groceries on the counter. Then I go find Robert.

He is in the living room, pacing from the stairs to the French doors to the back yard. He turns around and sees me. He stops as if the mere sight of me paralyzes him. He is still wearing his work clothes, blue pants, a striped shirt, and a knitted blue tie. His eyes are dark, and his face gray and sagging. He looks infinitely sad and tired and all misplaced there in the sunlight from the garden.

"What happened?" I ask, knowing the answer will change me. Change us.

"She's dead," he says. "My wife is dead!"

It takes me a few seconds to process what he's saying. He just stands there nailed to the ground now, with tears streaming down his face. I walk over to him and try to hug him, but he is putting up his hands, which I, in turn, end up grabbing and we stand there as though we are waiting for the music to start so we can dance. I look him in the eye.

"I'm so sorry for you," I say.

That is the truth. I hope it sounds genuine because I am sorry for him. I want to hold him, to help him, to scale the wall he has just put between us, to be by his side as an equal partner. But he is not letting me in. He looks away. He is lost in his sorrow, trying to keep it in and let it out at the same time. That takes all of his efforts. He pulls away from me and sits down on the couch with his face in his hands. He sobs quietly for a bit, but then he wipes his eyes and looks up.

"I have to tell the boys when they come home," he says to no one.

He looks at his watch.

"They should be here any minute," he says. "Oh, God."

He hides his face again. I am still standing by the French doors, awkward and unneeded.

"Do you want me to be here when you talk to them?" I ask.

He startles and looks up at me. He must have forgotten I'm here.

"No, no…" he says as if he doesn't want to bother me.

"Okay," I say. "I'll keep my kids away to give you some privacy."

"Thanks," he says, distracted and lost in thoughts again.

I go back to the kitchen and unpack the groceries—two gallons of milk in the fridge and cereal boxes in the pantry. Chicken breast and broccoli also in the fridge, rice in the cupboard above the stove. Keeping the house going is the least I can do.

I am impatient and ashamed about it. I want to know what is going on, what happened—all the details. I want to know that we are going to be okay,

Robert and I. But this is not the time for me to ask. It is not my place. I am suddenly just a guest here and have no right to intrude on the host and his grief. I am an inconvenience if I am not careful. I don't want to be an inconvenience. I wonder if I should take the kids somewhere over the weekend just to get out of the way.

But I don't want Robert to look back on this day and think I wasn't here for him. So we are going to have to stay. I start making PB & J sandwiches and tea. When I am almost done, I hear the kids at the front door. Brayden and Lily are responsible for picking up Maya, Ben, and Harry at their elementary school when middle school lets out. It is a way to bond the kids that they walk home together.

Backpacks are being dumped on the floor in the hallway, and shoes kicked off without untying the laces. I walk out there to corral mine to the kitchen. Robert is standing in the doorway to the living room, looking like the death he is about to announce.

"Harry and Bray, can you come in here?" he says. "I need to tell you something."

I motion for my babies to follow me. Lily tries to catch my eye, but I hold her off until we are in the kitchen, and the door is closed.

"What is going on?" she asks. "Are you guys splitting up?"

There is a trace of hope in her voice.

"No," I say. "Harry and Bray's mom died, and Robert needs to tell them by himself."

All three kids stare at me. I can see Lily regrets her comment, and Maya starts to cry. Ben tries to read on my face for how he should react to this.

"They need a little bit of privacy right now," I continue, "but then you are going to have to be their friends even more than usual. Understood?"

They nod.

"Have a sandwich before you go start your homework," I say.

I am interrupted by a piercing scream from the living room.

"No, no, NO, Mom!" Harry wails, and it sounds like he falls over.

We all stand frozen in the kitchen. Even Ben, who has never turned a sandwich down, seems to have lost his appetite. Maya cries harder. Lily's face is tense as if she was hurt. That is how I feel. Hurt and hurting. I feel so bad for Robert on the other side of that wall. It isn't enough he has to weather the blow to himself; he has to be the rock to lean against for the boys.

Everything is quiet but for Harry's violent sobbing in there and Maya's crying out here. It is as if moving will make it worse or somehow not honor this somber moment. In the face of death, it is difficult to do ordinary things. It has the air of diminishing the tragic event. Doing mundane tasks makes death mundane.

But if death stops time, then death will have won. It feels like that right now. Death has won. Death has taken over. Death holds us hostage. And it is hard to release ourselves without being disrespectful. I don't want to be disrespectful, but I also don't want to be ruled by Robert's now dead ex-wife. I accepted— even welcomed— her place in our relationship when she was alive, but right now, it is a bit much.

I want this to be over with. I want us to go back to normal. I want this hurt and hushing gone. That is not for me to ask. And it has only just begun.

Moment 35

South Pasadena, CA
Friday, March 31st, 1978, 11:20 PM
I am 33 years old

I come into our bedroom after having brushed my teeth and put on my nightgown. Yes, I wear nightgowns now. Who would have thought I would ever become this respectable? Robert is already in bed, staring at the ceiling. His face is gray and serious and a little puffy and blotchy from tears.

His wife's memorial service was today. Over the past two weeks, she has been more of a presence in our lives than when she was alive. She is even here in the bedroom with us now. It is, in fact, getting crowded in between our sheets. Betty has shown up too. She is my wing-woman, although she is giving advice meant for a much stronger person than I am.

"Pull up your big girl pants, Livvy!" she instructs me. "Stand in your own magnificence!"

I know what she means. At least I think I do. She wants me to claim my own space here instead of trying to blend in with the wallpaper. But that is hard when all the air gets sucked out by a dead person.

The dead are untouchable. We will be stricken down by lightning if we say anything bad about them because they can't defend themselves. Well, I think she is doing a pretty damn fine job at that. She has a free run at pointing out my faults and illegitimacy. I am the one who can't defend myself. Because how petty is it to be jealous of someone dead?

She crowds out my room with her misery and depression and guilt and shame. That is all Robert sees. That is all Robert hears. That is all Robert feels. She wraps him in this heavy dark blanket while looking over her shoulder, taunting me. And I am powerless. There is nothing I can do about it. Except stand in my magnificence, as Betty says.

I have to find it first because I seem to have misplaced it. If I ever had it. Was I ever magnificent? I can only remember glimpses of that. The wonder of giving birth to the kids. Finding the courage to leave Jonathan and get clean. The pride of getting a degree, of being independent.

But none of that can compete with Robert's wife. She has been sainted since she died. All her dark spots have been erased, forgotten. And I am profane for bringing them up. I guess that is what Betty is telling me—do not compete. No one likes a whiner.

I am not whining. But she did leave the boys. They did divorce. There was a reason for that. They agreed. That's all I am saying.

It doesn't matter. Because right now, all that shines is her death. She committed suicide. She collected pills at the institution until she had enough to overdose. It took months, probably since Robert asked her if the kids and I could move in. Robert hasn't said it out loud. Yet. But he has pieced together the timing as if it means something.

Maybe it does. Maybe him asking did start a chain reaction in her. Maybe she felt it was a relief. That she could finally let go because he would be well taken care of. That her job on this earth was done. That is not the version of the story he subscribes to. He is guilt-ridden because he drove her to this. He afforded himself something he shouldn't have. Therein lies the difference between him and me.

I do not believe in longevity for the sake of longevity. If you feel your purpose is fulfilled, you should have the choice not to stick around. There is no point—in my opinion—to stay as a bleak reminder of what once was. What my mother did was based on her stupidity. Her misconception of reality. But it was her choice and hers alone.

That is not what Robert thinks. To him, everything just became final. Hope disappeared. Light disappeared. His boys drowned in sorrow. And while his wife took the pills, he was the one who gave them to her. He pushed her. He killed her. And I'm the reason why.

He can barely look at me. I am afraid that he thinks I'm not worth it. That he has considered me temporary until she felt better. That he had hoped that asking her if I could move in would jolt her into action, into recovery. I am a walking insult. That is where we are at.

I didn't know where to sit at the memorial service. I didn't even know if the kids and I should go. I asked Robert about it.

"Of course!" He said.

I didn't dare ask for more details.

"Why do we have to go, Mom?" Ben asked while I was tying his tie before we left.

"Because we have to pay respect to Harry and Brayden's mom and because we support each other," I answered.

"But we didn't know her!" Ben pressed on.

"No," I conceded, "but that doesn't mean we can't do it for Robert and Harry and Brayden."

"Why?" Ben asked again.

"Because we're kind of family now," I said, hoping I was right. "That's what families do."

"So, do we have to sit with them in church?" Ben wanted to know.

And that is where I came up short.

"We'll have to see when we get there," I said. That was the best I could do.

It ended with a practical solution. The church was small, and the pews short. Robert and the boys, his parents and her parents, and her spinster sister sat in the first pew. The kids and I in the second pew. Friends of the family in the pews on the left. The old Hanson gave my arm a squeeze before we sat down. That helped. Her parents looked at us as if we were dog shit that someone dragged in on their white carpet. That didn't help. But beggars can't be choosers, and this event wasn't for us.

That is what Betty is telling me. Do not be a beggar.

I have that thought in my head as I get into bed. I set the alarm. That's when I remember it is Saturday tomorrow, and we don't have to get up early, so I turn the alarm off again. Once in the dark, we lay there, Robert and I, like two dolls having been tucked in by a little girl, staring into space. I can hear from Robert's breathing that he is not asleep. I decide to step into it.

"Hey, you," I say.

It is quiet for a bit. Then someone or something scrambles with a trash can. Maybe a raccoon.

"Hey," Robert says.

That has to be a good start, hasn't it? Or the calm before the storm.

"I'm so sorry for you and the boys," I say for the thousandth time in two weeks.

"I can understand if this changes everything," I say for the first time ever.

Quiet again. Then Robert sighs and rolls over on his side to face me.

"What do you mean?" he asks.

I think about how to phrase it so I don't sound ungrateful or as if I want to end it because I am not, and I don't. But I also don't want to stay if I am suddenly the symbol of what went wrong in his life. I know I can make it on my own. I draw a breath and say,

"I can understand if you think she killed herself because I moved in."

I pause.

"I don't want to be a constant reminder, so if you want us to move out, just let me know."

I stop there and can hear the blood pulsating in my ears. My cheeks are burning. I have said what I needed. Now come what may.

Robert sniffles. I didn't hear him cry, but he must have. His voice is thick with tears when he says, "Is that what you think? That I blame you? Us?"

He turns over and flicks on the lamp on his nightstand. He then looks at me with red puffy eyes.

"Livvy, she ended her life because she was ill," he says. "You didn't do that. I didn't do that. She wanted it to end because she was ill. It was nobody's fault. It was her illness."

Now I am crying too. I didn't realize how much I needed to hear that. Fear and worry must have built up inside me over the past fourteen days, but it is released now.

"I know I'm not the closest person—she told me that many times when we were married—but I do love you, and I want you to be here," he says. "The boys need you. I need you."

"Okay," I say and smile a little through the tears.

"Death is a big thing to take in," he says, "and it will take us some time to get back to normal. I hope you understand that."

"Okay," I say again.

I do understand.

Moment 36

South Pasadena, CA
Thursday, April 9th, 1981, 8:20 PM
I am 36 years old

"I want to go live with Dad," Lily says to me.

I read *Sophie's Choice* by William Styron on the couch in the living room. Robert has taken the boys to baseball practice, and Maya is at a classmate's house studying for a math test tomorrow. The house is quiet except for Lily's new radio playing in her room upstairs. She stands in front of me with her hands on her hips and a look on her face like I am so way behind the curve because I haven't arranged this for her yet.

"Why?" I ask.

"Because I want to!" she says with her teenage logic.

"I know you do, but that's not a good enough reason for me," I say and return to the book mainly to annoy her.

"But Dad says I can," she presses on.

"Yeah, still not gonna fly!" I say from the book.

So this is an idea that she and Jonathan have cooked up. They must have talked about it at her birthday party last weekend. Lily is fifteen going on twenty-eight. Over the past two years, she has acquired a substantial attitude and several opinions about my shortcomings as a mother. That is normal, I guess, but quite a change from the first thirteen years of her life. Most of the time, I feel like I have lost touch with her. That she is out of my reach. She looks at me with such disdain and judgment that if I were her, I would want to move out as well. In fact, I was her, and I did want to move out, only I didn't have anywhere to go.

I try not to let it get me down. I try to be the grownup. I try to be the mother. But it is hard to be responsible for everything from unwashed t-shirts to The Cold War without buckling a bit from time to time.

For some reason, she gets along well with Jonathan. Maybe it is because he isn't trying to be her parent. More like an uncle. Except her real uncle is more committed to her welfare. Lily gets Jonathan in a way I never did. He is letting his guard down with her. He is teaching her tricks, I think.

She looks at me angrily and makes a little "hmmmfff" sound and stomps back upstairs to her room.

"I want five good reasons in writing!" I yell after her, just before she slams the door so hard the house rattles.

I sink back into *Sophie's Choice* and ponder the similarities. She is with this guy who is like day and night charming and loving and then violent and paranoid. She is afraid of him but can't leave him out of guilt. She punishes herself and thinks she deserves all misfortune and pain coming to her. I didn't punish myself with Jonathan. That was all voluntary. At least in the beginning. I was in love and swept away and was willing to ignore his flaws and drawbacks. Falling out of love with him was so much slower than falling in love. It wasn't like the pro side of the list got that much shorter, just that the con side grew longer and longer and kept piling up until I had to go for the kids' sake. And for my own sake. I was burning my candle at both ends. I could only do that for a short time and still have a candle. It doesn't mean I don't miss the candle.

I could be punishing myself with Robert. Well, maybe not punishing, but being cautious not to let myself be consumed by fire. He is good at that. Slow burn. Nothing crazy. He is good for me. Keeps me in check. Doesn't let me get ahead of myself. He is good for the kids. Present. Responsible. Kind. Engaged. To me.

He proposed, and I said yes. It was a Tuesday after work. He drove us down on Arroyo Drive and stopped the car, where there is a view of the hills on the other side. We got out of the car, and he got down on one knee and said,

"Will you marry me?"

And I said, "Yes."

And that was it. We drove home to the kids and told them at dinner that night. Lily got angry. Ever since Jonathan got better, she has hoped we would get back together. She thinks she deserves that because everything is about her. She can be so mean to Robert. I can hear Jonathan's tone in her voice. She refuses to acknowledge Robert's boys even if we have all lived under the same roof for years. She pretends they are guests at the same hotel as her. I have tried to talk sense into her, but I will not justify myself to her, and she won't grant me even a little happiness. We are at an impasse.

So maybe it wouldn't be so bad if she went to live with Jonathan for a while. I know she would be able to handle it. My doubts go to Jonathan. I am not sure he is ready to have a teenage girl live with him. And I am afraid he will get her into trouble. She is so ready to try everything, and I'm afraid he'll let her. And if she goes on a sour note with me, I am afraid she will be too proud to ask to come home again.

She storms down the stairs again and throws a folded piece of paper on the coffee table. I think she wanted to make it dramatic and with a bang, but the paper floats lightly down without a sound. Then she runs upstairs and slams her door once more.

I unfold the paper. On top, it says *5 reasons I should live with Dad* in her neat and girly handwriting. Below she made bullet points with numbers. They say,

1. I hate you
2. I can make my own decisions
3. You don't want me here anymore

4. Dad takes me seriously
5. I can go to high school there

She signed the note with her name and a little heart to dot the 'i', followed by xoxo. In spite of the blow of the first bullet point, I can't help but smile. She is still my little girl. She will always be my little girl.

I get up and go to the desk in the corner and get a pen. On the other side of the note, I write,

1. I love you
2. I know you can make your own decisions, but I am here to help you
3. I would like you to stay here because I love you and you are part of this family
4. I take you seriously too
5. If you really want to go, we should sit down and talk about how that can work

Love from Mom

I fold the paper up the other way and go upstairs and push it under her door. Then I head downstairs to make myself a cup of tea. I trust Lily. She is responsible and has a good sense of what is right and wrong. She is not a scaredy-cat, but also not foolhardy. If she feels strongly about going, I shouldn't stand in her way. I shouldn't hold her here for my sake. She isn't here for me. I should be there for her. She is the child. I am the mother. She shouldn't be on the hook for securing my happiness, and she isn't. She should do what makes her happy.

I don't think that will be living with Jonathan, but she needs to figure that out for herself. The more I tell her so, the more she will be drawn to it. That is how teenagers work. That is how I worked. And high school might not be such a bad time to make mistakes. So however much I want to scoop up my little girl and coddle her forever, I think I need to let her go. Literally.

The kettle has boiled long ago, and my tea is both done and cold in the mug. I put the water on the stove again and turn it on. As I turn around to fetch another teabag from the cupboard behind me, I see Lily standing in the door to the kitchen with our correspondence in her hand. She is in her socks, which is why I didn't hear her come down the stairs.

"Hey, Babe," I say, "Do you want a cup of tea too?"

She nods and sits down facing me at the table in the breakfast nook.

"I really want to go!" She says.

"I know," I say and sit down across from her with the two tea mugs. "I just want us to talk about it like civilized people.

"And I don't want you to go because you don't like it here. I want you to go because you think you're gonna like it there."

"I do," she says and sips her tea. "Dad says the neighbor has horses I can ride and that he will take me to school every day or at least to the bus stop."

Jonathan now lives in Lone Pine, California. A sleepy town where people drive through at high speed. He tries his hand at art and crafts he then sells to the tourists who do decide to make a stop there. I don't know how successful he is and haven't cared about that until now. We might have to chip into the household.

"So how about you stick it out here until the school year is done?" I suggest. "It'll only be a couple of months."

"Sure," she says. "I want to finish it with my friends."

I have to let her think she is getting her way, even if I am getting mine. She can be so stubborn and hardheaded, and if she feels like I am taking charge, she will dig her heels in.

"And if you have to miss Maya's birthday, I am sure she is okay with that. It might be the last time we spent the night at Disneyland anyway."

That is the first time I see a flicker of hesitation in her eyes. She loves our annual weekend at Disneyland more than anything. The rides. The fireworks.

The performers and dancers. Even the last couple of years, where she has been too old for the whole experience, she has left her sassiness at the parking lot and dived in headfirst.

"Maybe I wait to go until after her birthday," Lily says. "I don't want to disappoint her."

Sure Baby. Whatever you say.

"So, why do you want to go?" I ask as calmly as I can.

She thinks about this. I can see she struggles to find the words.

"I...it's just that...what I mean is...I'd just like to try something else than this." she ends up blurting out. "I mean, this is fine, I guess. But I'd like to stay with Dad as well."

I can feel she is not done yet.

"...and now that you and Robert are getting married, you won't get back with Dad, I guess..."

So that is where we are.

"Lily Pad, my love," I say, "even if Robert hadn't proposed or I hadn't said yes, I wouldn't be getting back with your father."

"You don't know that!" she says with defiance. That is what the teenage is—one moment almost a grownup, next moment a child again.

"Yes, I know that, Baby," I say. "See, your father turned out to be no good for me. That is not gonna change. But that doesn't mean he can't be a good Dad to you."

"He has really changed," she says to herself. "And I think it would be nice to try something new."

"So, what will you do if you don't like it there?" I ask, hoping that mature Lily sticks around.

"Then I'll come back home," she says.

I know I shouldn't be that way, but I feel a pang of triumph when she calls this house her home. I have not been all wrong.

"Well, that might not be that easy if it's in the middle of the school year," I say.

"And you should also think about your Dad's feelings," I add for good measure. "You wouldn't like it if a boyfriend one day moved in with you and then out the next day, would you?"

"Moooommm…I know all that!" She says and rolls her eyes. The teenager is back.

"Well, young lady," I say, collecting the tea mugs to put them in the sink. "Then you hop up to bed if you are done with your homework. You can call Dad tomorrow when I get home from work, so I know what you say to him."

Not that we talk a lot, Jonathan and I, but I assume he is still a night owl, and while his wildest party days might be over, I don't know which Jonathan will come to the phone at this time of night. It worries me that I think that way, but I can't help it. I am in turmoil over letting her go, and I need some time to sort it out. I also want to talk to Robert about it. Not that I need to answer to him, but I would be odd if I didn't. I am afraid he will think it's irresponsible. I think it's irresponsible.

Moment 37

South Pasadena, CA
Tuesday, February 2nd, 1982, 6:25 AM
I am 37 years old

"I can't wake him up, Mom!"

At first, I don't understand what she is saying. I am barely awake. The words don't compute in my brain. I look at the alarm clock on my nightstand. It shows 6:25. It must be dark where she is, too, I think. Why is she up at this hour?

"Honey, why are you up this early?" I ask.

"Mom, Dad is on the floor, and I can't wake him up," Lily says. Her voice is shrill and panicky.

"I must have heard him fall," she says with more after-thought.

"Is he bleeding? Is he breathing?" I speak my thoughts as they enter my mind. "Baby, you need to call 911. Tell them you need an ambulance. Give them the address. Then call me back."

"Okay," she says now on a mission.

She hangs up, and I let the emotions flow over me. A wave of worry. Worry for my baby who has to deal with this. Worry that it will make her grow up sooner than she has to. Just like I did.

A wave of guilt. I put her in this situation. I allowed her to go live with him. This is all my fault. I should have gone with my instincts. I should have listened to my gut because the gut is always right. I wanted to teach her a lesson. I wanted to make her appreciate me more. Bring her closer. Instead, it drove her further away. Put her in trouble that she had to deal with on her own. I knew it wasn't right, and yet I didn't bring her home again. I didn't help her.

A wave of anger. Immense anger. At Jonathan. Why does he keep pulling shit like this? It is all about him and his needs. That is what it comes down to. He doesn't care about anybody else. He doesn't even care about his own daughter. She is just another servant who has to pick up after him. He has no shame. He has no shame. The anger turns to me. I should never have trusted him. I should know better. After three kids, I should know better. Back to him. Stupid bastard. How dare he put Lily in this situation? She doesn't need to see him like this. No child should have to see their parents like this. No child should have to pick their parent up from the floor. It is not good for them. I know.

"What was that all about?" says Robert from his side of the bed.

"That was Lily," I say. "Jonathan has done it again. He is on the floor, and she can't wake him up."

"Oh, shoot!" says Robert with fervor.

He never curses. This is as close as it gets. Right now, it annoys me. That he can't let himself go just a little bit. That he can't be a little less correct and a little more human. I know it is unfair, but it sets an impossible standard for the rest of us—an impossible standard for me. No matter how much better I get, it is never enough. I am still the uneducated orphan mother out of wedlock he took in. I am still the victim. Always the victim. Well, fuck him.

Luckily the phone rings again, and I almost drop it in my eagerness to pick it up.

"Yes, Babe?" I gasp into the receiver.

"Hi Mom, it's me again," Lily says from far away but calmer now. "I called the ambulance. They are on their way. I rolled him onto his side, so he doesn't choke."

"Well, you just stay put, Baby." I say, "I'll be there as soon as I can."

"No, Mom." She says. "I have to go with the ambulance. I don't want him to wake up alone. I'll call you when I know what's going on."

Then she hangs up. She might as well have shocked me with a cattle prod. My baby just left me. My baby just left me for the second time. And I have no right to sit down and sob over it because I brought it on myself. This is my punishment for pushing her out. This is my punishment for being so irresponsible. This is my punishment for punishing her.

I didn't have many noble intentions when I let her leave. I thought I did. I told myself I did. I made it sound to myself as if I did. But I didn't. I wanted to show her that the grass isn't greener. I wanted her to learn that Jonathan might be shiny and charming, but he is no prince or king or father. I wanted her to know he is not one to be admired. He is not worth it. I wanted her to be miserable at Jonathan's. And she was.

The first couple of months were fine. She spent a lot of time outdoors, horseback riding, hiking, swimming, making new friends. She started her sophomore year of high school in August. The school was very different from here. Slower. Old stuff for her. She got bored, called her summer friends babies, started to hang out with a different crowd. High school dropouts. Punks. I began to sound like my mother. Judgmental. Anxious. Lily began to sound like me. Defiant. Stubborn. The trench between us grew deeper.

One time I called, and she was stoned. Slurred her words. Spoke really slowly. Lost her trail, then giggled it off. I asked to talk to Jonathan. She put the phone down and went to get him but must have forgotten on the way. When I finally got him on the phone after having screamed for ten minutes to be picked, up he was stoned too. Of course, he was.

I wanted to go get her right away, but Robert held me to my plan to let her make her own mistakes. I got so mad at him. He did not budge. Said if I went right then, she would resent me even more and not learn anything but to keep me out of her business. Said I would send her right into the arms of Jonathan. Said I had to trust her to make the right conclusions from her experiences. Easy for him to say. Neither of his two super nerds would know one end of a bong from the other.

Lily came home for Thanksgiving changed. Weary and disillusioned. It broke my heart. I skipped the scolds and reprimands. I told her I loved her, and she was welcome to come home. Anytime. She looked straight at me and said,

"I can't. Dad needs me!"

She had drawn her own conclusions, alright. That weed was not for her. That she didn't like to lose control over herself. That others shouldn't either. That her Dad had a major drug issue. That she was the one to get him out of it.

I tried to tell her no one could get Jonathan out of his drug problems but himself. She didn't want to hear that. She dismissed it as another one of my mother-lies. Something I said because it was convenient for me and because I wanted things my way. She is a smart cookie, that Lily. She went back to Lone Pine after the holidays to prove me wrong. Fire in her heart. Determined to do her enlisted job.

From what I could hear on our weekly calls, she hasn't had a lot of luck. She has sounded tired and tense, but not willing to talk to me about it. She will never admit defeat. Maybe today is the day.

I don't want to be smug about it. I don't feel smug about it. I feel sorry. Sorry, she has to go through this. Sorry, I am not there with her. Sorry, I was right. Assuming I am right.

"I can take the kids to school," Robert says. "I don't have to be in the office until nine."

He swings his feet out of bed and sits up with his back to me. His shoulders are a little hunched, and the light blue PJ makes him look old. That and the gray streaks in his hair. He could be 85 sitting there. He could be my father. In many ways, he is.

I often wonder if that is why I said yes to marry him, why I am together with him. Because I didn't have a father and he is the next best thing. I sometimes find myself taking Lily's side in their disagreements. Like I am a rebellious teenager too. He can be stuffy and stiff. That is his normal mood, I guess. His Monday to Friday mood. On the weekends, he makes an effort to loosen up, but I can tell it is out of his comfort zone. There is a fine line between silly and laughable, and he mostly ends up on the wrong side of that.

He can be a killjoy. Last spring, Ben and Harry—Robert's youngest—joined the school basketball team and wanted to practice at home. So Robert got them a hoop for the driveway but didn't leave it at that. He also made them read all kinds of boring theory about the game and spent every night after work outside yelling at them and drilling them through pointless exercises until the semester was finally over and summer took mercy on them.

It is as if he doesn't get lightness or ease. Everything has to be so serious or not at all. But he cares. He cares more than anyone I know. He is a good father. He makes us all feel safe. And that makes up for the lack of fun and impulse.

He is not romantic by any stretch. I miss that. I miss the extravagant gestures. The flowers. The weekend getaways. The champagne. The indulgence. The indulgence of ourselves. Robert doesn't let go of the world. He never sheds his duties. His feet are firmly planted on the ground at all times.

I have never seen him out of control. Not even when he got the news about his wife's death. It was like an underwater explosion. He just took the news in swallowed them and let them do their damage inside. Nothing showed but a few more hard lines on his face and a deeper furrow in his brow.

He was always devoted to his wife. He still is. It doesn't matter they got divorced. Or that she was ill. He never lost respect for her. He never stopped caring about her. I am not jealous. Not at all. It takes the weight off my shoulders. She is the one who is glorified. She is the one who was like no other. She was the first. I am second in line. I am the consolation prize. And that is fine.

It works both ways, I guess. I stand in her shadow, and Robert is Jonathan's counterpart. They are night and day, and I chose the day when the nightlife didn't work out. He is my second choice but not a lesser one. He is the choice I made when I got smart. There is no pressure for Robert to be like Jonathan. Quite the opposite.

It makes sense to marry him. We make sense together. It is all very sensible. There is something in it for both of us, and we have thought about that. He brings security, reliability, care. I bring...I bring a need for that, a purpose. He can fix me, and I can fulfill his need to fix. It makes sense.

Only in my weakest moments do I want something else. Only in my weakest moments do I see his grandfather PJ and salt and pepper hair. Only in my weakest moments does he repulse me. And those moments pass. In fact, it already has.

"Yes, that would be great," I say. "I don't know if and when I'm gonna go up there, so I'm gonna call in sick and wait for Lily to call me."

Moment 38

Santa Barbara, CA
Saturday, July 17th, 1982, 3:45 PM
I am 37 years old

My hands are clammy. This is a big deal. Even if it won't change anything, it still changes everything. It is a milestone. A breaking point. An end of an era. An acceptance of my fate.

I didn't think I would be nervous. I was rather hoping I could take it easy and just enjoy the day. Celebrate the occasion. Yet here I am. Sweaty and frazzled. Maya is fussing around me, rearranging the curls on the side, adjusting the small white daisies that are stuck into the braid across my head to keep my wild hair away from my face, smoothing my dress in the back.

Maya likes creating. Colorful things. Warm things. Beautiful things. That seems to be her mission. To create something pleasing to the eye. She is still finding the lines and paints within them. She doesn't upset. Not yet. But one day I hope because I know she has it in her. For now, she chooses to go by the book. To show she has got it. She can follow the rules as well as anyone. But not break them. Not yet.

Lily sits on a chair and assesses the result. She makes it clear that she is against the whole thing, but if I am going to go ahead with it, I might as well look my best. She will not participate actively. This is her non-violent resistance. I want her here but not in this way. I can hardly ask her to be grownup. She has no problem with that. She is already way ahead of me.

Ben sits next to Lily in his ill-fitting suit. It was difficult to get something that would hold his girth and not have sleeves and pant legs that trail a foot behind him. We had to pick it from the men's section and then have it altered so he can never use it again. He is busy picking his nose. Charming. He will walk me up the aisle in a few minutes. He was so proud when I asked him. Finally, there was a job for him. Finally, he could do something good. Finally, he was part of the family. Finally, he had responsibility. And he takes it very seriously. We have been practicing in the driveway. It hasn't been pretty. Ben not so much walks as stumbles forward in a confusing heap of feet that seems as wide as they are long. I will be lucky if we reach Robert without one of us taking a fall.

That is what it feels like. That I am setting myself up for falling. That I am giving up my last bit of resistance to let myself fall face forward into this marriage in one of those trust exercises where I just hope someone will catch me. Robert will catch me. I know that. He always does. And I am grateful for that. It would be easier if he didn't. It would take the weight off my shoulders. It would justify my doubt.

Right now, I have nothing. I can't think of a single reason why I shouldn't marry Robert. Except that I don't want to. I can't articulate what it is that I am giving up, but it feels like something I shouldn't.

It is not my independence. Robert is okay that way. He is mindful of our differences. He doesn't expect me to bow to him or agree with him. He expects me to bow to and agree with reason and practicality and common sense. That is hard to argue with.

It is not another chance at the wild life. I have done that. I don't want to do that again. I can't remember when I last partied all night or had too many drinks or just let myself go and did something new and unexpected. Everything is as expected. And I am willing to pay the price to forego the roller coaster ride that was my life before. Or so I thought. I just didn't think it would be so black and white. Comfort or exhilaration. Reliability or excitement. Dullness or surprises.

It is not that I'm waiting for something better to come along. How is that supposed to happen? We have our whole life together, Robert and I. We are hermetically sealed against any outside influence or disruption. And that is a good thing. I know I should appreciate this more because it is as good as it gets.

It is not that I don't love him. I do. He is kind and warm and cares deeply for me. It is not that. I love that I get to have that. But is it really me that has it? Or is it the me that I have turned myself into to protect myself? I think that is the me who loves Robert. Not the 'me' me.

I don't like that my life is reduced to a bunch of ungrateful shoulds. I should love him. I should appreciate him. I should snap out of my pouting. It is a little late for all that now. I can't back out fifteen minutes before game time. That would be wrong. That would be cowardly. That would be regrettable. Because what then? Leave him? Give it more time? I can't say what it is that needs more time, what I want to change, what I want. Just that I am not sure about this, not really feeling it. It feels too much like defeat right now. That I am late to the party and this is what I get. And marriage shouldn't feel like that. At least not in an ideal world. But this is not an ideal world; this is the real world. And I am not ideal. It is not like Robert is getting a great deal either. What with me being lukewarm and resigning to the whole thing. With me being lukewarm and resigning to everything.

I am talking myself in circles. I need to pull up my big girl pants and not think too much about it. I have come this far, and there isn't any point in stopping now. I have a good life. The kids have a good life. It might not be what I had hoped for or dreamed of, but it is so much better than what I feared. There is something to be said for that. So I will stow away my reservations and complaints and get it over with.

It is not like a lot will change. We have a well-tested formula. A way of being together. Stay the course. Do as always. That is our mantra, our slogan. This day is no different. It doesn't mark a milestone. It marks a process. A process that we have and that is working and that we want to celebrate. We have spent years honing the process. And now we have it down. We feel secure enough in the process that we are willing to share it with the world. Commit to staying with it.

It really doesn't make a difference. Except that, today, I have to say out loud that I want to live my life the way that I have lived my life for the past five years. That I want to continue until death does us part. That isn't something I have done before. That is something I have avoided doing before. I have just taken one day, one week, one month at a time, not fixed what wasn't broken, not questioned it. And now, fifteen minutes before closing time, I start to think I should have. That maybe it is worth giving some thought.

I never thought I had options. I never thought I had a choice. I never thought. And now, because I never thought about them, my options are running out. Not seeing my options made them go away. Like houseplants die if I don't talk to them. That is my problem. Today, I sign my choice away. I let the world know I do not want it. Only I am not sure. I am not sure what it is I am about to give away. Because I start to doubt, I even know my options. My understanding is limited. And it is much too late.

One of the church people knocks on the door to the room to say we should get ready. Lily and Maya pick up their purses. Maya gives me one last look-over to see that everything is how she wants it. It seems to be. Then the girls leave to find their place up in front with the family. It's just Ben and me.

"Are you scared?" he asks me.

That is the most insightful question he has asked me his whole life. I wonder what gave it away. He is still on the chair where he probably left his boogers under if he did not eat them. He doesn't think I notice he does that or he doesn't care. It could be either. My sweet man child in his new grey suit with a vest and white shirt and black tie and soft white flower boutonniere. He looks five and fifty at the same time. He has peach fuzz on his chin and upper lip. It is too dark to not notice but too light to do anything about. It looks like he didn't clean his face for three weeks, which might be accurate. Apart from that, his face is still baby-like. The chubby cheeks have not changed a lot from those early years, and neither has his appetite, and that shows. His fingers are like sausages with dirty nails, and the vest has gaping mouths between the buttons when he leans forward like now.

"No, I'm not scared," I lie. "What would I be scared about?"

Maybe if I can get Ben to tell me it won't seem so bad.

"I dunno," he says like he also has no idea what made him ask that. "Like you forget what to say or something?"

My mistake, I see. I assumed he was talking about the concept of getting married but forgot that his twelve-year-old brain is calibrated in a different way. To fart noises and belches and mumbling and grunts. I do like that he is concerned about me. Like we are in this together. Like we will guide each other through this. Like we are a team. And we are. Ben will forever be on my team. If there ever was a momma's boy, he is it. I love that, but it worries me. I love that he will never be too big for a hug or holding my hand, but fear it means he will never be big enough to let me go.

He is not capable of surviving in the wild, I think. When in trouble or doubt, he looks to me or his sisters. Of all of us, he suffered the most when Lily moved up to Jonathan. He not only missed her; he could barely function without her. He was late to school, couldn't find his way home, and tuned out of so much of sixth grade he had to repeat it this past school year. He was not embarrassed about that. To him, it was just a fact of his life. Without his sisters and me, he can't be.

In all the ways my children are like me, Ben's are beyond my reach. He has sides of me that I don't acknowledge or won't get in touch with. I go out of my way to ascribe them to Jonathan, but in my most honest moments, I know that I can't. The codependency, the neediness, the impotence, that is all me. I hate that about myself. And even if I love Ben as much as his sisters, if not more, I also hate him. Why couldn't he take a little more initiative and commitment and resiliency with him into his genes? Why did he have to sit back with just what he was dealt? Why doesn't he ever fight for himself? It is as if my mother passed through me to Ben. Perhaps that is my punishment.

Since I couldn't love her, I have to love Ben with all her faults. Loving him is easy, but it is such hard work.

I look in the mirror. My wedding dress is poofy with big shoulder pads and a plunging neckline. There are not a lot of frills to it. A simple design. It looks a little like Princess Diana's, but not nearly as big or elegant. The poor woman's Lady Di dress. They didn't say that at the store, but they were thinking it. I am glad I didn't go for a big train or gloves because it is hot in here. It looks like the dress is wearing me more than the other way around. Even the dress knows I am not sure about getting married. It is propping me up, keeping my back straight, and my shoulders from sagging. It keeps me from running away. My white shoes are pointy in the front and have a low kitten heel. They could take me out of here. I like them very much. And Betty is with me. I wear a diamond necklace of hers with matching ear studs. They add class to the ensemble without taking it over. Just like Betty would have. As always, when I am in doubt, I hear her voice in my head.

"Don't sell yourself short, dear!" She says.

She has a firm opinion about marriage. She never remarried after her husband died.

"Why would I?" she often asks me. "I did not need to be married to have men. And they were just after my money."

Robert is not after my money. I am not after his. I am after his… I think about it for a moment.

"You don't have to let him own you to be with him." Betty points out.

As if I didn't know that. And I should be able to explain myself to her. Only I can hear her cutting me off at every turn.

I want safety.

"You already have boring safety!" she says. "Nothing but boring safety!"

She is right. I do feel safe and cared for. I want to give it back. I want to thank him.

"Oh, then blow him once in a while," she says with irritation. "That's not a reason to marry him. Besides, isn't he still married to his wife?"

Ouch, that hurt Betty. Yes, he is still married to his wife, even if she was sick, even if she was gone, even if she is dead. She will be with him forever. The best love he ever had. The first love he ever had. The only love he ever had. He doesn't compare us. That is good because I would not measure up. I can never live up to that.

"Well, there you have it!" she says as if I just made her point.

I know everything she says is true, but it is not enough. I can't take her words to Robert and make him understand. They would only hurt him. And I don't want to hurt him. I want to love him. That is the least I can do.

"You can hear yourself, right?"

That is the last Betty comment I will allow myself today. Yes, I can hear myself, but that doesn't change anything. I tuck Betty away. She will have to wait to come out until we are back from the honeymoon.

I catch my engagement ring in the light. It is new and shiny. Not too big, not too flashy. Robert's wife had his grandmother's ring. I guess she still does. It wasn't among the things Robert kept after her death. But I don't know.

I remember the lady at the dress shop telling me I have to take off the engagement ring before the wedding, so I do and exhale. My hand looks finer, more delicate, lighter without the ring. I feel lighter without the ring. Less constrained. That should tell me something. But I refuse to listen and slide the engagement ring onto my right hand for safekeeping until after the wedding. The wedding ring has to be closest to my heart. So does Robert.

However, that space is already taken. My children are closest to my heart. They are my biggest love. We are both going for seconds then. And that is okay.

"Come on, Ben Ben," I say like we are late for school in the morning.

I give myself one last look in the mirror and then step over to open the door and let Ben go out first. Outside on the covered walkway, I grab his hand and drag him with me as I hurry to the stairs in front of the church. On top of the stairs, the doors open like the people know we are there. I still don't know what to call them. Ushers?

I am not catholic. I am not anything. This whole church thing is for Robert. He wants everything by the book, as always. So we have gone to counseling with the priest who will marry us. He is an old man but kind. He doesn't have a problem with me not being catholic, which is good. He has explained what will go on today. And what he sees as the meaning of marriage, which is two people being committed to each other as equal partners. He is not preachy. He has a sense of humor. He is very down to earth. I like him. I see him in his priest garb up there at the other end of the aisle with Robert waiting for me.

Ben and I trade places, so I am to the right of him, and we start to walk down to the Prince of Denmark march being played by the organ and a trumpet. Ben keeps a close eye on his feet while he mumbles,

"Left right left right left right" to himself with the music to not mess it up.

Now that we are in it, I trust him and let myself be led by him while I smile at our guests. We had to give up on the tradition of one side of the church being for the bride and the other for the groom because I can fill less than a row with my guest. James is the only one. I didn't want to invite Jonathan, and I am sure even if I had, he wouldn't have come. But James is here. He didn't respond with a plus one, but I don't know what that means. I am not jealous anymore. He is a brother to me. I want him to be happy. I want him to find someone who loves him for who he is and not for what he does for them. He watches me come down the aisle with a smile on his face. That warms my heart.

Ever since they met at the hospital seven years ago, Robert and James have become friends. They couldn't be more different, but they are very alike. They have great respect for each other and seem to have formed an alliance for the kids and me. Funny how that goes.

The girls from the office are here. They whisper and giggle without taking their eyes off me. They are most likely getting back at me for not involving them in the wedding preparations. But why would I? I have my own girls, and they need a part in this. They wait for us to the left in their light green dresses looking both older and younger than they are. Maya is beaming proudly at her creation of my look. Lily is sullen but unable to hide a little excitement. That will soon be gone.

She will soon be gone. Head out to live her life in her own way. As any healthy teenager, she feels weighed down, shackled really, by my supervision. We have to redraw the map of our boundaries on a daily basis. She pushes through to gain ground. I overreach to protect her. Back and forth it goes.

But bit by bit, she comes loose. She detaches from me. Not by action but lack thereof. She doesn't involve me. She doesn't talk to me. She doesn't reveal her thoughts to me. The indifference leaves me breathless. The inaction paralyzes me. The absence overwhelms me and pins me down. I can't defend myself against this non-attack. I can only wait for it to be over so I can heal and then—hopefully—get to know her again.

Harry and Brayden sit with Robert's parents in the front pew to the right. It is hard to read what they think of us, of me. They accept me, I guess. Because I am not their mother. They already have a mother. Since I have never tried to take her place, they accept me. This must be strange to them. As if they are forced to watch something that is irrelevant to them. That does not concern them.

We are almost at the altar, Ben Ben and I. It is a short walk. Robert smiles at me and reaches out his hand. All I have to do is take it. Ben lets go of my arm and shuffles over to his sisters happy and relieved to have performed to the best of his abilities. For a moment, I am untethered. I could fly away like a balloon released into the air.

Then I grab Robert's hand, and the feeling passes. I take him in. His brown eyes holding mine. His salt and pepper hair. His broad shoulders and wide chest that he has firmed up for this day. Ben's suit matches his same gray tone, a vest, and a black tie. The white shirt is the same color as my dress, and the boutonniere with soft white flowers and green leaves matches the girls' dresses. We are all coordinated to show we belong together. We want to belong together. I do feel part of the family when I am holding Robert's hand. He is the circuit in which I come alight. It is a physical thing because my mind can't be trusted. It is all over the place, ready to jump ship any second. But my body is at ease here. Nothing is required of it. It can just be. It belongs.

The priest greets us, and we sit down on chairs next to him. It does feel good to be here with Robert. Just the two of us together. The rest of the world drowns out of our bubble. There is a series of songs and gospels and readings and prayers and standing up and sitting down. I just follow Robert, who knows this. We never let go of the other's hand. It feels so safe to be here. It feels so soft to be here. It feels so right to be here.

Then comes our intentions and vows.

We have come here to be married without coercion, freely and wholeheartedly. Yes, we have.

We are prepared to follow the path of marriage to love and honor each other for as long as we live. Yes, we are.

As the knight in shining armor he is, Robert had a vasectomy after Harry, so we skip the part about accepting children lovingly from God.

We do take each other to be our lawful spouses to have and to hold from this day forward for better, for worse, for richer, for poorer, in sickness, and in health, until death do us part. Yes, we do.

We receive our rings as a sign of our love and fidelity in the name of the Father, the Son, and the Holy Spirit.

There are more prayer and singing and kneeling and blessing. I let myself be carried away by it. I don't think about the meaning or purpose. I just float along with the sounds and sensations. Do as I am told. Embrace the love and let myself be embraced by love. Make promises. Vow to keep them. That is the path of least resistance. That is the path of no resistance. I surrender.

I get my prince. It is nothing and exactly as I dreamt it. We are not young or innocent. We are deliberate and mindful. We are not free or in need of saving. We are strong and respectful. We are not hasty or taking a leap of faith. We are experienced and certain. I could not ask for more. I shall not ask for more. I will not ask for more.

I have the satisfaction of having made the right decision. It goes a long way. Now that I have said yes, all the reasons to say no fade away. I have chosen to disregard them. I will not hold them in regard.

I am relieved. So is everyone else it seems. A wedding is a day to be happy to celebrate to forget about doubts and reservations and just be in it. We allow ourselves to just be in it. We— the newlyweds—commit to just be in it. On this day, we agree to not only be together for as long as we live but to carry the torch for everyone else. We agree to set the example. We agree to do it right. And it feels good. It feels like we can do it.

We walk out of the church as husband and wife and stand on the steps to have our picture taken. By ourselves and with the kids. All of them. Also Harry and Brayden. People throw white rose petals at us. It adds a glow of innocence and fairytale. That is Lily's doing. She wants to save the pigeons from death by constipation from rice. We are all immortal right now, both people and birds.

Moment 39

South Pasadena, CA
Monday, September 17th, 1984, 11:20 AM
I am 39 years old

"How could you do that?" Robert asks me his voice filled with outrage and disbelief.

We are in the living room where all the important conversations of our lives take place. We were actually at the office this morning, but then Robert came up to my desk and said, "I need you to go to a meeting with me. Right now!"

He drove us home again and directed me through the back entrance and into the living room. He paces from the French doors to the hallway, as is his habit, and I sit on the couch and watch him pace. I am surprised at his strong reaction. He is much angrier than I thought he would be. Honestly, I didn't think he would find out, so I didn't expect him to react at all. And certainly not this way. He is kind of hot when he is angry, but I try not to let that distract me.

"What does it matter?" I say in an attempt to make the whole thing go away as fast as it came. "It's not that Chuck Beckett needs more money anyway!"

"That's not for you to decide!" I mouth the words as Robert says them.

"Do you know what you've done? How serious this is? I could lose my license if anybody finds out!"

He is quite mad. He talks to me in the same manner he talks to the kids when they have done something wrong. Not that his boys do that often, but mine provide plenty of opportunities to bring out the stern father act. Something about it makes me take on the role of the moody teenager.

"Well, no one's gonna find out!" I say as if that is a defense.

I wouldn't accept that response, and he doesn't either.

"That's not the point, is it?"

He stops to catch my eye. He needs to assure himself that I get the graveness of the situation. That I understand and will behave like a grownup. Judging by his expression, I haven't so far.

"How could you?" he says again, not as a question but as an opinion. He returns to his pacing.

"Come on!" I say. "Don't tell me you've never thought about it."

I am getting a little annoyed here. He needs to come down from his high horse. I refuse to believe he has never entertained the thought. He has probably been too scared to do it. Too righteous. Too flawless. Too straight and narrow. But he must have thought about it. Of all the cases that have crossed his desk over the years, there must have been some where he had the urge to set the record straight.

That is how I look at it; I set the record straight. This was how it was meant to be, and I just helped make it that way. Sometimes, the universe needs a little nudge, and in this case, I was the chosen nudger. And Betty helped too.

About a year ago, the office got this new client, Mrs. Cynthia Beckett. She was in her eighties and felt it was time to bring her affairs in order. She would have her caregiver Monica take her to the office every other week or so to do her will because she wasn't great with short term memory. Each time it was the same thing. She would make an appointment with Robert at 10 AM and have Monica drive her and help her into the office in the wheelchair. Robert and Mrs. Beckett would talk privately in his office for ten-fifteen minutes, and then I would be called in to take notes and write up the documents for her signature afterward.

Mrs. Beckett was quite wealthy. She was not missing anything but a little love and attention. Her son Charles Beckett is a hotshot in Hollywood and rarely came to visit his mother.

"Oh no, he is very busy." Mrs. Beckett would say with pretend understanding and a strong resolution to not feel sorry for herself.

"Oh, yes, he is very busy!" Monica would say with sarcasm and strong empathy for Mrs. Beckett.

Monica and I often talked while she waited for Mrs. Beckett, and I waited to be called into Robert's office. Not about the will, of course. There was strict confidentiality, and I would never ever break that. About everyday things. Things we have in common. Kids, being single moms, taking care of old ladies, not have our lives turn out the way we thought they would.

Monica has two kids, a boy who is now five and a girl who is three. Monica is younger than me, probably no more than 26 or 27. She had this shithead husband who not only ran away with her best friend two years ago but took everything with him down to her wedding ring she kept in a small dish next to her bed at night. He emptied all the bank accounts, the jar with change in the kitchen, and took the car. To add insult to injury, he found the best friend's kids more endearing than his own, so they got to come along, and he is now playing happy family with them.

So Monica had to find a job to support her and the children, and that is how she ended up at Mrs. Beckett's. Lucky for her. Lucky for them both. Monica is caring and beyond grateful for her job. Mrs. Beckett really liked Monica and had nothing but respect for her and her situation. And Mrs. Beckett wanted to help Monica in any way she could. There is no doubt about it.

Given the nature of the law firm, there are quite a few older clients. And they often change their minds about who gets what. Some children know this and try to get on the good side of their parents by smooching and suddenly visiting them every week. Charles—Chuck—Beckett was not one of those. To him, fame and image are far more important than wealth, which is, of course, easy for him because he is already loaded. Mrs. Beckett, however, really didn't know what to do with her money except giving some to Monica and some to the Humane Society—she apparently loved cats—and then leave the rest to Chuck.

That is where the whole thing started. Every time Mrs. Beckett drew up her will, it was the same—except for the amounts. It was always Monica, the cats, and Chuck but sometimes Monica and the cats, each got $100,000, sometimes $50,000, sometimes $10,000. It would even change during the meetings. Mrs. Beckett was not good with numbers or remembering, but it was clear what her intention was.

The last time she came in, she really had trouble. She started out by saying $100,000 for Monica, then changed it to $10,000, then back to $100,000 when I tried to confirm, and five minutes later, she said $10,000. That was the last amount she mentioned. When I typed up the will for her signature, I added a zero. I didn't even think for a second when I did it. Why would I? It was clear what she wanted, and I knew what that money would mean to Monica. My heart did skip a beat when I brought the documents in for her signature in front of witnesses, but she only skimmed them through and signed. She was tired by then, and her eyesight was far from perfect. Robert and I then signed as well, and that was the last time we saw Mrs. Beckett. I took it as a sign that she was happy with the way the will was written up and forgot all about it.

Mrs. Beckett died a month ago. The office began to process the estate. The will ended up on Robert's desk this morning, and he remembered. He remembered the amount, and he realized what I had done. And now, here we are.

"No, I've never thought about committing a crime and dragging you down with me!" he yells at me. "And honestly, I never imagined you would either. If I had, we wouldn't be here!"

The words hit me like a hammer. The words knock me out. The words rattle my core. Because this isn't about me helping a friend to get back on her feet. This isn't about me righting a wrong. This is about Robert and me. This is about our marriage. This is about our trust in each other. Without realizing it, without thinking, I have undermined that trust. I was so focused on how easy it was that I didn't think about what it would mean.

I wanted Monica to have what I have, but in the process, I broke it. I feel like I backed over someone's cat in the driveway. I have done—maybe irreparable—damage, and I did not mean to.

"I'm sorry," I say and feel a tear sliding down my cheek. Now I am the one to try to make eye contact so he can see I am genuine.

"Well sorry isn't gonna cut it," Robert says now a little calmer.

"Then tell me what will," I say. "I didn't mean to hurt you. I love you."

I don't say those words often. I don't say them nearly enough. And I don't appreciate my love for him enough. I thought I was better. I thought I was smarter. For some odd reason, I thought I didn't have to. It isn't until now when a piece—or maybe all—of it is lost, I see what I should have done. I never thought I would be the perpetrator and not the victim. I thought my usual victim role rendered me guilt-free. But that is not how it works. How arrogant of me.

Robert sits down in one of the armchairs as far away from me he can get without leaving the room. He rubs his face in his hands and sighs. After some thinking, he says,

"Well, for a start, you will have to resign."

I am the defendant. He is the judge. That is the verdict.

South Pasadena, CA
Saturday, December 8th, 1984, 8:45 PM
I am 40 years old

I pour myself another glass of red wine, thinking maybe I shouldn't. Ah, who cares? I look around, and no one cares. They are all absorbed in their quiet conversations, and most of the kids retreated to their rooms upstairs after they ate. Lily is home from college for the holidays. Brayden too.

I put this party together for me—my 40th birthday. I hate turning forty, but I thought I could at least have a decent party to get the decade going. This is not a decent party. I must have invited the wrong people or served the wrong food and drinks or something because no one is dancing or laughing or drinking. Instead, Lily got them all serious by bringing up the Union Carbide accident in Bhopal. It is a horrible thing, but it doesn't get any less horrible by ruining my birthday.

Lily just can't help it. She is such an activist soul. And I am proud of that, only not on my birthday. This is all she has been talking about for a week. She is raging against corporations that kill and maim innocent people in the name of profit even if it is on the other side of the earth. She has the fire in her. That is the one good thing I gave her. I used to have it too. I just spend it on less worthy causes like Jonathan and drugs.

It has not added to the cheer that Robert is his cautious self in cases like this, not wanting to judge the situation before all facts are in, not wanting to accuse anyone until there is proof, not wanting to denounce the principles of free enterprise. And even if he would never admit it, he gets a kick out of baiting Lily. The more upset she gets, the calmer he is taking the opposite viewpoint, playing the devil's advocate until she is reduced to the screaming, crying teenager that she is; stomping back to her room slamming the door. He likes that. Showing her who's boss. It doesn't bother him one bit that he confirms all of her opinions of him, and she gets angry and likes him even less. He wears that like a badge of honor. It makes him feel big.

He still hasn't forgiven me. It is a slow process, and some days, I just want to give up. There is a limit to how much I want to please him, and he is toeing that line. He is almost into the area where it is no longer anger and disappointment but punishment. Like I can never be good enough ever again, and he keeps holding that over my head like a sword. Will it come down on me? I don't know, but I better be good, so it doesn't.

I resigned from my job at the law firm. My lifeline. My independence. My identity. I had to. Robert made me.

"I don't trust you anymore!" he said. "I can't risk you doing something like that again!"

I wouldn't. I have learned my lesson, but that is beside the point. The point is the trust is gone. He didn't want to fire me, so I had to resign myself with some story about me wanting to spend more time at home with the kids and us trying to balance a family life.

That hurt double. Not only did I lose the job I love, but I also can't get another. So I am stuck here at home. Day in day out. It is boring. I don't really know what to do with myself. And Robert, for sure, isn't helping. He acts like I am a child who has to sit in my room and think about what I have done wrong. Whenever I come up with something to do, he looks at me with that Daddy look of 'who are you to think you deserve to have any fun?'

Then I get contrary. I want to have more fun than I've ever had before. I want to be outrageous and reckless and full of life and show him he can't bring me down. Hence this party for my birthday.

I just felt like going all out. Good food, nice drinks, music, and dancing. Great guests. The guests make the party. That is what Jonathan used to say, and there was always a party around him. I think that is where I went wrong tonight. I don't have any party friends anymore. I guess I never did. They were always Jonathan's friends, the party people. The people who could liven up the room by just walking in the door. That is not who is here tonight.

I had to scramble to find someone to invite whom I am not related to. I asked a few people from the law firm, but many of them declined with vague excuses. I guess the tension between Robert and me is tangible. I invited some of the neighbors, but none of them is really outgoing. We live in a quiet neighborhood where everybody keeps to themselves. I asked some people from Palm Avenue, and those who came are uncomfortable with me not being one of them anymore. They think I have gone posh by abandoning them and moving in with Robert in the first place. And then there are some parents from the kids' schools who we've stayed in touch with. No one is really close except with themselves. No one is inclined to step out of their bubble and meet new people. No one wants their prejudice or preconceived notions shot down. It is all very slow and tedious.

I was hoping the drinks might help with that, but no one seems to dig in—except for me. I take a large sip of my wine and head for the nearest group working on my best opening line.

"Did you see the Serious Moonlight concert with Bowie?" I ask the 64-year-old bookkeeper from the office, Mrs. Cook, and an older gentleman standing next to her whom I can only assume is Mr. Cook.

She looks at me like I have just asked her if she ever encourages her husband to go commando for better access. She then turns around to the third person in the group, Ms. Little, a spinster in her mid-50s, who helps with the phones and says,

"I find the best way to keep pests out of the roses is with a blend of baking soda, vinegar, oil, and dish soap. Just dissolve it all in water and spray it on the leaves once a week. Isn't that right, Hans?"

I take another sip of the wine and float over to the next group. Here Robert is explaining why re-electing Reagan as president is the best thing to happen to the US since sliced Wonder Bread and beer in a can. I take pity in the couple of twenty-somethings, Moira and Pete, who are currently renting the house on Palm Avenue and who look like if they voted at all that it wouldn't have been for two aging white men in favor of nuclear weapons and maintaining income inequality. Still, I don't want to get in the middle of that. Robert and I have had too many discussions about his anachronistic and unacceptable political views for me to ruin my birthday with another.

So I move on. Move on to better things. I find myself next to the stereo where someone has found it funny to put on Wagner's Tristan and Isolde and turn the music all the way down. I switch to the radio—KIIS FM—instead where they are recounting the top 40 hits of the week. Pat Benatar's We Belong is on, and I turn it up and have some wine and start to dance by myself by the speakers. Everyone moves uncomfortably out of my way as if I have a contagious disease and continue to talk a little louder over the music.

The next song comes on, and it isn't one that I know, but now I have gotten into the dancing, and it is difficult to just stop and walk away. Also, I want to show these people how stuck-up they are for not letting loose when they have the chance. I don't care—it is my party. So I go back to Robert and grab him by the hand and pull him into the middle of the room with me and try to make him dance. He is stiff as a board and mightily annoyed with me. His brows are heading for the bottom of his nose. He ends up standing more or less still while I dance around him and move his right arm up and down while trying not to spill the rest of my wine in my left hand.

Moira and Pete come to my rescue. They seem so grateful to get a break from Robert talking that they come to join us. It is a good transition place. Then they can walk off and talk to someone else afterward. They don't seem to know the song either, but who cares we are dancing!

A slow song comes on after that, and I get closer to Robert forcing him to wrap his arms around me because I am still holding the wine glass. We sway from side to side to the music without moving much around.

"Can we please stop this?" he hisses at me. "You're embarrassing!"

I ignore his comment and send him a seductive smile instead. I fiddle a bit with his tie to see if I can loosen it, but he pushes my hand away.

"Livvy, stop it!" he says and looks around to see if anybody has noticed.

Now I am the one getting annoyed. I stop and take a step away from him. I am a little unsteady on my feet. I empty my wine glass and put it down on the coffee table with a clank so that everybody hears. Then I kick off my high heels and feel the rug with my bare feet.

"Hey, listen up!" I call out and look around at the shell-shocked faces. "This is my birthday party, and I get to do pretty damn well as I please! If I embarrass you, you are free to leave. Otherwise, have a drink and get dancing!"

Robert looks at me in horror and then storms out. Who is the teenager now? The Cooks and Ms. Little also head toward the hallway and their jackets, mock yawning and 'calling it an early night.' I don't care. I go get another glass of wine. I know that now I really, really shouldn't. I lean my back against the wall and look at the six or seven people who are moving to the music.

I think about what has happened to me. When did I become the loudmouth? That was never me. Maybe those years with Jonathan have rubbed off on me. I have seen him work parties from polite chatting and maybe tapping your right foot to jumping in the pool naked and making a bonfire out of the patio furniture in thirty minutes, so maybe I learned something. I am also aware that back then, I was the quiet, cautious one who did not want to stand out in the crowd, and that is not the case anymore. I am the one who sticks out like a sore thumb here. I am the one who is different. I am the one who is alone.

I am alone. I have managed to push everyone away. My husband, my children, the few friends I once had. I have taken what they had to offer and then turned my back at them. Especially with Robert, I have pissed in the nest. Bitten the hand that fed me. Poor him. And poor me. What am I going to do now? I will have to walk it back. I will have to eat my words. I will have to apologize. I will have to put myself aside and get with the program. I owe him that much. I owe him everything. But it will have to wait until tomorrow. I can't do it right now. I am going to take these few hours to remember what it was like back when it was easy, and I hadn't messed up my life yet. On that note, I toast myself and walk over to turn the music further up.

Moment 41

South Pasadena, CA
Friday, May 17th, 1985, 6:15 PM
I am 40 years old

We sit around the dining table for dinner. That rarely happens anymore. Lily and Brayden are just home from their first year of college. The rest of the kids keep their own schedules most of the time and are not interested in eating with Robert and me. Some days, even Robert and I don't want to be eating with each other, so it just turns into a quick sandwich at the kitchen counter. And a glass of wine for me.

Since I had to stop working last year, my day has a set routine. I get up early in the morning—before anybody else—and clean up in the kitchen. Erase the traces of the day and night before. I make my coffee and sit at the kitchen table for a bit. I take in the day. Think about what I have to do. I have to plan it out. What I want to do. How I can fill up my time. Then I put out cereal for the kids, and another pot of coffee for Robert, and I get them out of bed. They are all out of the house before eight, and then it turns quiet. Sometimes too quiet. I put on the radio to feel someone is there with me. That I am somehow connected to the world. Even if it is just by a thin thread. Other days, I am not ready to be connected. I need a day off. I need to feel it does not concern me. If the world doesn't want me, I can do without it too. I shower. I assess my body. I am not fat. Too thin, if anything. Thighs and tummy and breasts are sagging a bit, but I can cover that up. And we never make love with the light on so it doesn't matter. It is all in my head. I can drown it out. I run my errands before lunch. Get groceries, go to the library, take the week's newspapers to Robert's dad in the home he now lives in, get the dry cleaning, get my hair done, get my nails done. Sometimes, I have lunch with a girlfriend somewhere on Mission or Fair Oaks. We have a salad and a glass of white wine, maybe two. Then a cup of coffee if I can't avoid it, and then I head home to sit down and read and maybe doze off for twenty minutes or so. The kids show up at home anywhere between 3 and 7 PM. I have a snack waiting in the afternoon until 5 PM. After that, they will have to wait for dinner. No one cares anyway. I read some more or do crossword puzzles or do laundry or come up with another chore that can last me some hours. Then dinner rolls around, and I can have a glass of red wine with that—two if dinner requires preparation beyond boiling a pot of water for macaroni. After dinner I watch TV. Not the news because what is the point? Drama series, sitcoms, that sort of thing. Sometimes, if there is nothing on, I just sit in the kitchen and nurse another glass of wine with my book if Robert is out doing something. Mowing the lawn or fixing something up in his woodshop or watching Harry play basketball. Harry is good at that. His varsity team wins almost every game and then goes on in tournaments across the county and state. He will amount to something. There is no doubt about it. And Brayden is doing remarkable too. It shows.

 I look at them, sitting around the table right now. Brayden in his nice khakis and light blue polo shirt that accentuates his blue eyes behind his metal-rimmed glasses. I can't see it, but I know he is wearing burgundy loafers. Just like his dad. With that little tassel that reminds me of a testicle bumping back and forth. Harry, just a tad younger and sportier, in his school shirt and shorts and sneakers. He doesn't need glasses yet, or maybe he does. It is hard to tell if he keeps his school work to a minimum because he can't read or because he is too smart. Either way, all is forgiven due to his vast talent for throwing and catching a ball. Both he and Brayden are a good bit over six feet tall, so they tower like a wall on one side of the table. Ben looks so small and pudgy next to them. He is only five foot ten and looks even shorter when he sinks into the chair like now. He is not smart. He is not sporty. He is not going anywhere. He likes heavy metal and smoking weed. And if left to his own devices, that is what he'll do indefinitely. If he is not holing up in his room with his other pale, pimpled friends, he takes his bong to their house for days on end. I had to ask Robert to stop being on his case and quit comparing him to Harry and Brayden because Ben will never be like them. Ben's world will never look like theirs. Not by a mile. Ben is all alone in the world now that Lily is off at college. He was confused and needed help before, but got completely lost this year because his sister moved away. She used to help him. After she moved back from Jonathan's, she replaced her desire to save her dad to save Ben. And she did a great job. Sat with him every day to help him with homework. Got him started on after school activities like comic drawing. Gave him some confidence in his abilities to be active in the world. But that went away with her. Now I can barely get him out of bed in the morning, and half the time, I am not sure where he goes once out the front door. Lily feels guilty about that. I know. But she has her own life to care about. And she is so excited about college. Meeting new meaningful people. Getting into movements. Finding her place and voice in the world. She will speak up. Sometimes a little too much, but that is to be expected. She is young and fresh and needs to flex her voice. She is not jaded yet. She will chase every cause from polar bears to penguins, from plastic wrapping to gun control, but especially, gender equality. I think she scares strong men away. She is much too heady. Too independent. Too amazon. She attracts puppies and lost causes. She nurses them back to health if she can, and then they leave her. At least for now. Only her baby brother Ben will stay with her forever.

But Maya is the center of attention tonight. She and her new boyfriend, Derrick. Whom she met at church. Where she started going last year. For some reason, Derrick sits at the end of the table. That is just how it ended up, I guess. We are not big on set places, just Robert and I together, Robert at the end, me to his left. Regardless of who else is home. Derrick and Maya mirror that. They look like a married couple too, what with their nice sensible clothes and purity rings. I can't believe she is my child. My girl. She reminds me of my friend Amelie from high school, only without the rich parents and equestrian skills. Very careful to make sure she does the right thing. Very careful to follow the rules. Very careful not to step outside the lines. Where did the girl who loved coloring all over the paper go? The little beam of creativity who didn't care how it was supposed to be done, she just did it. What did it take to break her down? To make her conform? To beat her into submission? Because submissive she is. She is the opposite of Lily in that regard, and that might be where it is coming from. Most of her sentences start with "Father Luke says…" or "The scripture says…" or these days, "Derrick says..." Her voice has disappeared. It has gone into hiding. It is as if she decided that forming her own opinion was too much of a hassle and that she could do just fine without.

So here at dinner tonight, we get to meet the man, or rather the boy who is in charge of her. Who directs her life with the help of God and abstinence. The girl is barely seventeen, and she has already given up on rebellion. Or this is her rebellion. Choosing the straight and narrow because the rest of us did not. Because I did not. You can hardly get more straight and narrow than Robert and his boys. But they are more on the reasonable side. The jock side. The working-hard-to-be-successful side. Is this Maya's riot against me? Is this her way of telling me that I should have kept my knees together? Could be. One thing is for sure. I have to be careful not to make too much fun of this guy because then he might stick around. That will be my punishment. That this is not a phase, but the path she chooses for herself.

I have gone out of my way to cook a nice dinner. A roast with mashed potatoes, baby carrots, green beans, and a bordelaise sauce. All from scratch. Then an apple pie with vanilla ice cream for dessert. Robert and I share the rest of the red wine with dinner, and I have another bottle ready, if necessary, which I think it will be. For me. Everyone else can have their favorite soda fresh from the Soda Stream machine. Better not upset the pure souls with serving alcohol to minors. It all does make an impressive display at the table, and most of us are ready to dig in when Maya says, "Derrick and I would like us to say grace before we begin."

Her voice is light and slightly apologetic, but there is no doubt she means it. Derrick has already folded his hands and either closed his eyes or is focused on the cloth napkin in his lap. This is serious stuff. Ben looks genuinely annoyed that his meal will be delayed by several minutes, but otherwise, we collectively decide to play nice and follow suit.

"Bless O Lord this food to our use and us to thy service and keep us ever mindful of the needs of others. In Jesus' Name, Amen." Derrick's voice thunders out.

It seems too forceful for his figure. Too intense for his frame. Roles are reversed. Robert is no longer the head of the table of this house. There is a new preacher in town, and everyone is scrambling to rise up for or against him. I know which side I am on. Little prick! Thinks he is so much better than us.

I start to scoop mashed potatoes onto Robert's plate and there is almost an audible gasp and stolen looks to see if Derrick will permit this. I look him straight in the eye to let him know who is in charge, and he gives me the tiniest nod of concession. For now.

Really, really mature, Livvy, I say to myself. How grownup to enter a pissing contest with an eighteen-year-old nerd with mother issues! But I can't stop myself. Something in me wants to provoke him. Make him cry. Expose him as the fraud he must be, so Maya can see that neither Derrick nor God is the answer.

Is that what my problem is? That this manling believes in something and I don't? That the Peewee Herman wannabe down there thinks there is something that will save him from disaster and destruction as long as he sleeps with his hands above the covers? *Honey, no one can save you but yourself*, I want to yell at him. And Maya too. Look out for number one baby, because no one else will.

Part of what irks me is that Robert is pleased with this. In his own kind, but patronizing way he thinks Maya has made an excellent choice or had a spot of good luck. It is like early admission. Robert thinks that Derrick is about as well as Maya can do. That I shouldn't be so judgmental. Such a hypocrite. I am not the judge here. Or I am not the only judge here. And I will not be put in my place by him. He can't have it both ways. He can't have both the Madonna and the whore. In private, he savors the whore, he savors me, but he has no respect. That is not what he wants his stepdaughter to be.

I don't remember ever being this resentful before. Well, maybe towards Jonathan's parents, but that was a long time ago. And I was so eager to fit in back then. To be Jonathan's favorite. Just like Maya wants Derrick's approval now. I resent that she has to ask. I resent that she figures she needs this nobody's permission to do anything. I resent she feels she has to hold herself back because he is the one who gets to lead. To walk in front. To set the direction. Why can't she do that?

Unfortunately, she takes my cue and starts filling up Derrick's plate. Like he should be exempt from such a mundane task. Like a virgin washing Jesus' feet. Or sucking his dick. That is disturbing and low even for me, I know.

I dial myself back. I focus on getting the green beans to go around on both sides and for Ben to get some on his plate. If given a choice, Ben will only eat meat. I think that is where his energy goes. Processing protein. It slows him down like a sloth. Or a koala high on eucalyptus leaves. The contrast of him in the room is almost too big. It is a blaring example of the 'One of these things' song on Sesame Street he used to watch at the neighbor's house on Palm Avenue. Where did the time go?

Now we are here. A bunch of youngsters, so unlike us parents, it is hard to believe we made them. I should speak for myself here. Robert can't nor would ever run away from those two on the other side of the table. But Lily, Maya, and Ben, they could just be strangers off the street. I have no claim to them. Not really. Not anymore. They are beyond my control. They will have to turn into the people they will be. And I will have to live with that.

Moment 42

South Pasadena, CA
Sunday, September 16th, 1990, 7:35 AM
I am 45 years old

"I had a vision of love" by Mariah Carey sings in my head. Over and over again. There is nothing else but her voice and the feeling of being in one of those spinning teacups at Disneyland. I am dizzy. And queasy. I look around to figure out where I am. I am in my bed in our bedroom. Alone. Robert's pillow and comforter are gone from the bed. When did that happen?

I seem to have traveled far to get here, but I don't really remember the journey. Something is different. And it is not just that Robert isn't here. Robert doesn't matter. I am different. What happened to me? I can't remember. There is a hole in my memory. Like I am waking up from a coma. Am I waking up from a coma? Was I in an accident? I can't remember.

I try to dig back to the last thing I can remember for sure. Sending Lily off to school in second grade. On grandparent's day. She was dressed in her finest dress. Cream white with pink and lavender flowers. White socks in black Mary-Janes. A red cardigan because it could be chilly in the morning. She didn't want to wear the cardigan because it didn't match the dress. But it was the one she had. We talked about how all people have grandparents because they have a mother and a father who has mothers and fathers too. She was with me that far. She understood I am her mother, and Jonathan is her father. She was so hopeful he would come and visit again. She would like that. She had a harder time coming to grips with Jonathan and me having parents. How could she not? She had never met my parents or Jonathan's dad and could barely remember the prissy lady who was Jonathan's mom. She knew none of them would come and see her perform in school that day. She said that was fine because her friend Anna-Lisa had offered to share her grandparents, and she had four. Lily figured that would be two for each of them, and she was hoping she got to pick first. Ah, the mind of a seven-year-old. When was this? Last week? Last month? Last year? It was for sure, a while ago, because we lived in a different house. Not this house. Not this home.

I take another spin in the teacups while Mariah Carey sings. It is hard to hold on to everything at the same time. I make a short list of things I know. There is Lily and Maya and Ben. My children. There is Jonathan. He has a magnetic aura, but I know I can't go there. There is Robert, who saved me. Who took me in. Who cared for me when I was sick. Whom I owe my life. Who lived in a house next to a garage. That he owned. Wait. That wasn't Robert. That was…that was George? Jerry? Jim? No James. James was his name. Yes. But I am not with him. I am with Robert. I think. I am. They are almost the same. Almost the same. Except, Robert is more grownup. James is like me. A person trapped in a body. Haphazardly. With no control. Robert has control. He has intention. Right now, it is to not be with me.

What time is it? I had a vision of love. When was that? Love is red and pink and purple. Like Lily's dress and cardigan. Like fire and velvet. It envelops me. It embraces me. It drowns me. I can't breathe. I cough. I fall awake again. The room is spinning with teacups.

I am drunk. That rarely happens anymore. I walk a line. It winds through my day. I start off with resolve to keep the drinking to a minimum. Because mornings are bad. My body aches. My mouth tastes bitter and dry. My mind beats me up. Yells at me. I disgust myself. I can't stand to be with yesterday's broken promises. It takes every bit of my discipline to get out of bed and begin a new day. To not just repeat the day before. To earn it. To not have a glass until I deserve it. I have to wash the curtains in the living room. Or get groceries for the whole week. Or change the sheets in all the bedrooms. No one can say I don't keep up my part of the deal. To be a housewife. And every day just before lunch, my rules, my principles, my framework starts to slide. Maybe I can just get groceries for today? Or we can go out for dinner. The curtains in the living room have waited so long it doesn't make a difference if I do it tomorrow instead. Ben can sleep in his sheets a few times more if he comes home. I lower the bar. I reward myself for less. I have a glass of wine with lunch. Even if the lunch is a yogurt at the kitchen sink. And I vowed I would never drink alone. And I still have to pick up Robert's dry cleaning. I can drive on one glass. You can barely see the scratches from the trash can on the front bumper. There really is no room in the alley behind the dry cleaner's. They should get that fixed. Because I only had one glass. To the rim. That I might have refilled. I hate myself. I hate myself from the outside because I am not stupid. I can see what I am doing. I can see the slippery slope, and I am almost at the bottom of it. To hell with it. Today is already gone. Tomorrow then. Day in and day out. Week in and week out. I long for the weekends. I dread the weekends. Robert is at home. To keep me company. To be on my case. At least on the weekends, we have social events. People to see. That gives me cover. That gives me excuses. That gives me reasons.

And then comes Monday when I try to be good again. But I am no good. Neither on Monday or any other day. I had a vision of love. I need some water. I need to clear out the sludge from my mouth. I need a shower. A cold one. I need to get sober, so I can start the day. Or at least not be this drunk. It is all about hitting the right spot. The right spot is where I have had enough to be lenient on myself. Comfortable in my own skin. Forgiving of my sins. Where I am smart and charming and sexy and…me. If I go too far. If I pass the right spot, it gets worse. Sometimes. That is why I don't drink alone. That much. Because I lose my outside perspective of myself. Then I am trapped in my drunk body, and that's horrible. I don't want to be trapped in a drunk person's body. Not even if that person is me. I take pity on myself. I wallow in it. I fall into a dark pit. I obsess over all the things I could have done with my life if I had been smarter. Brighter. Less gullible. Not had loved Jonathan. Not had had three kids. Not had married Robert. Not had screwed everything up for myself. Not had taken up day drinking as a hobby. It goes in circles. I drink to find the right spot, but if I drink more than that, I have to keep drinking. Over and over. Nothing comes from that.

I had a vision of love. And then it got away from me. Why is that song stuck in my head? Something with a party. In a ballroom. So probably not a birthday. It doesn't feel like it was a birthday. Pinker than that. But not a baptism. That wouldn't be a party. At least not the ones I have been at lately. Who is a grandmother at 44? I am too young for that. I think I am too young for that. I thought I was. But somehow Derrick and Maya didn't take that into consideration. Maybe it was even to spite me. I would not put it past Derrick. So now I'm a grandmother. You would think Maya had learned something from me. Are your kids not supposed to be smarter than you? She claims to be. Because she has God in her life. God and Derrick and a baby and another one on the way. And little else it seems to me. But that is not for me to say. I just don't want her to make the same mistakes I did and then regret it later. Because then, she is stuck. Like me.

I sit up on the side of the bed to prove myself wrong. I am not stuck. I have the full use of my faculties. I have a vision of love. Damn song. Damn floor. Flying up in my face like that. Must have made a racket in the whole house. And it hurt. I was so unprepared that my nose took the fall. Do I have a nosebleed? I move over on my right side and onto my back. I feel my nose with my left hand. Shit, it hurts. And bleeds. Perfect. Just perfect.

I think through my options. I should really get to the bathroom. I need toilet paper to stop the bleeding, and now I also have to pee. But if I can manage to fall down just sitting on the side of the bed, there is probably no way I can get up and walk to the bathroom. That leaves me with crawling on all four, which might make the blood drip on the rug. The rug will stain. It will stare back at me every time I go to bed and get up in the morning. I don't want that. Who thinks about that while drunk and hurt? I am crazy. Crazy boring.

I roll onto my left side and try to scoot towards the bathroom door to keep the blood on my nightshirt, which I don't remember putting on. It is a ridiculous way of getting myself around, and I can't help but giggle a bit. At the same time, the pain in my nose is so fierce it draws tears. It might be broken. Nice job. I see myself with my nose in a cast. I giggle again. It sounds like a hippo snorting.

We were at Courtney and Matt's wedding! That's where we were yesterday. At the Castle Green. More than 150 guests. Sit down dinner. Open bar. Courtney's dad Carl had gone all out on his only daughter's wedding. Nothing was spared.

I did not spare anything either. There was a lovely ceremony at 3 PM, then a champagne reception, then the dinner. That went on forever with speeches and toasts. They kept filling my glass. I don't remember a lot after the main course. We were at a table, Robert and I, with Carl's other golf buddies. We all know each other. The husbands are all lawyers, the wives all well-preserved. Mindless talk. I didn't eat anything all day. That will have to be my excuse.

I had a vision of love. But it is not the one who flings the door open and says,

"Oh my God, Livvy, what happened?"

Robert looks genuinely concerned. It must be the blood.

"I fenn down!" I say, and it sounds all wrong because my nose is swelling up, and my head pulsates with pain.

"Let me help you," he says and steps over behind me to get me off the floor.

The floor is not my friend. Robert bends down and puts his arms under mine and lifts me up as if I am filled with feathers. All blood rushes to my feet, and I don't feel too good.

"Robert!" I say to explain, and my legs give out. It is a good thing he is holding me up; otherwise, I would have hit the floor again. He sits us down on the side of the bed. I hang on him, and he stretches out his arms to get a better look at my face.

"I need no pee," I slur.

"Let me first get you some toilet paper for that nose," he says, "can you sit up by yourself, or do you need to lie down?"

I answer by lying down on my side with my feet still on the floor. Robert gets up, and I can hear him unroll toilet paper for me. It seems so easy when he does it. He comes back and hands me the paper. I put it under my nose and wince at the pain from the touch.

"We need to get your nose looked at," he says. "Let me get dressed, and I can take you."

"Mmmmnnnnhhh," I reply, and if it didn't hurt so much, it would be funny. I lift up my legs and roll onto my back.

He walks over to his side of the bed and takes off his pajamas. He walks over to his closet and gets out a pair of khaki chinos and a polo shirt and a pair of socks from his closet. He rarely wears shorts unless he is doing sports, and he would never be caught dead in a pair of jeans. He always looks preppy. He is sweet. I like it when he pampers me like this. It doesn't happen often. I feel safe with him. If only it would stop hurting.

Why isn't he mad at me? It strikes me like a lightning bolt. If I lost it last night. If I was very drunk last night, he should be mad at me today. That is how it usually goes. I drink, he scowls. So why isn't he mad at me? Maybe he was drunk, too. That's not very likely. Maybe he forgot in all the commotion. Maybe he is saving it for later.

"Okay, let's get you into some clothes," he says back at my bedside.

He looks a little helpless as if he isn't sure where to start.

"Nhere are nome nweatpants n the drawer," I say and point.

He rummages around. He finds an old pair of orange sweat pants I got on some vacation because I ran out of clean clothes. Those were not what I had in mind, but nose bleeders cannot be choosers because it hurts too much to speak. He also finds a purple sweatshirt that says South Pasadena on it like it is some kind of renowned college town, which is hardly the case. I don't have the energy to protest that either.

"If you need the restroom, why don't I help you out there before you put on the clothes?"

That seems like a good and efficient idea. Like Robert himself. I nod a slight nod and blink my eyes to give my approval. I make my way up to a sitting position, and the room is spinning a little less now. But just a little. Robert puts my left arm around his neck and shoulders and lifts me up. He is strong and tall. I am a ragdoll bouncing around on his side. He slowly walks me out to the bathroom. I tippy-toe along, barely touching the floor. Take that floor—I don't need you! He sits me down on the toilet with both his arms under my arms. It is awkward because I'm not 85. The reflex of sitting there is so strong. It takes all my focus to not pee in my panties. I motion him to let go of me so I can pull up my nightshirt and get my panties down to my knees. He is right in front of me, willing me not to fall over with his stare. I let go of my bladder and pee up a storm. A warm smelly yellow creek fills the bathroom and goes on forever. I thank the Universe he isn't looking me in the eyes, but rather somewhere between my chest and my lap the same way you would a three-year-old on the potty. I even expect him to say "good job!" when I am done, but he doesn't. Instead, he gets me some more toilet paper to wipe myself, which I manage to do with one hand while keeping the other full of toilet paper under my nose. It's confusing, like patting my head and rubbing my tummy at the same time. I have the urge to giggle again but give myself a firm no on that one.

"Can you stand up?" Robert asks. "Then I can help you with the clothes."

His voice is tender and warm. I get hangover horny. That makes my nose throb a little less and other places more. He pulls me up and closer to him. He smells like sleep and cologne. Like lying down together on the bed and see what happens. I find his eyes with mine, but he doesn't connect with me. He is in caregiver mode and all about the business. No sex there, just strength and helpfulness. I try to look enticing while I pull up my panties and hold my nose, but there is no response. After a long inhale of him, I let it go, and my nose takes center stage again.

He lets down the toilet seat and sits me down again. Then he gets my clothes and dresses me like I am his child.

"Let's get you to a doctor," he says and takes me to the emergency room.

Moment 43

Pasadena, CA
Sunday, September 16th, 1990, 1:15 PM
I am 45 years old

"You have to stop," Robert says.

Not in an angry or irritated way. More like he is concerned. For me. For him. For us.

"I know," I say.

And I do know. I have to do better. I want to do better.

We are on our way back from the emergency room at Huntington Hospital. Robert is driving. That keeps his eyes on the road while he talks to me. I sit next to him. I lean my forehead against the side window. My nose is the shape, size, and color of a beefsteak tomato. However, it is not throbbing anymore. The pain meds have kicked in. This hasn't been a good day so far. Since my nose wasn't bleeding that much or about to fall off, we kept being bypassed by more serious injuries. No one spoke to us after the initial triage around 8:30 AM. We hardly spoke to each other. We just sat and waited. The ER is cramped and outdated. I guess they are building a new one. Robert got us water from a vending machine, but that is all. My hangover is worse than ever. I am tired and cranky and hurting and embarrassed and pissed that we spent all of this time getting the message that my nose is broken, but there is nothing they can do about it, except to give me some ibuprofen that I could have gotten for myself at the drugstore. And if I don't like the way it grows back together, I can ask my own doctor for a referral to a plastic surgeon. That is all.

I still can't remember what happened last night after the second serving of the main course. Robert hasn't said anything, and I'm not one to ask him. I can smell myself. I need a shower. I need something to eat. I need to get my act together.

"I know," I say again and sigh.

I can feel Robert is uncomfortable with this conversation. He has to search for his words, which is not like him.

"I don't want to have to carry you home like I did last night." he finally says.

I get a small rush of relief. We are just talking about last night. That is good. I can fix that. I can manage that.

"I understand," I say. "It won't happen again!"

Phew. I feel like I dodged a bomb and got away with a flesh wound and a broken nose. It could have been way worse. He could have asked me to fix my life. To stop being bored. To do something meaningful. To love him. Monumental tasks that I don't have the strength to take on. That I wouldn't know how to approach. Where I would surely fail.

But dial it back that I can do. I have the discipline for that. I can restrain myself. I can control my impulses. I can be normal. I can hold it together. I can blend in. I can work on not embarrassing him. I just need to distract myself.

Maybe if I went for a long walk in the morning. Like three miles or something. Walk for an hour. That is an hour done right there. Boom. Instead of showering after Robert leaves, I could just put on sneakers and go for a walk. Or run. I have seen other people do that. I could just start with walking and see how it goes. That would make my day one hour shorter. Things would maybe solve themselves if I got into a good drill. It's not too late. I can do that. I think I can do that. I should start that tomorrow. If my nose doesn't hurt too much.

"Good!" Robert says.

I have his stamp of approval. We are good. We are fine. I am glad.

"I'll tell Carl that you didn't eat anything yesterday and are coming down with a bug or something." he continues.

I hadn't thought about that. I hadn't thought about there were other people at the party yesterday. People we know. People Robert knows. People, he has to apologize to. Apologize for me like I am an unruly child, he can't keep under control. Like I am the wild woman he has taken in out of pity. Is that true? Did he marry me because he felt sorry for me? Because he could save me? Because he felt obligated to?

Who does he think he is? I don't want his pity. I don't need his pity. And I would rather go without it. I can take care of myself. I always have. I will never be able to live up to his expectations. Certainly not if he expects me to be the nice and quiet suburban housewife. I think we have established I'm not. So he'll just have to deal with that.

"Don't lie on my behalf!" I say a little snippy.

"Well, what do you suggest then?" he asks, even terser. "My wife likes to drink, and she can't control it?"

Wow. That hurts. That hurts a lot. I'm not even going to think about whether that is true or not. Because it's not. It's not true. I can control it. I will control it.

Moment 44

South Pasadena, CA
Thursday, November 24th, 1994, 7:40 PM
I am 49 years old

"I don't want a fucking birthday party!" I yell at Lily and push my chair back to stand up. My legs are heavy from sitting down and unsteady from the wine, so I have to grab on to the edge of the table as if I have something to say. And I have. I have had it. I have had enough. She opened the tap with another inane question about bamboo shoots instead of a flower arrangement, and now, it all seems to be gushing out.

"Why can't you get that into your head? You are supposed to be the smart one!" I hear myself continue.

The dining room is quiet now. The only sound is from the kids' table in the corner where one of the grandkids tries to get the last bit of ice cream off his plate with a spoon before he licks it. Lily stares at me from across the table in shock. That feeds my fury further.

"Don't look so surprised, my dear. That's what I've been saying for the past month now, and if you took the time to listen instead of just going on and on and on about this stupid thing, you could have caught on a lot sooner. But I guess that is where you come up short, on the listening and catching on."

That is mean, and I know it. Back in September, Lily was left three feet from the altar by her fiancé because he was not at all who he made himself out to be. He didn't have a Ph.D. in linguistics, was not the heir to a substantial Austrian fortune, had just turned 45, and neglected to mention that he already had a French wife whom he loves very much and who is also a con artist, and they are on the Interpol list of criminals who are to be arrested on sight.

What hurt Lily the most wasn't that she was duped, but that in the end, he didn't love her. She was willing to stay with him even after his lies were revealed. She saw him as someone to be rescued. Someone she could reform and rehabilitate. A worthy and exotic cause. But he said no thanks and disappeared from one day to the next, leaving her devastated. So she needs another charity. She might have checked in on Jonathan to see how he is doing. Same or worse, I would guess. She takes Ben out for dinner once a week to try and get him started on something—anything—but that hasn't worked yet. And then she came up with this idea of a fancy dinner party for my fiftieth birthday.

I don't want that at all. There is nothing to celebrate. There has been no accomplishments, no milestones, no turning points, only a slow descent into a state of indifference. I am painfully aware of what my life has become. I don't need to be reminded. I have tried to tell her. I have tried to say it nicely. I have tried to ignore her away. I have tried and not succeeded. Now the time has run out. The party is on December 3rd, and there is no way I am going.

Lily's face burns with hurt and embarrassment, and I see a glimpse of a warning sign on my inner radar screen, but then Robert puts his left hand on mine to signal me to stop, and that is the wrong thing to do.

"No, I will not fucking stop!" I shift my wobbly focus to him. "For once, I would like to say what I think, and I am sick and tired of you telling me what to do! You always do that. Quit your job. Be a housewife. Behave yourself. Don't do this, don't do that. Like I'm a fucking child. Like I'm your little orphan experiment. Like I should be grateful for all the wonderful things you've done for me even if they're killing me inside."

It's not that I want to say this out loud, but one word takes the next and the next, and it is an almost physical release. My endless stream of berating self-talk must have switched from inner monologue to outside voice. I ran out of space to bury the corpses. The drain is clogged and the toilet overflowing.

Robert removes his hand again to make it clear that I am on my own. As if I didn't know that. I am always on my own. Robert and I live under the same roof but in different worlds. His is filled with work and golf and dinners at the lodge. Mine is filled with thoughts and loneliness and day-drinking.

"Do you think I'm like this because I want to? Do you?" I spit-ask him. "Don't you think that if I could snap out of it, I would've done so a long time ago? You of all people should be able to see depression when it hits you in the face."

And just when I thought I couldn't go any lower, I prove myself wrong. Nice one, Livvy! My vile and ugly demon has definitely taken the wheel and is going at full speed towards the edge, tearing into as many as possible on the way.

Derrick makes as if he is going to stand up too. He seems to think this is his cue to step in and perform an exorcism.

"Sit down, you little prick!" I say. "You don't get to say a single thing to me. I don't care for your sermons and sanctimonious shit."

One of their many kids snickers at the s-word until Derrick stabs him with a look.

"That's right! Shit, fuck, cunt, dick, motherfucker!"

Apparently, I'm possessed, and I'm not done with him yet.

"Everyone knows what you are, a pathetic loser hiding behind God and big words. You are just a piss ant and a nobody who thinks you can make yourself bigger by bullying everyone around you. Don't think I don't know what you are. Oh yeah, Maya tells me things!"

Maya shrinks with every word. I couldn't have hit her harder if I used my fists. She shields her face with her shoulders and tries to disappear into her sensible cardigan. She looks exactly like my mother on those bleak afternoons in the kitchen in Bakersfield, and it doesn't make me any less angry.

"Why don't you stand up to him? If he likes you to whip him as much as you say, why don't you whip him back into last week and make him wear a condom? You used to be so creative, so artistic, so wild. Now you're just wasting away from letting him screw you even before the last baby has been weaned off."

I shouldn't have said that, but it's true. They have four kids age seven or younger who all look like Laurel without Hardy and have old-world names like Elisha and Jeremiah, and I am sure, the next one is about to be announced any day now because according to Maya, Derrick is not keen on keeping it anywhere but in her.

I have no right to talk. I did the same thing. Kept having kids to not face me. Look how that turned out. Here I am at 50, with next to nothing to show for it. All because I let men take advantage of me. Brad. Jonathan. Even Robert. Isn't each generation supposed to be an improvement from the one before?

The silence is crushing. Everyone at the table is staring down at their hands to avoid looking at each other or attract my attention and get a salvo. Except for Ben. Ben looks me straight in the eyes. Not with confidence and defiance, but sorrow and despair. He always was my mirror. The one in the furthest corner of the smallest room that I never dared look into because I knew what I would see. He is the cry for help that I never could make myself let out. He is everything that is weak and trapped and vulnerable about me. He is my child, but I was never his parent. He is too close and far away at the same time. Too alike for me to reach. I cannot fix him because that would mean I could fix myself, and if I could fix myself, I would have done it. It's not that I haven't tried. Both fixing him and myself. It's never good enough. We are beyond repair, him and I. Like cheap shoes and eggs. Yellow yolk on the shirt of life. We will never come off in the wash. Without a word, Ben asks me why, and I don't have an answer for him.

Brayden, who is on my left side, gets up and grabs my lower arm with one hand and my shoulder with the other and tries to make me sit down again. I am not having that, so I wrestle myself free of his grip. My chair falls over in the scuffle. I end up staring at his chest because he is six feet two, and I am not.

"I think you have said enough now." I hear his voice from up there in the clouds.

I think he is right, but I realize I don't know how to leave. There is no elegant way out of the crevice I have backed myself into unless I want to go Thelma & Louise style. We all wait with bated breath while I think of something.

"Fine!" I say, but it is not.

I walk into the hallway and out the front door.

Moment 45

South Pasadena, CA
Monday, June 28th, 1999, 4:10 PM
I am 54 years old

The phone rings. I debate whether I should answer it. I don't feel like talking to anyone today, but since it is Maya's birthday, maybe I should pick it up. We really should get caller ID. That would make it so much easier. I grab the wireless phone from its holder on the side table and say,

"Hello?"

"Hi Mom, it's me," I hear Lily say, her voice all wrong for a birthday conversation so that can't be it, but now it's too late to hang up.

I look out the French doors into the backyard. Some critter has mauled her namesake flower, the Gloriosa Lily, again. Warm red flower petals with a sun-yellow edge are spread all over the flower bed and the lawn in front of it. For some reason, the animal only goes for these flowers. I'll have to mention it to Robert so he can get it cleaned up.

"Lily, sorry dear," I apologize to her as if the flower destruction was a personal attack on her. Or maybe it's because I always have to make amends to her. The older we get, the more our roles seem to reverse. And I hate the parallels to my mother and me, but I can't seem to get in front of it. The power has somehow shifted. If it was ever mine, it has slipped out of my hands. Lily is the grownup. She tells me what kind of parent I should be. She raises me. She judges me. To stand up to her, I take on the teenager role.

I ignore her. I roll my eyes at her. I think I know better. But I don't. I don't think I ever did. I just pretend.

"Oh, so you already know?" Lily says.

She is confused. That doesn't happen often.

"Know what?" I ask, now worried and imagining all kinds of terrible news to hit me in a second.

"Dad died." She says.

Now I'm the one who is confused. I can't really grasp who she is talking about. If Robert died, I am sure I would be the first to know. Why would they call Lily? It doesn't make sense.

Then I remember. She never called Robert Dad. She refused to. She was always big on calling things by their proper name. Maybe that's why she got into communications. To force the world to be precise. Accurate. Truthful. She means Jonathan.

Jonathan has died. I don't know how to feel about that. It doesn't resonate inside me. It is a sad but impersonal fact about someone I once knew.

"Oh," I say and understand that Lily isn't calling to let me know of the fact. She is calling to process the news for herself, and I am the context she feels is the most appropriate.

"Yes, just after lunch," she says, "he was rushed to the hospital on Friday. A neighbor found him passed out and called it in. He was very dehydrated. The doctors tried to save him, but he never woke up. We have been here all weekend."

I read the same old subtext into this. I am the one who should've been at the hospital. I am the one who should've taken care of him. I am the one who should've saved him. It is all my fault. I am a bad mother. I am a bad person. We have been through this a thousand times. Just now, with a fatal ending.

After I married, Jonathan got the hint. Not in the least because every time he would call me or show up to ask for money or a roof over his head, I would involve Robert and Robert would involve James. Jonathan can—

could— only work his magic on one person at the time so the three of us banding together made him give up on that stream of funding. Instead, he hit up Lily. Lily with the big heart. Lily, who believed if she saved him from the immediate crisis, he would get back on his feet and better. Lily, who believed that every time would be the last, and even if it wasn't, she couldn't let him fall. Lily, the humanitarian, who believes in help without judgment. Or at least, no judgment of Jonathan. I, on the other hand, am a different story. I am deemed strong enough to be judged and shamed and guilted.

When I let her know—maybe about ten years ago—that I didn't want to hear about him anymore and when he flaked out on her, she shouldn't come crying to me, she didn't speak to me for a year. That was her punishment for me. And she's still at it. This is the first time in a decade that Jonathan has come up, but she has never once passed on a chance to express how she feels about me.

I have no doubt she stayed in touch with him. They were always close. I don't know why that is because Lily is not that like him. Maybe she is trying to prove that to herself. Maybe she thought if she saved him, she would save herself too. Or maybe she just loves him.

I realized a long time ago that no one could save Jonathan. He didn't want to be saved. This is how he wanted to go out. This is what he has been trying to do forever. Burn and crash. He was always meant to die young, and he regretted every day it didn't happen. I think it switched when his father died. Grief damages people. That was when he shifted from having a good time in the fast lane to attempting to drive himself to death. It didn't matter how many people loved him. He didn't love himself, and that's the only thing that counts.

He might have loved Lily a little, too. I don't know. But if he did, it wasn't enough to make him change his ways.

I feel sorry for her. She must be devastated. And I don't want her to hurt. She is my baby, even if she is a stubborn one.

"I am so sorry," I say again.

I don't want to sound condescending because I am not. That is why I don't add a 'for you' in the end. She doesn't need my distinction at this point. She lets herself go and sobs,

"He was...he was so small, Mom."

"I know, dear," I say, but I probably mean something different than her.

"You should have seen him, Mom." she cries. "He was so small."

I let her cry it out for a bit while I walk to the kitchen and pour myself a glass of white wine from the carton in the fridge. It's that time anyway.

"Did you tell Maya Bean and Ben Ben yet?" I ask, after taking a slurp of the wine.

She makes a noise to stop the sobbing.

"No," she says, her voice still thick. "I wanted to call you first."

I can see why. Jonathan was their father as well, but they were never as close to him as Lily. Maya will consider his death a rightful and just act of God since everything in her world is a rightful and just act of God. She has handed over her free will and personal opinions to the Lord and Derrick and relies on them to take care of her in every which way. Ben is no more self-guided than Maya. He has just given up. He decided he will never amount to anything and then sat back to wait for it to come true. He is caught in this chicken and egg loop, where he is neither.

"I can call them!" I volunteer without knowing why.

Maybe it is to get off this call. But Lily will not let me go that easy.

"No, no," she says and slips back into mothering me, "let me do that. I need to wish Maya a happy birthday anyway. I'm sure this will ruin it. But if you can call Uncle James?"

I hadn't even thought of that. Someone has to let James know. And that someone is me. Maybe that was her plan all along. She can be clever that way, my Lily. She is right, though. James should hear it from me. I am the one who is closest to him. I am the one who has Jonathan in common with him. We are at the same level of Jonathanness.

I haven't talked to James in a while. I have held back. I know why, but I am not capable of saying it or doing anything about it. Ben doesn't get his inaction from strangers. I judge myself too.

"Sure, I can do that," I say, but I am not sure at all.

"Thank you, Mom!" Lily says, now sounding a little lighter. "If you can let him know, Dad is at John F. Kennedy Memorial Hospital in Indio, and I'll call him later to discuss details for the funeral."

She is the organizer, that girl, and however much I dislike being told what to do by her, I don't want to do it myself.

"Okay," I say, trying to not be too snide about it.

"I better go," she says. "Love you, Mom."

And just like that, she is gone again.

I sit down at the kitchen table with my wine. I wonder if something has ended in my life, but it hasn't. Jonathan in my life ended long ago. It ended so hard that I haven't opened nor wished to open the door since then. His sporadic intrusions have been unwelcome, to say the least. Like a stomach bug and usually not lasting any longer.

Still, I have rarely wished him dead. I am sad to say that it would be too good for him. I have wanted to punish him for everything he did to me. For luring me in, for making me believe in him, for making me love him, for loving me in his own deficient way. He should be punished for that, and getting what he wanted and finding peace is no punishment.

I don't believe in heaven or hell or the afterlife, but if there is such a thing, I know that Jonathan has managed to trick himself into heaven. He has spun a tale to Saint Peter of how he is a victim who has survived for so long, despite the adversity heaped upon him, and Saint Peter believed him. There is no cosmic justice. I will go to hell for my petty sins; he will go to heaven on a monumental lie.

I have often wondered what made people believe him. It was as if they wanted to be conned, to be charmed, to be duped. They want to believe in fairytales. That the underdog can win. That there is good in people. And there is. Just not in Jonathan. The good there is in people has to be protected from people like Jonathan. Because he will ruin it. Look at me. LOOK AT ME. Here I am, on a Monday afternoon, drinking before 5 PM and wishing the dead father of my children something worse than that. He ruined me. And now I will never be right again. Once again, he broke something but didn't stick around to fix it.

I sigh. I take a deep breath in and let it out long again. How come I fall apart now? The whole thing is like an exhale. An exhale I have held back for more than thirty years. That is how long I have leaned against him, first to let him in, then to keep him out. That is how long I have been in his shadow. That is how long I have been under his cloud. There have been happier times in my life where I pretended he wasn't there, but now there is nothing. There is nothing to press up against. There is nothing to prove wrong. There is no purpose, no direction.

Moment 46

Fresno, CA
Tuesday, July 6th, 1999, 10:10 AM
I am 54 years old

We all scramble to our feet as the organ begins to play the intro to "The Lord Is My Shepherd." The choir starts on the first line, and the rest of us fall in as best we can. The church is filled to the brim. I don't understand how that can be. There should be no one but us. The nearest family. The ones who got the calls in the middle of the night when Jonathan was teetering on the edge. That wouldn't even include me anymore. Nowadays, the calls all go to Lily, who then contacts James. I think. I would be happy not to be here.

But I have to. It would not be right otherwise. He was the father of my children, but he never was a father to them. He once was my love. The sun in my solar system. And I thought no one else would come today. But here we are. All crowded out.

I am sure he would have liked it this way. He would have felt that this was nothing but proper. Even if his appearance and health and circumstances have been on a steady decline for thirty years, nothing had dimmed his mind and confidence. He was convinced he could still charm the pants off any woman he met, and that belief could easily have made it so. He must have judging by the audience here.

I wonder how many are Lily, Maya, and Ben's half-siblings. And why they never have come forward before, but I don't know that they didn't. Jonathan was never one for monogamy - not even on a serial basis—he believed in love for all as it showed up in his presence. And it seemed to do that all the time.

I do see Jessica here. Her hair still black, and her posture straight and proud. Were they married till the end? I think we would have run into her more over the years if they were, but then again, I only ever met her that once when I sought her out. No, Lily would have said something about it. Or not.

Considering how much she has been drawn to her father, we never talked a lot about him. She made up her mind about him before I could taint it with my feelings, and that kept it intact all these years. However, much I have warned her about him has only reflected on her opinion of me, not him. She has never taken my advice, and if she did, she wouldn't admit it in court.

I feel sorry for her today. She was so much closer to him than I, and seeing all these people here must hit her harder. She doesn't show it. She has her game face on. Maybe she has already said her goodbyes.

She was the one who drove him up here. She and Craig, her husband. The urn with the ashes in the backseat of their car. He was cremated in Palm Springs a couple of days ago. It was more practical and cheaper that way. Now he sits on a table in between the two front pews. There are white flowers around the urn and an old photo of him from back when he worked at his father's dealership. Handsome as hell. His death wish didn't show back then.

This is how he would want to be remembered. I think right now he is. All the people might have private memories of him that say something different, but this is how we all saw him to begin with. This is what lured us in.

"...And in God's house forevermore

My dwelling place shall be."

The music fades out, and we sit down again. I have Robert to my left and Ben to my right. Ben wears one of Robert's old suits, and it isn't good. I always thought Ben would grow into himself take on his own proportions, but now at 30, that hasn't happened yet. He is still uncomfortable—awkward—in everything but ripped saggy jeans and worn-out t-shirts. It is as if his self-awareness is too small to cover his whole body. He looks trapped in the dark gray suit and nearly white shirt as if the clothes have taken him hostage. Even more so because the shirt and jacket are very tight around his back and shoulders. He is a beige-pink Hulk without the power to break free. It makes me fuss over him. Fret and fuss.

Even if he has not said so, I know he wonders why he is here. He never had any contact with Jonathan. Never spent time with him. Never talked to him. Never knew him. Only through Lily and me. That might be his reason for being here. That his beloved sister-mother told him to be. Lily used to worship Jonathan, and Ben worships Lily. Grief by association.

Lily sits on the other side of Ben, then her husband, Craig. Then Maya's husband Derrick the Pious, and then Maya. What a crew. Lily is the foreman at the center. We are the workers at her command. We have not been trusted with much. Maya chose the flowers and the three hymns for the service under Lily's strict condition that "normal people"— meaning other than Maya and her husband—should be able to sing them. So we still have "All Things Bright and Beautiful" and "Amazing Grace" to go. Derrick is not happy about being told what to do by Lily or having to mingle with us heathens, but then again, Derrick is never happy because that can lead to sin. I can see him flogging himself in his monk cell at night or indulge in bondage with his fellow church people, but that is my warped mind running away with me. I am sure he is nice.

Father Bill turns around to face us. His hair is white-gray and Einstein crazy; he stoops a little, which makes his small frame seem wider than it is, and his movements all have a slight tremor. He has always been priest to the Burkes. He has married and buried Jonathan's parents, baptized and confirmed Jonathan and James, and must have mixed feelings of how much of his obligations towards the family are done, now that he can see his own end coming.

"We are gathered here today to pay our last respects to our beloved Jonathan Burke." he booms with more force than expected.

It hits me that Jonathan is dead to everyone here. That he has ceased to exist for everybody, not just me and the few people I know. That everyone here must be conflicted about this goodbye. That most of us have seen him at his best and some of us at his worst. It is a strange feeling of community and invasion of my privacy at the same time. I have always known that he wasn't mine alone, but it is boundary-crossing to meet the proof of it like this.

"Jonathan Burke was, as many of you know, the oldest son of Gordon and Mary Beth Burke." the priest continues. "The Burkes have been pillars of this church and our community as far back as I can remember, and it is with great sorrow that we see the family decimated in this way. Jonathan was known and loved by everyone here today, and it can be difficult to understand why his time on this earth had to come to an end."

I don't like the way he says it. I don't like that he glosses over the fact that Jonathan, with clear intention, drank and drugged himself to death. I don't like that Jonathan is glorified because he doesn't deserve that. However, Father Bill cannot bloody well say, "Jonathan Burke was a raging narcissist with little respect or feeling for anyone but himself, and he finally succeeded in killing himself as had been his goal for many years."

It would be a refreshing honesty if he did. It just bothers me that Jonathan is made into someone better than he was. That is what the church is to me. Not a place without judgment as it claims. But a place that turns the judgment on me because I am too small to see Jonathan in the light in which he is painted here. Such hypocrisy. Love thy neighbor. Well, in this case, the neighbor was a jerk and incapable of loving me back, and somehow I feel that was my fault.

I was never loved. Not by my father. Not by my mother. Not by Jonathan. Yes, my children loved me when they were young, but only because they didn't know better yet. Robert might think he loves me, but who he really loves is his wife, and I am just a close enough replacement.

And I am supposed to grieve over him. Him. I can only grieve for myself. For my misunderstandings. For my missed opportunities. For my misdirections. That is why I am here now. For me.

"...though Jonathan moved away from our community a while back, he was never forgotten, to which all of you here today are a testament. Please rise as we say the Lord's Prayer together."

I must have missed the good part of the speech if there was one. We stand up again and mumble as an echo to the true believers.

"Our Father who art in heaven

Hallowed be thy name.

Thy kingdom come.

Thy will be done

On earth, as it is in heaven.

Give us this day our daily bread

And forgive us our trespasses

As we forgive those who trespass against us

And lead us not into temptation

But deliver us from evil.

For thine is the kingdom

And the power and the glory

Forever

Amen."

Where was this Father when I needed him? How did he not lead me into temptation? There is nothing for me here, but painful reminders of the many ways I am not worthy.

We sit down again. I want to run for the door. The organ plays some sort of interlude to allow for quiet contemplations of Jonathan's life and love. To my surprise, Ben grabs my hand for support while he whispers something under his breath with his eyes closed. I guess this place takes hold of him too.

The music ends, and Lily makes her way to the table with Jonathan's urn and picture. She turns around and looks at people but not at us— her family—since we are to the side of her. She smiles a sad smile and unfolds a piece of paper in her hand.

"As some of you might know, I'm Lily, Jonathan's daughter," She says in a steady but quiet voice, "and over here is my sister Maya and my brother Ben."

She indicates them with her arm.

"My father was not a big presence in my life, and for that, I am sorry." she continues.

I try not to let the words sting me.

"But the time I did spend with him was precious, and he meant a lot to me."

She pauses to wipe the tears from her eyes so she can read her notes.

"Above anything else, he taught me I should live my life to the fullest. There is no reason to hold back on my love and passion. When we talked about big things like that, he would always hum this Doors song to himself,

'The time to hesitate is through

No time to wallow in the mire

Try now we can only lose

And our love become a funeral pyre'"

She pauses again to catch her breath.

"That was the way he lived his life. With love and passion and only regretting the chances he didn't take. I know that is how he wanted to be remembered, and I hope you will. Thank you all for coming, and thank you for allowing me to speak."

Rather than walking back to her seat, she sits down next to Maya and squeezes her hand. It is clear to me that Lily knew a different Jonathan than

I. A younger Jonathan. A Jonathan who had aspirations, perhaps on her behalf but aspirations nonetheless. She was a peer to him. Maybe even an upgrade. He saw his own qualities reflected and crystallized in her. I, on the other hand, was a mere vessel for her wonder. A suitable carrier. Once again, I am jealous of my own daughter. Jealous of everyone here. If it had not been for them, I would have been the only one.

We all stand up to sing "All Things Bright and Beautiful." I wonder if there is another song about who made all the things that are dim and ugly. It doesn't seem that they came off the heavenly assembly line. Maybe the backroom of Santa's workshop?

I have reached my limit. I can't be here anymore. It is too much confrontation. Too painful. I put the psalm book down on the pew and grab my purse at my feet, and while people are still singing, I edge my way past Robert and walk down through the church and out on the street and down a block where Robert parked the car. It is not until I get there I realize that I don't have a key for it. I switched out my purse yesterday and didn't think to bring car keys as Robert would be driving.

I stand by the car and can't make up my mind on what to do. I don't want to stand here until the service is done. I don't want to go back to the church. I don't want to go too far away so Robert can't find me. I just want to go home and be done with it. This is ripping into too many old wounds. Old ways of doubting myself. It just hurts too much. I want to go back to my life as it is now and then let the rest of them deal with this thing.

Lily has taken charge of the situation, and I should just let her. If she wants to, she can have it. I don't want to have to be invited to my own life. I don't want to share. That is what it comes down to. I don't want to share. Jonathan never gave me enough. Never loved me enough. I need the illusion that it wasn't because he gave it to someone else. I need the illusion that it wasn't because of me but because he couldn't give anymore. I need the illusion that I was worthy of his love.

But instead of granting me that, Lily is pissing all over it. Instead of being grateful that I brought her into this world, she turns around and tells me all the ways I did her wrong. Is that the gift of motherhood? Is it?

I don't regret having kids, but at this moment I do. I regret that after all these years, I still have to pay for my sins.

I walk further down the street and see a green area on the corner on the other side. I would be able to see the car from there, and there might be a bench to sit down on. I cross the street and walk up to a little white pavilion with benches inside. I sit down and discover that I still hear that damn hymn in my head. All things bright and beautiful. That seems to be the motto for Fresno nowadays. I haven't been here since the mid-seventies when Jonathan had one of his blackouts, and that time, we only went to the hospital. Fresno is all changed since I lived here. New city hall, new parks, new hospital, new arena. This is not what my youth looked like. This is so foreign to me that I might as well never have been here before. That is okay. I have no desire to go back. No more open wounds.

I watch the traffic go by. The flow changing with the lights. There is a bus stop on the corner, which breaks the rhythm because people have to get off. I let myself be absorbed by the cars until I catch sight of Robert next to the car. I get up and hurry over there while I wave so he can see me, too. He is by himself. Ben must have gone with either Maya or Lily. That is good. That means we can just take off.

Robert has seen me and waits by the open car door.

"Where did you go?" he asks as I reach the car.

"I couldn't stay," I say, hoping I don't have to explain it to him.

"Can we please go home?" I ask.

"What about the coffee thing then?" Robert says, concerned and hungry.

"I'm sure they can manage without us. And we can get something on the way," I say, crossing my fingers.

"Okay," says Robert and gets into the driver's seat.

I walk around to the passenger side and get in, too, thinking that there is love in my life after all.

Moment 47

Bishop, CA
Thursday, April 30th, 2009, 1:15 PM
I am 64 years old

We have stopped for lunch at Schat's Bakery, Robert and I. We are on our way to Lily's house for the weekend. I don't like to go anymore, but she was very insistent on the phone, so I didn't think we had an option. We could have flown in, but then we wouldn't have a car and couldn't leave when we want to. Driving is better, even if it takes longer. We will be there tonight.

We have ordered a ham and cheese sandwich and an egg salad sandwich to share and a slice of red velvet cake for dessert. They don't serve wine or beer here, so we will have to stop somewhere for dinner as well. The sign with our order number is on our table together with my lemonade and Robert's coffee.

"Mark is cheating on me!" says a woman at the table next to us to her friend and bursts into tears. She looks short and has dark brown hair in a bob, brown eyes, and perfect makeup.. Someone once told me that if you are going to cry in makeup, you just have to let the tears run and not touch your face until they have dried. Cheated-on woman is not taking that advice. Her friend is her exact opposite. Tall with long blonde hair, but I can't see her face from where I sit, and the tables are too close that I can ask Robert. Not that he would answer anyway. He hates being privy to other people's conversations and usually finds something idiotic to talk about to shut it out.

"Did you pack my red sweater?" he asks me like it's a matter of life and death. "You know I need it for the evening walks."

It is a matter of life and death then. When we are at Lily's, her husband Craig and Robert go on long evening walks in the hills behind their house to get away from the talking and us women. I think neither Robert nor Craig would survive without those walks. I know they bring flashlights and maybe also a beer for a break, but have no idea what they talk about or if they talk at all. I envy them. It must be so much better than the interrogations I usually go through inside.

The woman's friend has grabbed her hands over the table, maybe to stop her from rubbing her face any more.

"Oh no! I am so sorry, Gail!" the friend says. "Tell me as little or as much as you want."

"Well, have you?" Robert says with irritation.

"Yes," I say without being able to tear my eyes off Gail. "That and the gray one, too."

"The neighbor told me," Gail cries, "she couldn't stand to see her come over when I had night shifts. My own home, Bri! Oh my God, I'm so stupid!"

My heart goes out to Gail. It must be awful.

A girl with a tray edges her way to our table and almost throws down the sandwiches and cake. Robert thanks her loudly, so I can't hear how Bri responds, but she must have asked about what Gail wants to do.

"I just want to get out," Gail sniffles now a little calmer. "I don't care what he does, I just want to get out. Maybe I can go to my parents'. My Dad'll kill him."

"Do you want the egg or the ham and cheese?" Robert tries to distract me again.

"I don't care," I say, not to miss anything, "You choose."

"We can also split them both?" He plows on.

"Yes, fine," I say.

"Do you mind cutting them?" He almost yells at me.

I shoot him a look annoyed that he is keeping me from the drama of the day. This is better than TV. I manage to flatten both sandwiches beyond recognition with the dull knife and dump the halves on our plates and then return my attention to Gail and Bri while eating.

Gail cries hard again. Bri holds her hand.

"You know whatever you need, I'm here for you!" Bri says.

"I know!" Gail sobs. "Thank you!"

It occurs to me that I don't have any close friends. Not like this. The friends we have now do not share their problems, and they never ask about ours. Not relationship problems anyway. Only kidney stones and bypass operations. We see them for special occasions; 60th and 70th birthdays, gold or silver wedding anniversaries, dependent on what number marriage it is. Since our high-performance days are behind us, we now compete on the success of our children. Who got a promotion, who has a new car, who reproduced.

This could have something to do with our age, but it doesn't. I never had friends. James might be counted, but he was family by the time he was a friend. Betty was like a mother to me. The mother I never had. I haven't thought about her in years. Decades. I guess Robert is a friend but not a close one. We are from different species, him and I, and we don't speak the same language.

I am not friends with my children either. For that, we fight way too much to give up or acquire the responsibility of parenthood. Lily still wants to mother me all the time. Maya doesn't care. Ben will not let me go and grow up. Same old, same old.

I try to figure out if I miss it. Having close friends. But how can I miss something I never had? My troubles are nobody's business. I don't even want them to be my business. And I have enough of them to want to take on somebody else's, too.

But looking at Gail and Bri. The way they sit there next to us squeezing each other's hands. That gets me. That makes me see the hole inside of me.

Moment 48

Calabasas, CA
Thursday, April 30th, 2009, 8:35 PM
I am 64 years old.

"Mom, I have cancer," Lily says.

Geez, I think, why don't you just spring it on me? Then my brain goes blank. I look around to figure out where I am and what just happened. Ten seconds ago, I was on the back patio at Lily's house with a glass of white wine and some salted almonds and bushes in bloom and hummingbirds buzzing around for nectar and the cat greeting me by leaning against my leg.

Now I am not so sure. It looks the same but feels like a parallel universe where reality has gone into reverse. Like I am the dumb bimbo in a horror movie who gets a ride from the serial killer assuming everyone is good until proven otherwise. Like I am about to die. I catch myself in that thought because that's not right either.

Lily is the one who is going to die. She just said that. I remember. Only I wish she hadn't. Why would she say a thing like that? Death is no joke. I can be difficult at times, but she shouldn't get back at me like that. I am bad, but I don't deserve that. It's not like her. She likes to provoke me. Push my boundaries. But that is usually with participating in drum circles or crystal readings and then pretending it has real meaning. This is out of character.

What if it's true? What if she really has cancer? That would be terrible. I don't know if I can handle that. I might just combust or keel over and die. Just like that. Disappear from the earth.

"Mom, did you hear what I said?" Lily asks.

I don't know how to answer that. I think I heard what she said but what if I am wrong? I can see she wants me to say something, but I need more time.

"Hhhmm?" I say and look at her face.

It doesn't look different. Maybe a few more crows' feet around the eyes, but that is to be expected. Her eyes are still sparkly and hazel like always. No makeup today, so I guess she didn't have to go into work. Maybe I didn't hear her right. She seems alright to me. Thank God.

"I said, I have cancer," she says. "They found a lump in my breast, and it is malignant."

I try to take it in once more, but it's like being the last person at musical chairs. It has nowhere to sit in my mind. It doesn't fit there. This is not how it's supposed to be.

"Are you sure?" I say, and I can hear how dumb it sounds, but these mistakes happen all the time. I look around for support. Someone to agree with me, but there is no one else here. Robert and Craig have gone on their walk to shake the ride out of Robert's back, and the kids are somewhere else. Even the cat has made itself scarce.

"Yes, I'm sure," she says with an overbearing sad smile. "We got a second opinion."

Well, get a third, I think, because this one isn't working for me. I can't get close to it. I can't get on the other side of it. I can't get with it. It gets stuck on me. It is a glob of green alien slime stuck on my shirt, and I don't want it there. It is the orange shirt from Nordstrom Rack that Lily got me at the Black Friday sale last year, and I don't want it to be infected with this. Maybe I should go take it off and wear something else that I care less about. I think I did bring a plain white t-shirt to wear underneath. That would be better.

I can't get up. It would not be right. And also, I can't feel my legs, so walking might be out of the question. Anger rises up in me. Frustrated anger. Frustration that I can't process this fast enough. That I don't understand.

That I know that there is something I should be doing, and it's not staring into my lap or getting another sip of wine like I'm actually doing. I should probably embrace my daughter, embrace the whole thing, and absorb it into my body, but I don't want to do that. I don't want it on me. I don't want it in me. I want to be safe. And this isn't it.

I am angry that I can't get past myself. Really angry. Beyond angry. I want to stand up and scream at myself. Scold myself. Let myself know what a poor mother I am that I can't handle this. Let myself know how utterly selfish I am to make this about me. So angry. Anger is blocking me like a wall. Only small and insufficient comments can make it through. Like I'm sorry, or that's bad, or poor you. Things I can't say to my daughter, who has cancer because they don't reach the knees of what I feel. And I can't tell the whole of what I feel because I don't want to put that on her. She shouldn't have to carry that. She shouldn't carry me. I should carry her.

I don't have the strength. My strength has dissipated. Because I didn't use it, I guess. It left when I thought I was done with it. When I thought I wouldn't be called upon again. When I thought I had succeeded in making my babies safe. I didn't understand that no one is ever safe. The Universe can punish me at any time without warning for thinking I know better. Because clearly, I don't. I say it anyway,

"I'm sorry!"

I know it doesn't cut it and search Lily's face to see if she does too. Yes. There it is. The disbelief of me thinking I can get away with that. The hurt that I can't step up. The disappointment of letting her down once more.

"I don't know what else to say." I try to explain. But it sounds all wrong. I would get really pissed at me if I were her. It bubbles up as redness on her neck and cheeks and fire in her eyes, and it is all she can do to not let it out of her mouth.

"I know it's a lot to take in, Mom," she says. "But I didn't want to tell you over the phone and just leave you hanging."

I wish she would have. I wish she hadn't cared about how I feel. I wish she didn't have me in this vice. I am paralyzed by her and her mothering me. She is the one making it about me, and I can't break free of that. She will not step down. We cannot be each other's mother at the same time. Only one of us can hold the spot. And Lily isn't moving.

She needs to make room for me. She needs to give it up. She needs to let it go. But instead, she says,

"If you need to talk to someone about this, I can find you a good therapist."

Always so helpful and not helpful at all. What am I going to say to that? Yes, and admit defeat? No, and be callous? Why does she have to fix everything? Why does she have to do everything better than me? I never get a chance to do it my way.

I don't want to talk to a therapist. He would judge me. Size me up and think I am a horrible person. Tell his wife about me when he gets home at night. Call Lily and let her know I am a lost cause. I want to talk to someone human. Someone with flaws and feelings. Someone who won't write me up and treat me like a case. A patient. A disease.

Most of all, I want to talk to Betty. I didn't understand why she popped into my head earlier today, but she knew this was coming. She knew she would have to be ready for me. She knew. That is what I long to do. Talk to my mother. Because that is what you are supposed to do when you are in trouble. Talk to your mother.

Moment 49

Calabasas, CA
Friday, May 1st, 2009, 2:20 AM
I am 64 years old

I stare at the ceiling in Lily's guest room. The shadows go on and off with some critter triggering the floodlights in the neighbor's driveway. It must be building a nest or feeding its family because it is walking back and forth a lot. Someone is on top of things.

Not me. I'm not on top of anything. I'm so far on the bottom of things that there is nowhere left to sink. My daughter has cancer, and I can't cope. I have been frozen since she told me many hours ago. I am out of order. Of no use.

I have tried to wiggle out of my suspended state but have had no luck. Wine hasn't worked, but then again, it never does. I talked to Robert as we were getting ready for bed.

"Lily has cancer," I said.

"I know," Robert said. "Craig told me."

I couldn't think of something to add to that, and Robert mustn't have found it necessary because he just continued to put on his PJ and then crawled into bed with the Wall Street Journal. I got on my nightgown and followed him. I didn't brush my teeth because leaving the guest room seemed unsafe. I didn't want to risk bumping into anybody or overhear any conversations. So here I am with bad breath and open eyes. Trapped in this room. This body. This mind.

I wait for Betty to find me. I don't know where she is. She should still be out there. She is no less dead than she was, so not a lot could have changed, could it? What if she has gone on to live another life somewhere else? Would her spirit still be available to me?

I haven't talked to her since our wedding. That was twenty-seven years ago. She didn't agree with me, and I shut her out. She said to not settle. She thought Robert was boring and too safe a bet. I got offended because she was right. So we stopped talking. Another relationship that I've failed at.

Now I need her to come back. I am willing to apologize. To concede. To take the blame if she'll just set me straight now. I can't remember what she sounds like. I picture her in my mind. Her face on the pillow in her room at the Williams' house. Her foul mouth. *Limp dick* that is what she used to call Robert.

"Are you still with that limp dick?" she says.

"Yes, I am," I say. "Good to hear from you, Betty!"

"Took you some time, didn't it?" she remarks.

She sounds a little huffy. She is entitled to.

"Are you getting laid?" she asks.

"No," I say.

There is no point in lying to her.

"Why not?" she asks like I knew she would. "You're not dead, are you?"

"No." I smile.

I smile for the first time in a long while. Years it seems, but surely that can't be true. My face is unfamiliar with the movement of the muscles. Stiff and rusty. I can almost hear it creak.

"I am 64," I say as if that explains anything.

"Bullshit!" she says. "I enjoyed a good fuck long into my seventies, and I wasn't as flexible as you. Is it because of limp dick? They have pills to fix that now, you know?"

Good old Betty.

"So why did you call me, dear?" she asks.

"Lily has cancer," I reply.

It feels good to say it. Not nearly as big as in my head.

"Wow, that sucks!" Betty says. "Did you have a good cry about it yet?"

No, I didn't, but now I can feel the tears coming. I let them run out of the lower corners of my eyes and sideways on my face down into my ears without wiping them away. I try to be quiet, so I don't wake Robert up, but usually, a freight train could cut through the bed without waking him up. He is a good sleeper.

"Yes, but that doesn't ring your bell." Betty points out.

I get it all out. All the hurt. All the self-pity. All the anger. Then I let my face dry and sit up to have a sip of water. I feel empty and better now.

"So, what do you wanna do about it?" Betty asks.

"I don't know" I admit. "What do you think?"

She doesn't say anything. That is what I feared. She doesn't know either.

"If it was you, what would you want her to do?" she asks.

"Not worry!" It just flies out of my mouth.

"Well, that's a start," Betty says with some skepticism.

"I guess I could offer to take the kids some time," I say without conviction.

"Really?" Betty snorts. "But, you hate those brats!"

I don't know how Betty knows this, but then again, she is in my head. And she is right. I am not a big fan of Lily's children, to say the least. They treat grownups like servants and only want to watch TV. They leave a trail of dirty clothes, dirty plates, and trash behind, and they speak only in derisive grunts. It would be like having Ben move home again, just without any gratitude. I shudder at the thought.

"No, you are right," I say. "But then what?"

"Maybe you can sit with her," Betty suggests. "Just like you sat with me in the end."

I feel inside if I can do that. I'm not too sure. It is different to sit with an old lady who is dying of age than to sit with a child dying of cancer.

"You don't know she's dying," Betty says.

"What?" I say, confused.

"You said 'to sit with a dying child.' You don't know she's dying."

I realize that is true. These days cancer doesn't have to be a death sentence. It can be treated. I just assumed to be on the safe side.

"Well, there's a cheery mom!"

Betty's sarcasm is endless.

"I don't want her to die!" I try to explain, "I was just trying to protect myself. Prepare for the worst, so I wouldn't get any surprises later."

"Okay," Betty says but doesn't mean it.

I feel forced and say, "Alright, alright! I think I can sit with her."

"There you go!" Betty approves. "Now hold on to that thought and go to sleep. We'll talk more later!"

And just as quickly as I summoned her, she is gone again, and I am alone in the dark with Robert.

Moment 50

Calabasas, CA
Friday, May 1st, 2009, 8:05 AM
I am 64 years old

"I'm sorry, Mom, but that's not good enough," Lily says.

She is at the stove, scrambling eggs to keep herself occupied. Her budding anger is another means to that end, but I'm not sticking my head in there. All I said was that I had a hard time taking this cancer thing in.

Lily turns off the burner with the eggs and faces me. I sit in the breakfast nook to the right with my coffee.

"I didn't get cancer to get back at you or teach you a lesson," she says a little louder and with a slight tremble in her voice. "I didn't wake up one morning and think it'd be a great idea to have some fucking crazy cells grow in my boobs to mess up your life. I don't think that way. You do!"

I wince and have to break her stare. She is too strong for me. She means this. I swear I didn't want to upset her, and now I am on thin ice. I deserve that. What a pitiful excuse for a mother I am.

"I didn't mean to upset you, Lily Pad." I try. "All I meant was it breaks my heart!"

"Oh, it breaks your heart?" she yells at me. "Well, then I'll stop it right now! Oh wait, I can't because it's FUCKING CANCER!"

Lily cries when she gets angry. Just like me. I bet she hates that. She has folded herself into her chest and sobs down her shirt. Her shoulders shake. I feel like I should do something, but I am afraid that it'll make her angrier. I get up from the bench with my coffee cup and put it in the dishwasher next to the sink. I take a quick glance outside the kitchen window to the driveway where Craig and Robert load the kids into the minivan to take them to school. It doesn't seem they heard any of the screamings. Then I walk over to Lily and put a hand on her upper arm. It is an awkward gesture, but it is the best I can think of.

"Get away from me!" she hisses. "Get away from me, you fucking cunt!"

I let my hand fall and think about how many of these conversations we have had in her lifetime. Hundreds. Thousands maybe even. But not for years, so I am out of practice. Her words hurt. Whether it is what she truly thinks of me or it is her fear and sadness talking, they still hurt.

A better mother would have hugged her. A better mother would have showered her with love. A better mother would have already forgiven her. That is not me. I need her to stay mad at me. I need her to stay right where she is. I need her degrading words. They are all part of my just sentence.

And in some way, she needs me too. She needs me as her punching bag. She needs me to not live up to her expectations. She needs me to let her down. That is how she gathers her strength. That is how she pulls herself up from the floor. That is how she keeps going. And I am more than happy to oblige it seems.

I walk out of the kitchen and down the hallway to the guest room. It is the only closed door. Lily and her family don't believe in them. I let myself in and close the door behind me. Then I sit down on the edge of the rolled-out sofa bed. Her words still ring in my head, and I am sure they will for a while. I am going to give her some space. I think she needs that. I just need to figure out what to do in the meantime.

I am almost done with the book I brought. *Fearless Fourteen* by Janet Evanovich. Just an easy read. The same storyline as the previous thirteen. Not hard to follow at all. But I relate to the main character. She reminds me of myself at that age but without my broken home, narcissistic boyfriend, and three kids. Stumbling through her life with no real sense of direction.

She never seems to age. If her life moves at the speed of the books being released, she should be close to forty now and in a permanent state of panic. I am putting too much sense into it, I know. I just enjoy the mindless entertainment. That someone is seemingly worse off than I. I guess I could read the rest and get it over with.

I still need to brush my teeth, but then I have to go back out, and I don't want to do that right now. I decide to tidy up the room before I do anything. I pick up Robert's reading glasses and Thursday's Wall Street Journal from the floor on his side of the bed. He still reads that front to back every day. Keeps him informed, he says. I don't know what he needs to stay informed about, it's not like he's doing anything. I am a little bit testy too, it seems.

I fold his PJ and put it back in our suitcase. Light blue with white edges it is. Every time I think he has worn through the last of these suckers, there is another one. It makes him look as old as he is. There is not a lot of sex in that. But then again, the same could be said for my off-white nightgown. And the granny panties and sagging breasts. I am one to talk. It seems by mutual agreement, we have let that thing go, and I hadn't thought about it for a while until Betty popped back into my head last night. I don't miss having sex with Robert. I miss being young and having sex with someone. There is quite a difference.

I move on to fold up the bedsheets and put them away so the bed can be turned back into a sofa. Just as I am about to do that, Lily interrupts me by opening the door.

"I've thought about it, Mom," she says like she just wants to give me some helpful advice. "I think you and Robert should leave!"

I turn to look at her puzzled.

"This is a difficult time for me, and you're not helping," she says. "I would like you to leave. When Robert and Craig come back."

"Okay," I say more as a comment than an agreement.

I do feel a surge of relief. Maybe this was what I was waiting for all along. To be let off the hook. Maybe this is for the best. Maybe it's easier if we put some distance between us. That can work.

"If that's what you want," I say, all too easily giving up the fight.

"That is what I want," she says. "Thank you!"

She steps backward and closes the door again. I know this is not what she wants. It is not what I want either. But it is the best we can do right now. Maybe it will work like one of those water injection things I heard about. Where water is injected just under the skin on the lower back to distract a woman in labor from the contractions. Me leaving will sting so much Lily forgets about the cancer—or at least doesn't think about it as much. I know I am making a virtue of necessity, but so be it. I need time to think too. Time to process this. Time to understand.

I continue with tidying up the room, erasing every trace of us, so it doesn't stick out like a sore thumb once we are gone. I don't want to leave anything behind. I pull away the curtains to let the sun in and open the window to air the room out. I take out Robert's favorite red sweater from the suitcase. He will want that for the car. If I am fast, we can be out of here by nine.

Moment 51

Elko, NV
Monday, June 8th, 2009, 10:10 AM
I am 64 years old

"Hi, Mom!" Lily says, determined to get it over with. "They want me to do some chemo to make sure it's all gone. I'd like you to come with me."

Her voice doesn't sound different, and that makes me breathe a little easier. I must have expected it to. We haven't spoken in over a month. Not since she kicked me out. I guess she has needed that time to fight for herself. She went and had her surgery, and Craig kept us up to date with text messages a couple of times a day. I have wanted to call, but every time I get close to dialing her number, something holds me back. Fear. Fear of being unable to cope. Fear of her dying. Fear of being asked to take part. Fear of her needing me. Fear of her not needing me. Fear of her having shown me the door forever. As long as I don't know any details, it isn't real. I can keep it at bay.

I haven't told anyone about Lily's cancer. Just another way of shutting reality out. What mother doesn't rush to her daughter's side when she is gravely ill? That mother would be me. I know I won't be able to defend that to anyone, so I just don't tell.

I am not going to question what made her change her mind. I am just going to be grateful she did. I take a deep breath and say,

"Of course, Lily Pad! When do you need me to be there?"

Moment 52

Los Angeles, CA
Tuesday, July 7th, 2009, 10:15 AM
I am 64 years old

"At home, the flowers behind the bench are still looking nice," I say and hear how ridiculous it sounds.

As if chemotherapy wasn't uncomfortable enough, we just can't seem to talk to each other while it goes on. It was the same the last time we were here. Somehow, the situation is too serious and too absurd for us to come up with anything meaningful to say. The world is ending, and we talk about peanuts at the bar.

Speaking of which, I have put myself on a regiment. If Lily can go through cancer treatment, I can cut down on the wine. I think. I am of no use to her if I am falling apart and letting myself go. So here is to me trying.

"That's nice," Lily says, distracted by the toxins flowing into left her arm through the IV.

All the stories about chemo making you sick as a dog are true. Lily had hoped that she would be the one person in the statistics that went unscathed, but she is not. She has barely gotten her head out of the toilet from the last time, and now we are here again. Her beautiful curly long brown hair has started to come out in big clumps, and it is just because of the holiday weekend, she hasn't gotten it all buzzed off yet. She wears a pale orange scarf around her remaining locks, and it makes her look like Rosie the Riveter, but without the strength and determination.

"That is a nice scarf," I say. "Where did you get that?"

"Nice smice!" Betty exclaims. "What the hell is wrong with you?"

Betty has been on my case. She keeps me straight. She doesn't let me take the easy way out. She mocks me and scolds me and calls me every name in her book. She can be mean. But I'm glad she's back in my head. I need someone to talk to. Someone who knows me. Robert is fine. He knows me. He knows me well enough not to criticize me even if he disagrees with the way I have been handling Lily's cancer. He would never ever leave his boys if they were in the same situation, which of course, they would never be because they are perfect. He stood by his wife as much as he could when she got sick. He still loves her. Not that he doesn't love me, but she has aged way better in his memory than I have in real life. That is another thing I can't fight against. I snap myself out of it.

Betty is right. I should think of something more profound to say.

My mind is blank. Just like every other time in my life when it has been crucial that I stepped up to the plate. Maybe in order to save herself from disappointment, Lily lets me off the hook.

"You don't have to say anything, Mom," she says. "Just sit here and be still with me."

Moment 53

Los Angeles, CA
Monday, July 27th, 2009, 10:15 AM
I am 64 years old

"I don't understand why I have to go through this." Lily cries, "I am not a bad person."

It turns out that chemotherapy is like drinking all night with someone you don't know. In the beginning, you are polite. Try to be upbeat. Make it a party. If you are lucky, you can get the person to laugh with you. You have a good time while you keep drinking. Around 2 AM, you are all laughed out and so drunk and tired, you can speak nothing but the truth. That is when you get close. That is when you reveal yourself.

Here on the third cycle of chemo, the clock has finally struck 2 AM. Lily lets her guard down and speaks her truth.

As usual, I am all out of words, and there is no wine to get me talking. I squeeze her hand as an insufficient alternative.

"Is it because I'm not good enough?" she asks the Universe and me as its representative in this room. But I must have missed that day of employee training and can only say,

"No, honey, you are good enough."

It comes out all wrong. Like she is fine when she is more than amazing. Like she is no worse than anybody else when she is so much better and braver. Like she is adequate when she is the strongest one here.

I am the one who's failing. More than anytime else, I am failing as a mother, as a friend, as a person. I am so ill-prepared for having her lean on me that I am no support at all. I should scoop her up in my arms and hold her until all the pain and nausea and tiredness and hurt and frustration and anger are gone, but my embrace isn't big enough. It never was. I never could protect her. I never could alleviate her of any burdens. I never could. Once more, all I can do is step away so she can get stronger by herself.

"Come on, baby, you can do this!" is my sorry excuse for a cheer.

Moment 54

Los Angeles, CA
Monday, August 17th, 2009, 9:50 AM
I am 64 years old

Lily's husband, Craig, and Robert drop us off at the curb by The Samuel Oschin Comprehensive Cancer Institute, even if there is a sign that says NO PARKING in the front. Lily and I get out from the back seat in the minivan after Lily turns around and hugs Ben as much as she can from the awkward position.

The men are taking Ben home. It can hardly be called that because he lives on the property of a friend of a friend in Sylmar in a shed with no electricity or water. Then they are coming back to get us after Lily's chemo.

Craig drives out there every few weeks and picks up Ben so he can visit his sister and spent a couple of nights at their house in a nice bed and have a decent meal. Longer than that, Ben gets cabin fever and wants to go back to the outdoors and his stray dog companions.

Ben has been here a lot. He is probably the one—apart from Lily's son Hannibal—who has taken the cancer the hardest. I am pretty sure he comes here to have Lily assure him that she will be okay and in some convoluted way, that works for both of them. They have their own language. Their own way of being. Their own logic emerging from forty years of closeness.

Ben is the one person whom Lily can't let herself be weak in front of. He would lose his faith in the world if she did, and he is already not fully attached to reality.

The two of them, Lily and Ben, are so at ease with each other. They slip into their designated roles when together, and it is as if nothing has changed since they were five and two. Lily cares for Ben, and Ben adores her in return. And I am not part of that equation. I am only second in line to be his mother which is my own doing. Ben is still a baby duckling who will blindly follow the person who loves him the most, and that hasn't been me for many years.

I have to admit that I gave up on him. I let him go when he was in his twenties because I couldn't bear that he didn't grow up. I thought that would perhaps push him in the right direction, but clearly, it didn't. It just meant that Lily had to step up harder. Poor Lily and poor Ben. Holding on to each other for life.

Lily sends Ben finger kisses as the guys take off and then, we go in for another round of misery and torture.

Moment 55

Los Angeles, CA
Tuesday, September 8th, 2009, 10:15 AM
I am 64 years old

Lily leans back, closes her eyes, and slows her breathing as it has become her ritual for these chemo cycles. She seems to have resigned herself the horridness of the days we are here and the weeks of suffering that come after.

Despite her monumental struggle, she keeps being the unifying force of the family. We have been closer together in the past three months than in the last ten years. I can't remember everyone stepping up like this since Jonathan's memorial service.

Maya has put together a prayer circle that meets every Tuesday to ensure Lily's speedy recovery. They even offered to come here for the chemo, but Lily politely declined under the guise of lack of space at the outpatient center. It is all that there is room for her to bring one person with her during these sessions. I think they don't want chemo to be a big deal. Also, Maya comes on very strong with her opinions on medical treatment versus the power of the Lord, and Lily doesn't want her kid sister schooling the very people she relies on for survival.

Maya has not gotten less devoted to her faith over the years. All her major life decisions are in the hands of her two masters, God and Derrick, and they are keeping her on her toes. With eight kids and her duties as the pastor's wife, she has her work cut out for her around the clock. At least half the children are teenagers, and from what I hear from the sideline, not all of them as devout as their parents.

Maya has also stepped in to help with Lily's kids. Anabel and Hannibal, who are now eight and six years old, are devastated that their mother is ill. Especially, Hannibal is hit hard.

He has the black and white mind of any six-year-old. Either you get over whatever cold you have in a few days, or you are going to die. And since his mother is not better or doesn't look better, he is convinced she is going to die. His worst fears are coming true.

Anabel and Hannibal haven't been raised in any religious denomination, but I think the rigidity of the rules and the lack of questioning and open-mindedness at Derrick and Maya's is a relief for Lily's kids. Good for them. They could really use a break.

It is hard to be a kid whose parent is ill. There are all of these unanswered questions. Not only about your parent but about yourself. There is no direction. No instruction. I remember that. How I thought it wasn't okay to be happy, to laugh, to be silly, to sing when my mother was so depressed. That must have been what she was even if no one ever said it. No one was there to say it. I was alone and out of context. My mother's normal became my normal, even if it wasn't normal at all. I just didn't know. I just didn't know that there were other ways of being.

Now, this has become normal too. Sitting on a hard chair and let my thoughts wander the hallways in my mind for a few hours while Lily takes her poison.

I close my eyes, too, and see how I turned into my mother. That isn't something I went for. It was just too hard to resist breaking the mold to undo the pattern that is coded into my DNA. I tried. I think I gave it a decent try. It is just too much of an uphill struggle. And I am tired. I can't be on my toes all the time and weigh every action and reaction in terms of what my mother would have done. It comes naturally to me to do like her. It is the path of least resistance. The fallback.

I see Lily slipping into my shoes. I hear her being close to giving up. Giving up the fight. The cancer is beating her into her place in succession. She thought she could break free and be herself, but no one is allowed to shed their ancestors. We all have to carry them.

I didn't do her any favors either. I let her copy me. I let her take over. At five, she was a better version of me than I could ever be. How she cared for Maya and Ben when I was high or exhausted. How she fed them and bathed them and sung them to sleep. I have never thanked her for that. Thank you doesn't cover it. Thank you isn't the right way to say it. How would that sound? Thank you for giving up your childhood so you could live up to a responsibility that wasn't yours. Sorry is more like it. I owe her an apology. I let her be me. I let her be me even if I should have known so much better. I let her be me even if I bloody well knew what it meant to be my mother.

"Don't be me, Lily Pad!" I whisper under my breath.

Moment 56

Calabasas, CA
Monday, September 28th, 2009, 6:25 PM
I am 64 years old

I look at Craig and Robert shoving in the last of the meatloaf and gravy with the same resolve and efficiency.

They are very alike. They have a practical approach to deal with things like this. Get organized. Get the logistics going. Get the garage painted and the running toilet in the upstairs bathroom fixed. I think that's the reason they get along. Robert drives me down here when it is time for me to sit with Lily, and then the two of them spend their days tinkering around the house and yard. That is how they deal with their feelings. Soothing themselves by hammering and raking and having a beer on their evening walk.

In some ways, I admire them. They don't have to talk much to be together. They are perfectly comfortable being quiet together. And an opportunity to use the table saw in the woodshop out back is worth more than a thousand words.

I can see it in Craig's face. How much Lily's disease weighs down on him. How much time has worn him out. How much sleep he is missing. And it's a lot. But Craig can carry himself. Himself and everybody else. In Lily's long line of boyfriends, in need of rescuing, he is the exception. That must be why she fell for him. Because he allowed her to stop rescuing every sorry creature that crossed her path. Including those who should have rescued her. Including her parents. Including her father. Including her mother.

I am grateful that she found someone who can rescue her. I am ashamed it isn't me.

"Give me ten minutes to clear this away and get the brews, and I'm ready for our hike," Craig says to Robert.

Moment 57

Los Angeles, CA
Monday, October 19th, 2009, 10:15 AM
I am 64 years old

"I'm not sure I can do this again," Lily says as tears roll down her face.

Her hair is all gone, and she is pale gray and way too thin. She doesn't look like a survivor. Her once beautiful breasts have yet to be reconstructed, but it is still too risky because her immune system is so compromised. Even if she doesn't look it, she is getting better. Even if she doesn't feel it, she is getting better.

"Ssshhh, Lily Pad," I say. "Just one more time. You just have to do this one more time."

That is easy for me to say. I am not the one who has been destroyed by the chemo. It has taken away my baby. All that is left is this alien who is at the end of her rope. And I am of no use to her. There is nothing I can do or say that will make it any more comfortable. Often I think I have had the opposite effect. I have made it worse because I just sit here with her.

She keeps crying in silence as if making a sound is too much effort. I lean in from the seat of my uncomfortable chair to take her hand. Too little too late. That is what it is. But it is all I have to give.

She has been so brave. Braver than I could ever be. She has done everything it takes. Everything that was recommended. Everything in the book. But the cancer treatment is only a fraction of the cure. She has lost much more than her breasts. She has lost herself. She doesn't believe in herself anymore, and what is worse, she doesn't care. No drug can bring that back. And I can't bring it back. I can just sit here as a stupid couch potato and spew platitudes.

I am afraid to show her how I feel. Afraid and ashamed. It was like when we lived on Palm Avenue, just the kids and I, and a rare thunderstorm would roll in. She would crawl into bed with me, small and scared, and I would put my arms around her and smell her hair and not show her how scared I was. Because fear is contagious. And I am supposed to be the grownup.

Moment 58

Calabasas, CA
Saturday, April 3rd, 2010, 5:50 PM
I am 65 years old

I fill my glass with white wine again. The bottle is almost empty. I hope we are leaving for dinner soon; otherwise, I will have to go lie down for a bit. I haven't really had anything to eat since this morning because...I don't know why, but Lily's house is so chaotic that it's hard to keep a schedule. We are supposed to meet the rest of the family at the restaurant at 6:30 to celebrate Lily's birthday, which was yesterday.

Ben will not be there. Lily says they might pick him up sometime next week and have him stay for a few days, but dinners like this are not for Ben anymore. As time goes by, he seems less and less capable of being around other people. Or interested. Part of me understands that. I am not that keen on it either. It is a physical discomfort thing for Ben. He gets fidgety and panicky if he is confined inside with people and then, he either leaves or has a breakdown where he withdraws into himself. He needs to be free. Not tied down to anyone or anything. Otherwise, he can't function. Function is not the right word. It doesn't describe what he is or does. Existing in a meaningful manner comes closer.

How did he get this way? There are many answers to that. Drugs, I am sure. Neglect, I am sure. Genetics, I am sure. I don't know how I could ever expect him to grow up to be a normal balanced person. Who was supposed to teach him to be that? I couldn't. Jonathan couldn't. Robert tried for a while, but never reached Ben. Lily is the only one who has ever dialed into the channel where Ben is broadcasting. The rest of us thought it would be somewhere else on the band and weren't willing to give up that notion. We were so stuck on what he was supposed to be and wasn't that we didn't make an effort to find him where he was.

Poor Ben, forever living in his parallel universe. Maybe his is the real one, and the rest of us are lost in no man's land.

I really need to get some food into me to keep these thoughts away. It is the same every day now. They are wolves that circle around me at the end of the afternoon, and if I'm not careful, they attack and rip me to pieces. There is a small space between the boring wasteland of sobriety and the full-blown horror of intoxication that I try to retreat to. It is really no more than a narrow ledge, and too little or too much will make me fall. And when I'm out of my element like now, it is so much harder to find.

I could eat a piece of chocolate. Or some cake. That could stabilize me a bit. But Lily has cut out all sugar because it fed the cancer cells so that won't be forthcoming. Once again, it is either her or me, and she wins. It is so unfair. I let my anger towards her bubble up for a second, but then I have to put it away again. It's no use. I can't let it out. Ever. Who in their right mind is angry with their daughter for being sick? No one in their right mind. And I want to have a right mind. Without that, what do I have?

I take another sip of white wine. More like a gulp really. I know I shouldn't, but what can I do? The thoughts are out to get me. I try to remember a time when they were not. A time when they were not all bleak and without hope. I can't. That might be my drunk brain not working too well because surely, I have had happier times. Times where I felt alive. Where I felt it worth being alive. I really have to get something to eat.

I stand up. Too fast I think. I get that rush of blood from my head and have to hold on to the edge of the table in the breakfast nook to steady myself. It is not going to work with the high heels I have put on for dinner. I will break my ankle before I reach the fridge. I sit down to take the shoes off and put them under the table so no one can see them. No one is here, I tell myself.

They are all trying to get ready. Who would see me? For some reason, it is important that there is a sound reason for me taking off my shoes. It can't be that I just kicked them off because I am tipsy. I have to be able to explain it. I stand up again. The difference in height takes some getting used to. I feel naked and free without shoes. I walk the five steps along the counter to the fridge. My body and mind work at different speeds, so my body reaches the fridge first. I stare at it for a bit before I open it. I can do this. I look inside. Try to match what I see with a taste in my mouth. I feel like good old string cheese. No frills string cheese. Processed out of taste and texture string cheese. I don't see any. There is an imploded wedge of brie. Brie de Meaux, it says on the crumbled label that doesn't cover it anymore. It stinks. Like cheese. It disgusts me. Why can't they have normal cheese? String cheese. I look around. There is a glass of dill pickles. Now we are talking. I hold on to the side of the fridge with my left hand to not sway too much and swing the door more open with my right hand so I can get my right shoulder in there and stop the fridge door as it swings back. It makes a little sound of jars and bottles rattling when it hits me. I must have swung it harder than I thought. I reach for the pickle jar on the top shelf but have to give up figuring out how to open it with just one hand while still holding on and keeping the fridge open at the same time. I curse myself. Pull yourself together. People do this every day. No one ever had trouble opening pickle jars and fridge doors. Not in their sixties anyway. I only had two, maybe three glasses of wine. It shouldn't be this hard.

I shift my tactics. Give up on doing two things at once. Let go of the fridge with my left hand and turn myself slightly to face the counter. I put the jar down on the counter. The fridge door closes by itself.

"Having trouble, are we?" a voice says quite unexpectedly.

It takes me a second to realize it is Betty.

"Go away!" I say. "I can't have you here right now!"

But that is the wrong thing to say to Betty to make her leave. She ignores me and says,

"Maybe if you hadn't downed four glasses in 20 minutes flat, you would be able to open the pickles."

She has her most helpful tone on. Helpful and sugar sweet.

"It wasn't four!" I say in my defense, but I'm not sure anymore.

"Whatever you say..."

I can feel her hold up her hands and step backward in mock acceptance like I am a child who insists on buttoning my shirt myself.

"I am not a child, you know?" I say.

"I know!" she says, amused.

"Are you going to open that jar?" she asks. "Because then you have to turn it to the left. Righty-tighty, lefty-loosy, remember?"

I look down at my hands and switch from twisting the lid right to the left. The lid comes off with a popping sound. There are three pickles left. I am so hungry. I put in my fingers and pull out a pickle.

"Are you going to eat it just like that?" Betty asks, making it perfectly clear what she thinks about my manners.

"Go away!" I say again and hold my hand up, so I can get the bottom of the pickle in my mouth.

"Classy!" she remarks.

I don't care. The pickle is delicious. Better than any pickle I've ever had before. I finish it off and go for a second one. Mmmmm. Yummy. Then, that one is gone too, and there is just one left. I can't help it. I have to have it. But my hand is not that steady, and as I raise the last pickle, brine drips on my white shirt.

"You got a little something there," Betty says, and I feel her point to my shirt. "Maybe you should go change that."

I lose my patience.

"Can you just get off my case for once?" I yell at her. "You bloody well know I didn't bring another shirt!"

Fucking Betty. Always knows better. She is supposed to be on my side. My side. Tears well up in my eyes. Damn. Now my mascara is going to run too.

"Are you okay, Mom?" Lily asks, rushing into the kitchen. "Why are you yelling?"

I want to explain, but I can't stop crying, and I am drunk.

"She's supposed to be on my side." I sob. "She shouldn't be so mean to me!"

I stumble through the s's and can hear how it must sound.

"Who, Mom?" Lily says, indulging me out of concern. "Who are you talking to?"

"She shouldn't be mean to me!" I say again.

That is all I can think of. Betty is supposed to be my friend. My mentor. My mother. I shouldn't have to take this shit from her.

Lily looks at the wine in the breakfast nook and puts two and two together.

"Are you drunk?" she asks, now not so concerned anymore.

"No!" I reply with fervor and conviction and walk back to the nook and bend down to get my shoes but hit my forehead on the edge of the table and have to sit down on the floor. I scramble around on my butt to reach my shoes, which I have managed to kick further in under the table. This is not looking good for me. I know.

Lily takes in the whole scene while her face hardens.

"Maybe you should go lie down, Mom," she says slowly as if her mind is racing at 200 miles per hour, but she has to be careful what comes out.

"Yes," I say in a little girl's voice.

That is for the best. Have a nap. Forget all about this. Pretend it didn't happen. But I don't know how to get up from the floor. I don't trust myself standing up. The room is spinning, and I have a bad taste in my mouth from the pickles. I look at her, and she looks at me. None of us say anything. I lose again.

She steps over and grabs my arm with both hands. One on the forearm, one under my armpit. She lifts me up but does not let go of my arm. She is surprisingly strong, considering how thin she is. Like a workhorse. That makes me proud. She steers me down the hall and into the guest room where she lets me sit down on the sofa bed that I have made ready for Robert and me, so we don't have to deal with the bed linen when we come back from dinner. But I am not going to dinner. I am going to sleep. I lie down on my side with my feet still on the floor. I don't know how to make it right. Lily turns off the overhead light and closes the door.

Moment 59

Calabasas, CA
Sunday, April 4th, 2010, 7:35 AM
I am 65 years old

I tiptoe into the kitchen. I hope no one is there. I am not that lucky. Craig is out there, scrambling eggs and frying bacon for everyone. There is coffee in the pot. I can count on him for that. Regular everyday coffee, not all that stuff with milk foam and cinnamon. I also need a glass of water. But not food. Not right now.

"Good morning," I say to break the ice.

"Good morning," he says, and no ice is broken.

I get a mug in the cupboard above the coffee machine and fill it up. I look out the window into the driveway. Our car is boxed in by Lily and Craig's minivan, which they took to the restaurant last night, so no chance of a quick getaway. I turn around to see Craig load the last pieces of bacon onto a paper towel to dry off and turn down the heat under the eggs. He then leaves the kitchen without a word.

I sit down in the breakfast nook with my coffee. I have forgotten the water but will get it in a minute. I just need to collect myself. I have been awake since five, thinking about what to say to Lily. I am pretty sure she won't let it pass, so I have to have something ready.

I really don't know what happened. It is not usually like that. I have more control. It was just a stupid mistake yesterday. I miscalculated. I let myself go. Maybe she'll understand. The past year has not been easy for any of us. Well, her especially. But it has been stressful for me as well. She has to understand that. And yesterday. Yesterday I just wanted to celebrate her birthday. I got a little ahead of myself. I didn't mean any harm. No one was hurt. I wonder what she said to the others. She must have said something. I hope she just said I wasn't feeling well. That is the truth. Sort of.

I hear her steps down the stairs. Craig must have told her I was up. Stupid fucker. He couldn't leave it alone. He had to tell her. And now, it is too late for me to go back to the guest room.

"Good morning, Mom!" Lily says in her mother-voice from the hallway to let me know she has seen me. "How are you feeling this morning?"

"I'm okay," I say.

She enters the kitchen and gets herself a glass of some green juice from the fridge.

"Good!" she says. "I was worried about you."

Ah, guilt. There you are. I almost thought you wouldn't show up today.

"I am fine!" I say with emphasis, trying to keep the annoyance out of my voice.

"I know you think that," she says and sits down across from me at the table. "I'm not so sure."

Here we go. I brace my core for the punch. I am fired up. I can feel my heartbeat in my ears swooshing away. My face must be bright red.

Lily looks me in the eyes as if she is trying to read my thoughts. I always thought she could do that. That I'm easy to figure out.

"I know it's uncomfortable, but I have to ask because I love you," she begins.

And because you are nosy. And because you think you know better. And because you judge me. And because...because.

"How much do you drink, Mom?" she asks. "Do you drink too much?"

"No!" I say with as much conviction as I can muster.

She searches my face again. She must be looking for giveaways. I hope there aren't any.

"Robert says you drink wine every night," she says, pretending she didn't want to have to.

Thank you, Robert. That is a nice way to treat your wife. Tell on her. Snitch to her daughter. Thank you!

"Not every night!" I defend myself. "We didn't have any on Tuesday, and since when having a glass of wine with dinner is forbidden? I'm a grown woman. I can take care of myself!"

I can hear I talk way too much to sound credible. I need to dial it back.

"I just worry about you," she says.

Any trace of tenderness or trust or intimacy that we might have had, her and me, is gone now. So gone, I'm not sure it ever existed. The window has closed. It must have done so while she regained her strength after the chemo. She is back in the saddle, my mother-daughter. She is back. What can I do but fall back into my role as well?

"Don't!" I say angry and resentful and sad and hurt and lonely. "It's none of your business, missy!"

I haven't called her that in thirty years. Back when we fought about stuff she had done wrong. Back when she was the one who got in trouble. Back when I was the parent.

"I think you get so defensive because I'm right!" Lily says.

I don't know what to say. Maybe she is right. So what? That doesn't mean I have to take this from her. I can just stand up and walk away. I can do that right now.

I stand up and walk back to the guest room. Robert is awake. He looks at me with raised eyebrows to figure out what's going on. I shoot him the angriest look back and start to pack our suitcase. I don't care about folding anything. I just throw it in. I am so angry I need a release. I curse the fact that I can't leave on my own. I need someone to move the car, and I don't want to drive it all the way to Nevada by myself. But I need to go. Now. And I can sit shotgun for ten hours without saying a word.

"Can you please get up?" I say. "We're going home!"

Moment 60

Elko, NV
Wednesday, July 14th, 2010, 4:20 PM
I am 65 years old

"You must be one thirsty lady or live with a couple of drunk water buffalos!" The cashier says to me with a smile as he packs my eight half-liter boxes of Merlot into a double paper bag so the handles won't break.

The comment surprises me so much I can only stare him in confusion and then disbelief. His name tag says Carl, and I think that is an old name for someone who still has pimples. That thought rings a bell in the back of my mind. It is not the first time I have had it. Then I realize that Carl was working the cash register yesterday, too.

I see how it is. Damn you, friendly customer service! And completely oblivious to his major doo-doo, he says, "That'll be $20.11, but you remember that, right?"

He looks at me for approval and possibly a pat on the head for a job well done. He has no clue. I throw my pre-counted bundle of two fives and a ten and a one-dollar bill on the belt in front of him and grab the bag and storm out of Raley's to the car with my ears and cheeks on fire and my eyes on the ground three feet in front of me.

I have parked in my usual spot almost all the way down the aisle to the right of the store entrance. There isn't a lot of foot traffic there. As I'm speed-walking and cursing my way down there, I switch the grocery bag to my left hand so I can find the car key in my cardigan pocket with my right hand. It is sweltering hot outside, but without the cardigan, I wouldn't have anywhere to put my stuff, and I have given up on handbags since I seem to lose them.

I fumble with the car door. Robert didn't want to spring for another remote key last time I had to have it replaced, so now I have an old-fashioned one that has to go in the lock. Cheap bastard! He is like that Scrooge McDuck the kids used to watch on TV.

I put the grocery bag on the passenger seat and turn on the car to get the air conditioning going. As I relax into the seat, I let my right hand grab a box of wine and give it to the left hand so it can twist off the top. The first sip is always the best.

"Whatya doin' there, pardner?" Betty says in a silly accent, but I know she is dead serious.

I turn on the radio to KRJC Pure Country to drown her out. Out blasts a song about taking a girl on a ride on a big green tractor, which I don't think is about tractors at all. Betty is having none of that and starts singing along,

"Mmmm hmmm huh big green tractor

Dum dee dum dee dum go faster

Down…woods….out to pasture

La la la la la, why are you drinking?"

"I don't want to talk to you!" I say and turn off the radio again.

"Suit yourself. I'll be here all week," Betty replies.

She hums the country song to herself and pretends to mind her own business. She is annoying. I am annoyed. That must be the theme of the day.

"Look," I say, "why don't you go find someone else to spook? I don't need you here."

She sends me her most overbearing smile.

"Oh, dear," she says, "you're so funny. You know I can't do that. I can only talk to you, sweetie."

I take another sip of the wine.

"Okay, why don't we get started before you get sloshed?" she asks with infinite patience.

I say nothing. Nothing at all.

"Why are you drinking?" Betty asks again.

"What else am I supposed to do?" my gut answers.

I seem to have been taken out of this conversation, so I take another swig of wine while they carry on.

"Well, that's a mighty crappy answer," Betty says. "Why don't you try again?"

"I don't have anything else to do!" my gut says.

"So, you couldn't think of anything else to do on a Wednesday afternoon than to sit in your car and mope while your liver disintegrates?"

She gets on my nerves, that Betty.

"No," I say to end the conversation.

"How about a good roll in the hay with that stallion of yours or line dancing at the Y or making yourself a fool in front of your daughter?" she presses on.

I wince at her comment about Lily. I haven't talked to her or any of the kids for that matter since we left Calabasas in April. I haven't called anyone, and no one has called me. It is as if someone chopped off my right hand, and I learned to make do with the left, but now Betty has jabbed the stump with a fork. It fucking hurts.

And Robert and I don't talk too much either. I avoid it, and he takes the hint and stays away. I can't remember when he last gave me a hug or a kiss. So I am O for two on Betty's suggestions, but she already knows that. That is why she asked.

"Leave me alone!" I say.

"C'mon, Livvy," she says, "pull yourself together for once. Drinking in your car while listening to country. That's a new low, even for you!"

"Leave. Me. Alone." I repeat.

I am done with her. I don't need her to mock me. I don't need her to yell at me. I don't need her to hurt me. I can do all of that by myself, no problem.

"Yes, but you're not gonna, are you?" she says.

But that is where she is wrong. I curse and berate myself every moment of every day. That is why I drink. Because I can't stand listening to myself. Neither my scolding nor my excuses. So I drown them out the only way I know how.

"LEAVE ME ALONE!" I yell so loud the car is shaking and a man getting into his car in front of me looks up in surprise.

I give him the finger, and with an insulted stare, he gets into the car and drives off.

Betty is gone too. Betty is gone.

AFTER

Moment 61

Mojave, CA
Thursday, November 25th, 2010, 1:50 PM
I am 65 years old

"Are you going to tell me what this is about?" Robert asks.

We are just turning onto the road again after having stopped for lunch, a crappy greasy burger at Primo. We have hardly said a word since we left Calabasas in a hurry. I have been putting it off, and Robert knows me well enough to give me time. I guess the time is now.

I think about what to say and how my voice will sound. I often do that. Check if it is different after not having spoken for long stretches of time. Like Tuesdays, when Robert is at the club all day. Or Fridays when he cleans the garage and takes the yard waste to the city dump and then washes the car. We must have the cleanest garage in all of Elko County. That is one of his obsessions. More than ten years since he retired, and his days still run on an exact schedule. He is a creature of habit. That is what keeps him sane, he says, but considering how much it dictates our life, maybe sane is not the right word.

Even in my mind, I procrastinate. What am I going to answer him?

"Lily completely overreached and got on my nerves, so I just wanted to go home!" I say and try to make it sound like it has nothing to do with me. That is difficult because it has everything to do with me.

"She does it because she loves you," Robert says. "You know that, right?"

Of course, he knows what went down. He probably knew before we left Elko. But he isn't stepping into the fire himself. He gets other people to do the hard parts so he can be the quiet, wise man in the situation. Still doesn't take a case he can't win. He is a lawyer, alright. I change tactics.

"How long have you known they were going to do this?" I ask.

"Oh, a couple of weeks," he says. "Lily called me."

Sneaky bastard. Well, he kept that under wraps.

"Why didn't you tell me?" I ask, not knowing whether I am more disappointed or impressed.

"That would kind of defy the purpose of an intervention, right?" he says. "Besides, I promised I wouldn't."

And what about the promises you made to me, Robert? I want to ask but don't. What about how you promised to take care of me and stick up for me? That must have gone out the window. Maybe you left it at the city dump with the leaves from the oak tree.

"So you think I have a problem, too?" I ask.

I know what I want him to say, but I also know that it isn't what he is going to say. Could he just for once be on my side? Please! How on earth do they imagine they can get me to do anything if they all gang up on me? I have never ever ganged up on them. I have always, always stood by them. All of them. Never judged. Because I know better. I know that I am not in a position to do that. Ever. And this is the thanks I get. The thanks for keeping them alive. The thanks for saving them.

"I think it's controlling you more than the other way around," he says. "And I can't remember when I last saw you happy when sober."

Oh, come on, Robert. Why can't you just be black or white for once? Either you think I am a drunk or not. Which one is it? Because I can't deal with this in-between. Maybe you are the reason why I am not happy. Did you think of that? Maybe you are the reason.

"Wow, don't make it too clear for me!" I say, venom in my voice.

I can see that shot reaches one of his ships. His jaw stiffens, and he leans closer down to the steering wheel. That is fine with me. Right now, I want nothing more than to hurt him. Pull him down from his high horse. Burn the bridges between us. And have a drink.

I know there isn't a lot of chance of that now. I should have gotten a glass of wine with lunch. I don't even know if Primo Burgers has wine. Then we could have gone somewhere else. Maybe I can suggest we stop at that Indian Wells place to talk about this? Can I make it to Indian Wells from here? How far is it? An hour? Are they even open on Thanksgiving? He will see right through me if I say anything. Do I care? It is not like he doesn't know.

"All I'm saying is that I want you to be happy, and you aren't right now," he says. "Maybe not drinking will fix that."

"Maybe not being with you will fix that!"

It just flies out of my mouth before I can do anything. I am so damn angry. And thirsty. Do we have a bottle of water in the car? Maybe if I drink enough water, we can stop so I can pee and get a real drink. He can just drop me off. I can figure it out by myself. I have done that before.

"Maybe it will," he says. "But I don't think so."

Oh you don't, do you? That is pretty damn rich coming from the most boring man in the Universe. Who died and donated you a spine? Fucking fucker.

"Do we have any water?" I ask.

That's all I can focus on. Fighting with him will have to wait till later. I swear I am going to lose it if I don't get something to drink right now.

"I'm really thirsty," I say, "do we have like a bottle of water or something?"

"Not unless you brought the rest of yours from lunch," Robert says, not worried at all.

I know I didn't, but I still look around in the side pocket of the car and in my bag and under the seat.

"Why do I always have to remember every single little thing?" I rage on. "Why can't you think ahead just for once?"

I don't expect him to answer and he doesn't. Instead, he sinks even deeper into his seat and stares at the road. I, on the other hand, am getting more frustrated by the second.

"God, I need something to drink!" My voice expands, "I am just so THIRSTY!"

I bang my fists on the dashboard and start to cry.

"Can we please stop?" I sob, "I just want something to drink…"

Robert lets me cry for a bit. Then he says, "How can you say you don't have a problem? It's not even two in the afternoon, and you're falling apart."

"I know!" I sniffle. "What's wrong with me?"

This sounds like an admission, but I'm not ready. I feel so tired. Exhausted. And sick. Like I have the flu coming on. Just so tired. Maybe I am getting sick. But I know I am not. There is no straw left to grasp. None. I don't know what to do.

"I don't know what to do," I say. "Please help me!"

The tears come back even stronger. It feels so good to let them go. And I cry for everything and everyone. Myself. Lily and her cancer. Ben and his miserable life. Maya and her God complex. Jonathan and how he still haunts me. James because it never worked out. Robert and his grief. Betty and her strength. Monica, whom I haven't thought about since 1984. My mother. My father. I cry for all of us. I cry for a lifetime.

As I cry, something comes to the surface. Or someone. Someone I had forgotten. Someone I wanted to forget. Someone I had buried. She is vulnerable. Naked. Exposed. But she wants to be here. She wants to step in and take over. Should I let her?

She is already half out, enough that I sense it would be easier to be her. It wouldn't require anything of me. I wouldn't have to pretend. I wouldn't have to live the half-life I have for so long. I wouldn't have to numb myself to be able to stand myself. I have already let go of the railing behind me. All I have to do is find something in front of me that I can hold on to. I can't go back in the box.

Robert hasn't said a word this whole time. That is okay. He doesn't have to say anything. I wonder how he knows that. Maybe he doesn't. It doesn't matter. After all, I am alone in this. Thoughts and memories and instincts from more than forty years ago kick in. The same feeling of having to break through the wall and come out on the other side unless I want to die. I check myself. Do I want to die? Is it a waste of time to try and get better? Is it worth it? I don't want this to be the ending. If this is the ending, I have just wasted all these years. That is too much for me. That is just plain stupid. If I die tomorrow—which I might from how I feel right now—if I die tomorrow, I want to know I died from life. Not from some vegetative state. Not from a self-induced coma. There is a difference in the pain. Mere existence is a dull pain. Real life is a sharp pain. I want to die from the sharp pain. If I can. I want to die from the sharp pain.

But first, I have to get better. First, I have to break through the wall. First, I have to get worse to get better. First, I have to be born again.

I know how it's going to go. In some ways, that is a comfort. I know I'm going to hit my worst. I know I'm going to want to quit quitting. But that is about as low as I can go. To want to quit quitting. I can't lose more than that. And I think I know what I will gain. Myself. It might not be much, but it is enough. It is enough. Maybe there will even be time to win someone else back. That is the pie in the sky. That is aiming too high for now. I can't think about that right now. First, it's going to get worse.

Moment 62

Elko, NV
Sunday, December 5th, 2010, 12:10 PM
I am 66 years old

"Hello, I'mOliviaandI'manalcoholic. It has been 11 days since my last drink." I say. I can't believe that it has been that long. I can't believe that it hasn't been longer. I can't believe I am saying these words. I can't believe it makes such a difference to say them. Not that it makes the monster go away, but it is definitely not under the bed anymore. It doesn't scare me anymore. At least not enough to make me run away.

It is also my birthday, but I don't say that. I can't remember when I last felt my birthday this acutely. I have just been born again. Not like Maya, who claims to have been born again to God, but born again as a baby who has just left the dark cushiony comfort of her mother's womb. It is painful and scary and cold, and the light is too bright, and I feel like crying all the time.

I don't know what to do. I know what I shouldn't do, but that's about it. If I ever had instructions on where to go from here, I forgot them. Last time I got clean, I had a purpose. I did it to be a mother to my children. To give them a chance of survival. It was an act of putting on my own oxygen mask first, but with the distinct goal of enabling them to breathe. Leaving Jonathan was a requirement for me to succeed. Nothing else. I couldn't have done it with him.

This time, I have no obligation to anyone. Only myself. I am doing this for me. Not Robert, not the kids. I haven't even told the kids. They don't deserve to know. I still have too much anger in me. This isn't submission. This isn't obeying their command. This isn't to please them. It is in spite of them. It is a rebellion against them. It is to show the Universe and myself that I am something more than a mother and a wife and a victim. This is so I can breathe.

But I'm not there yet. I have only just begun. Even if I have the fire in me, it is just a tiny flame that has to be protected and nursed. Like a baby. I need someone to care for me. Someone to support me. Someone to tell me that I am on the right path. Last time I could just look at the kids' faces. That was enough for me to know how I was doing. I need more this time. I have baggage, and it's heavy. That's why I am here. To get help carrying it. To learn how others are carrying theirs. To put me in my place and remind myself of who and what I am.

I spent the first week after Thanksgiving dying. Shedding everything I was and knew and took for granted. It was a difficult ending. I filled myself with grief. Not for the life, I lived, but for the life, I lost. I mourned the me that could've been but wasn't. Someone who passed away too young and innocent. The loss of a child, really. I wailed and screamed and tore my heart out for her.

I had Robert lock me in the guest room and throw away the key. I asked him to stay away, no matter what he heard. He was kind enough to oblige. He is kind. He doesn't know what is going on, and yet he accepts it. I needed to be alone. And not the kind of alone that I have been all my life—muted and afraid. The kind of alone where I could wake up and face me. The kind of alone where I could open my wounds and let them drain. The kind of alone that would let me feel.

For so long, I have mistaken the throbbing pain for a heartbeat. I have been infected with guilt and shame and the burden of my ancestors. The pus was oozing, and if I were not to go into septic shock and die, I had to get it out. My goal is to live. Not exist. Not persevere. Not survive. But live.

In between the battles, I have been thinking about if that was my mother's goal too. To rid herself of her demons. To flush out the pain clogging her system. To come out on the other side as someone else because she could no longer be who she was. I would like to believe that was the case and since she isn't here to tell me that is what I choose. In that light, it doesn't matter that she failed. She had the right intentions. I can draw strength from that. I can trust that. I can move forward from that.

"Hi, Olivia!" The group answers.

Moment 63

Elko, NV
Sunday, December 12th, 2015, 12:15 PM
I am 66 years old

"Hello, I'm Olivia, andI'manalcoholic. It has been 18 days since my last drink." I say.

This is my church now. The ritual is everything. I am nothing but its loyal servant. This is where I hand myself over to someone or something else. This is where I exhale. It is a break in the struggle, in the clenched fist, in the hyper-alert watching of myself.

This is the only place I know what to do, what is expected of me, which thankfully isn't a lot. All I have to do is show up and say my name. I can do that. It is the rest I have a problem with. I have a problem with admitting I have a problem. Which is surprising, considering that I am already here. Telling everyone why is just a tiny step further than I have gone before. It is not like I am the only one here.

Bob, the chairperson of most of the meetings I've been to, says that is perfectly normal. The mind has all sorts of ways to deflect and deny. Once the words are spoken, there is nowhere to hide. Then I am no longer here by accident or to help others or to see how it is for future reference. When I say I am an alcoholic, I speak my truth.

I have gone to meetings every day since I could get myself out of bed. Some days, I have even gone twice. Because it is an hour break from my life. When I am not here, everything is painfully close. Home, Robert, my past. I have the urge to run away. To get as far away as possible. But it is not possible. I can never run away from what I'm trying to run away from.

I can barely stand being at home. I can barely stand Robert. The person that belongs with him isn't me anymore. I wonder if it ever was. I might just have molded myself into someone whom I thought he would like. But I could only stay in that contorted position for so long. After a while, I have to break either me or the mold. I chose to break me. I chose to pacify me. I chose to cut me.

It is easiest to put the blame on Robert. To think that getting away from him would stop me from drinking. But it isn't Robert's fault. It is just another act of denial. He's not the drinker. He is not even the reason I drink. I am. And wherever I am, the desire to drink or drug or numb will be there too. I will never be rid of it. I will never not be an addict. I will never be healed.

Those are harsh words. It is a bleak outlook. And in order to make it, I have to learn everything over. Not only do I have a problem to solve, but I also have to solve how to solve the problem. Old ways are not an option anymore. I don't know any new ways. I sit and wait for them to reveal themselves to me. For the fog to lift. For the hangover to break.

"Hi, Olivia!" The group answers.

Moment 64

Elko, NV
Tuesday, December 21st, 2010, 12:20 PM
I am 66 years old

"Hello, I'm Olivia, and I'manalcoholic. It has been 27 days since my last drink." I say.

I can't believe it has almost been a month. Every day is still new and never tried before. Every morning is unfamiliar, and I scramble to figure out where and who I am. Every moment is a choice I have to make. Most moments, I choose to not make a choice. Just wait it out and see what happens. Gather information. Gain experience. Some moments are bound by the choices I've made before. My past is full of chicken and eggs, and I can't tell them apart. Did I love Jonathan because he chose me? Or did he choose me because he knew I would love him? Did I have the children to give myself a reason to leave him, and did I leave him for the kids? Why did I marry Robert? Why? Is safety more important than love? Is it too late to find out? The questions swirl in my brain, and I have to open the drain to let them out. Come back to the empty tub. Start from there.

I'm kidding myself if I think this is just about not drinking. I know that. Yet, that is all I can focus on right now. That is such a big task; there is room for nothing else inside me. Or I won't let there be any more room. Not drinking isn't easy, but it is a non-action. Taking action is way harder. Anyway, it doesn't matter. They say here that I shouldn't make any big or rash changes too soon. My life does not need to change, I do. But how do I distinguish the two? Am I not my life? My head hurts from thinking about this. Something needs to give. I feel something needs to give. I breathe through it. Like I did when I was in labor. Like I did when I had the abortion. Like I did when I detoxed. If I just breathe, I will make it through. I will know what to do. I will come out on the other side. Shiny and new. Like Baby Jesus.

I still haven't told the kids. Nobody called on my birthday. Not that I know of. Probably on Lily's orders. But then, I'm not picking up the phone either. And I don't know what Lily and Robert talk about behind my back. Who would have thought they would gang up together? United in their disapproval of me. My anger is bubbling up. Breathe, breathe!

I can't blame them. Or rather, I won't blame them. They have both done what they could without sacrificing themselves. I couldn't help my mother from being depressed. I couldn't help Jonathan from being Jonathan. I haven't helped Ben. It took me 25 years to help myself to anything other than a drink. I roll with the punches, but it hurts. I have to be enough.

As of now, Christmas is off. Robert might go to Brayden's, but I am going to stay here. Right here. Where I belong. With my kin. My fellow drunkards and misfits. Bob, who is fighting to have his kids back. Lady Marion, the young damsel in distress. She reminds me of Ben. Same ineptitude, same needs, same tenderness. Jack, who is not going to make it because he thinks everything that happens to him is somebody else's fault. No, Jack, it is your fault! You drove your car into the Dairy Queen while you were drunk. Seamus, who comes for the shelter as much as anything else. Staying sober while homeless is a challenge. Jessica, who has nothing in common with Jonathan's wife except for an abusive husband. She hopes if she gets sober, he will stay. She hopes he won't take the boys away from her. She hopes she might be able to stand up to him. She hopes but knows it doesn't work that way. An unlikely group of friends, yet that is what they are. We do not have much in common but way more than anyone would think.

"Hi, Olivia!" My friends say.

Moment 65

Elko, NV
Saturday, December 25th, 2010, 12:05 PM
I am 66 years old

"Hello, I'm Olivia, and I'manalcoholic. It has been 31 days since my last drink." I say.

Merry Christmas. Except it is not. It might never have been. I have a hard time remembering a Christmas that was truly merry. When there were no failed expectations, no unmet needs, no disappointment. Never with my mother, not with Jonathan, almost but not quite with Robert. Over the past month, I have let go of my expectations. I take it day by day, hour by hour, sometimes minute by minute. Today is no different.

Robert was moping this morning. He hasn't said anything, but he thinks I keep him prisoner in the house. Because I don't go anywhere, but to these meetings, he doesn't either. He doesn't want to go alone. I don't know if that is true or he just doesn't trust me. Both, I guess. I don't trust me either.

His patience is wearing thin. He wants things to go back to normal. He is a creature of habit, and currently, I'm not habitable. He is annoyed. He doesn't understand what takes so long. He is impatient. He is also afraid. Afraid that I will change. Afraid that he will have to change too. He hates to change. To him, there was one little thing wrong with me, and it was just a question of getting it fixed. Like a missing button. I just needed another one sewn in. There is no reason to get an all-new shirt.

However, it is not a shirt but a sweater. And a thread has come loose. The deeper I go, the more it unravels. It's not my fault, but it is my fault. I want to do it right. I only get this one chance. And to do it right, I have to get all of it out. I have to pick me to pieces so I can discard the broken ones. I'm sorry it affects him, but there's nothing I can do about that. I have to stay the course.

He already knows everything he needs to. When I sit at the kitchen table and read in the Big Book, he sighs. When I tell him about the steps, he looks at me in pain. When I bring up my past, he squirms in discomfort. He can only take so much mumbo jumbo, and this is more than he bargained for.

We are drifting apart. I have to hold onto myself to not panic. I can't save us. I can only save me. I have to save me. I can live without him—I might even prefer to— but I can't live without me. I tried. I tried for so many years. It didn't work. That is why I died and ended up here.

"Hi, Olivia!" the group answers.

Moment 66

Elko, NV
Saturday, January 1st, 2011, 12:10 PM
I am 66 years old.

"Hello, I'm Olivia, and I'm an alcoholic! It's been 38 days since my last drink." I say.

It feels freeing to say the words out loud and well enunciated. I have decided to not hide anymore. It's time to move forward, and I can't do that if I have to drag my secrets with me. They are too heavy. Therefore, I am saying the words loud and clear. It feels empowering. Like I am stepping into the light. Like I have earned my badge. Like change is coming.

I tried to talk to Robert last night. I made Salisbury steak with mushroom gravy, scalloped potatoes, and green beans and put candles on the table. I am so hungry these days. It is like I never tasted food before. And I wanted to create a space for us. To tell him what is going on with me. To figure out where he is heading. Why he pulls away from me. It got very awkward and uncomfortable.

I said, "I can understand if you think that I'm changing because I am. But that's a good thing, right?"

He said, "I don't think you're changing!"

I said, "They say that sometimes, it's good if husbands and wives come to meetings too!"

He said, "I don't need that!"

I tried one more time and said, "If there's something you want me to do, just let me know…"

He got up from his chair and flicked on the light over the table, "I need some light so I can see what I'm eating!"

That was the end of the conversation. After the steak, he took his plate to the kitchen, put it in the dishwasher, and went to the den to watch TV. I ate the chocolate mousse by myself and went to bed to read, but couldn't focus and ended up staring at the ceiling instead until I heard the TV announce the new year.

I lay there with my hurt. Breathed through it. Thought about where it came from. Realized that I can't make Robert do anything he doesn't want to. That I can't wait for him to come around. I have to keep going no matter what it means for us. I am not supposed to hold up our marriage by myself. That is what we promised each other we would both do. And he has helped a lot. But. But I am too close to the other side to stop now. If I stop, everything will have been for naught. I will slide back where I was. I am running with a giant elastic band around my waist, and if I stop, it will pull me back to the old me. I don't want to be her anymore. She is dead. It is true I have no alternative right now, but I can't rush it. The new me will show up when she's good and ready. All I can do is make way for her to come through.

"Hi, Olivia!" My fellow greeters answer.

Moment 67

Elko, NV
Thursday, January 20th, 2011, 12:02 PM
I am 66 years old

"Hello, I'm Olivia, and I'm an alcoholic! It has been 57 days since my last drink." I say. "I will be the chair of this meeting!"

I am nervous and giddy at the same time. I have never chaired a meeting anywhere in my whole life. Looking at Bob, who usually does it, I figure it's not that complicated. I should have it down by now.

"Hi, Olivia!" The group responds.

I look down at my notes. I have written down what I should do, what to not forget.

"Let's have a moment of silence, and then we say the serenity prayer," I instruct.

I used to be so afraid of silence. In my life, silence has never brought anything good with it. The silence my dad left us with. The silence my mother forced on me with her depression. The tippy-toe silence of Jonathan passed out drunk or high. The silence of Robert's anger and disappointment in me. The silence of my children who don't think I'm good enough for them. But silence is new to me now. I can swim in it. Feel comfortable in it. Be weightless in it. I have come to see it as a room where I can sit and look at myself and my emotions without having to do anything about them. I can invite them in, have them sit down too, and we can communicate. They can tell me what they are all about. I am not required to react as long as I am inside silence. Right now, impatience breaks down the door and stomps in. I point to a small step stool in the corner, and it crouches down there looking kind of silly because it is so big and dramatic. I take my time to check if there is anything else in the wings, but nothing bubbles up.

I open my eyes and begin the prayer with,

"God,"

The rest of the group falls in,

"Grant me the serenity to accept the things I cannot change

The courage to change the things I can

And the wisdom to know the difference."

I have said the prayer so many times I don't really focus on the words anymore. Only on making the rhythm and sounds. That is the problem with all religion, I guess. After a while, the words lose their magic, and all you have left is the ritual. Then you have to assign meaning to it yourself. You have to interpret the scripture for yourself. Make up your mind. Find or be a prophet. I am no such thing. I can only go through the motions, not create new ones.

Thankfully, every meeting is the same. Someone reads from the Big Book, and we go around the circle, and everyone gets to share if they want and have been sober for more than a month. But when there are newcomers, it's different. More involved. More challenging. More painful.

And today, there is an older gentleman I haven't seen before. By older, I mean my age. His hair is white. His eyes are very blue. His elegant midnight blue wool coat is neatly folded over his knees. He wears a gray sweater on top of a nice button-down shirt—no tie— and darker gray pants ending in polished black expensive shoes. He is so classy and out of place that he makes me self-conscious about my own shabby t-shirt and misshapen cardigan. I even have a stray thought about what underwear I have on. Like that's going to matter.

I can feel myself blush, and my ears burn with a flash of nervousness and phantom exhilaration. I'm glad I put this in my instructions, and I skim through them to remind myself of the words I have to use.

"AA is a fellowship where we share our experience strength and hope with each other so we can recover from alcoholism," I say and look into his fantastically blue eyes. "You only have to want to stop drinking. It's free to be here, but we appreciate any contributions. Our purpose is to stay sober and help others avoid sobriety."

"I think you mean achieve?" he says in a velvety and deep voice.

His lips curl up in a little smile. Everyone else disappears from the room. I must look like a sweaty pig because I sure feel like one.

"What?"

I am confused.

"You said avoid sobriety," he says. "I think you meant to say achieve sobriety?"

"Yes, yes, of course."

"That's good because if I wanted to avoid sobriety, I could've just stayed home."

He winks at me. It takes me a second to process. So long, I think I might not have seen it right. But there is laughter and joking in those amazingly blue eyes, so maybe I did.

I return to my notes to collect myself, but I can't seem to make out my scribbles. Bob, who sits next to me, comes to my rescue.

"Maybe we should go around the room and introduce ourselves?" he suggests. "I can start. Hello, my name is Bob. It has been 436 days since my last drink!"

Bob stopped around the holidays too. He has been here the longest of all of us. Usually, people drop out or scale back on the meetings between nine months and a year when they have some solid ground under their feet. Or a lot sooner than that if they fall off the wagon. Bob is my rock, my mentor, the one who has taught me everything I know about AA and staying sober, but right now, I'm embarrassed by him as if he is my toothless hick of an uncle and the rich mine owner has come to town to inspect his property.

"Hi, Bob!" we say.

I am lost in my thoughts while Marion introduces herself, but come to as it is Blue Eye's turn.

"Hello, my name is Don," he reveals in that dark chocolate voice of his. "It's been two hours since my last drink."

Our gasp is audible. We stare at him in horror and jealousy. He is the voice from the other side. He is the voice of the living, and we the vampires take him in with thirst and pity.

"Hi, Don!" we drool.

Moment 68

Elko, NV
Thursday, February 17th, 2011, 12:15 PM
I am 66 years old

"Hello, I'm Olivia, and I'm an alcoholic! It has been 85 days since my last drink." I say.

Don sends me a smile, and my tummy flutters with butterflies. It is ridiculous. I have no idea what I think is going to come of this. And yet, I have started going to meetings where I know Don will be. We message each other several times a day, sometimes even an hour. Early in the morning, I get 'HOPE U SLEPT WELL!' Later it's, 'C U AT MEETING?' Sometimes I get, 'GREAT MEETING LOVE 2 HEAR U READ!' Then it's, 'WHAT R U MAKING FOR DINNER?' And before bedtime, it's, 'SLEEP TIGHT GORGEOUS!' I am not concerned about Robert finding out because he hates cell phones and only uses his for calling me if I am late for dinner, but I have put a lock on mine. I think the messages are innocent enough. There is nothing going on. I just don't want to have to explain it.

Bob pulled me aside after Don had been to a couple of meetings.

"You do know we don't recommend members seeing too much of each other outside the meetings, right?"

That bugged me. In fact, I got really miffed and said, "You do know I don't recommend you talking to me like that, right?"

Bob backed off and hurried out. On the way home, I thought about why I got so angry. I do know what the rules are. I also know why they are.

I have to be able to stay sober on my own, and it has to be a good experience. I can't be relying on another person and for sure, not someone who is trying to be sober himself. But that is not what this is. I am not reliant on Don. We are not seeing each other outside of meetings. It's not like we have ever had a real conversation apart from five minutes before or after a meeting. Exchanging phone numbers happened under the guise of being able to tell each other if meetings were canceled during a snowstorm. We mostly just message, smile, and look at each other. We are supportive of each other, and I don't see anything wrong with that. It's so nice to finally have someone acknowledge the hard work I put into this. Someone who is there himself. I can't help but think that is why Don is there. To acknowledge me. To show me that I am on the right path. To cheer me on.

Heaven knows there isn't a lot of cheer in Robert. He is grumpy and whiny and old. His back is acting up in the cold weather, and that isn't helping. I can't take that on. He has to do something about that himself. Go see a doctor. Get a massage. Try yoga. I smile at the thought of Robert in really tight yoga pants standing on one foot, with his hands together and his eyes closed. That is very far from anything that will ever happen. My point is that we are moving at different speeds. I am starting a new life, and Robert is stuck on the reason why. It is like everything is my fault because I was drinking. Dinner getting cold, the TV being on the fritz, us not seeing other people, the bad weather. But even if I was willing to entertain that notion, I am not drinking now. And that should count for something. That should count for a whole lot. That should count.

"Hello, Olivia!" The group sings, led by Don.

Moment 69

Elko, NV
Friday, March 11th, 2011, 1:40 PM
I am 66 years old

"Hello, my name is Don, and it's been two minutes since I grabbed your hands!" He says and looks me in the eyes. The shade of his eyes changes by the light, and now they are dark blue and soft.

We sit in the back of the Coffee Mug in a booth across from each other and have just ordered a late lunch. Robert is at the Lodge the whole afternoon, so I don't have to be home at any particular time.

This is the first time I sit this close to Don. This is the first time we are talking in person outside a meeting. This is the first time I am breaking the rules. When Don asked me if I wanted to get a bite, my heart did a somersault. It was a Bonnie and Clyde moment. I had the same feeling of fear and excitement as I had with Jonathan all those years ago. We walked the few blocks to the cafe at a brisk pace and only partly because it was cold outside. So this is how it starts, I thought. I have to remember this because this is the beginning. We didn't talk much on the way. I think we were both a bit nervous.

I'm glad she gave us this booth in the back, the hostess. I haven't seen her before, so maybe she is new. That is also okay. It would have been awkward if she knew I come here with Robert all the time. I couldn't really focus on the menu, but I've seen it a hundred times before. It just seemed wrong to order the cup of soup and half grilled chicken salad I always get. Sort of out of context. I ended up ordering the club sandwich with potato salad and a club soda. Don didn't even look at the menu but ordered a French dip with fries and a coke. As soon as the waitress turned away with our order, he took my hands.

I froze up and didn't really know what to do. Even if we are in the back, I am not that comfortable holding hands. What if somebody sees us? This is a small town, and Robert and I have lived here for a long time, and when or if he has to be told something, I want to be the one to do it. I want to be in control. Somehow having my hands enclosed in Don's doesn't give me much charge of the situation.

I don't want to be a tease. This is what I have longed for the past two months. Ever since Don was at his first meeting. It has been growing in my mind and my body. The promise of the situation. I have been savoring the experience. I have let myself dream. Of starting over. Of being with Don. Of a clean slate. Somehow the two have become synonymous—a new life and Don. Right this instant, I realize they don't have to be, it would just be so much easier if they were. At least in the short term. Like peeing in my pants—warm at first but then cold and sticky later.

I smile a weak smile and withdraw my hands under the pretense of looking for some tissues in my purse. The waitress returns with our sodas, and I hold onto mine to avoid more of the hand-holding thing.

"So, what do you say?" Don says. "Should we elope?"

I can see in his eyes that he is only half-joking, maybe even less than that. I thought it would feel a lot better to be asked that. More like a birthday present. More like a waltz in a big ballroom with glittering chandeliers. More like a fairytale. Instead, all I can think of is that I am not dressed for that, and I would have to get a toothbrush and some of the good night cream on the way.

"You could leave that deadbeat Robert and I could ditch the bitch at home!" Don continues and searches for an echo on my face.

"Robert is not a deadbeat!" I say.

Like all truths, it just slips out without me being able to stop it. He can't say stuff like that about Robert. He is not allowed. Only I can do that. And I don't want to. Because it isn't true. It is unfair and misunderstood. This isn't about Robert at all. This is about me. I don't want to get away from anyone but myself. And right now, Don. He doesn't understand. I stare at him with his blue eyes and expensive clothes. Really hard. And angry. Don leans back in surprise, but now my fuse is lit, and I can't let it go.

"Robert has been nothing but supportive and patient with me for the past 40 years!" I half-yell at him, "And you shouldn't talk about your wife like that either!"

I slam my palms down on the table for emphasis. Not hard enough to knock anything over, but hard enough to startle the waitress who has returned with our food. She looks at me as if to ask if she should leave again. I notice that other people are staring as well.

Okay, if they want a scene, I'm going to give them one. I stand up, which is difficult in the booth because the table hangs slightly over the seat, and I still have to get my purse and coat on the bench next to me. Yet I manage, without looking too clumsy, I think, and grab my stuff and walk out of the Coffee Mug with everyone following me with interest.

I have to stop right outside the door to put on my coat because it is freezing. Not the most dramatic exit. And I discover I forgot my gloves when the waitress opens the door and hands them to me. Yet, as I turn left and walk down the street, I know I did the right thing. I feel it in my body. There is an ease— clarity really—to it that hasn't been there in a while. A long while. Decades.

If I can't be with me, there is no reason to be. If I can't be me, there is no way I can fix that with other people around me. It doesn't matter if I am with Don instead of Robert because none of them can do what I need to do for myself. I need to choose myself first, and then the rest will fall into place or away. It will sort itself out. I will sort myself out.

Moment 70

Elko, NV
Monday, May 2nd, 2011 9:05 AM
I am 66 years old

"Hello, I'm Olivia, and I'm an alcoholic! It has been 159 days since my last drink." I say.

I feel so empty. Not helpless but empty. I thought I was going to be filled with something new, but then it turned out to be the wrong filling, and now only the walls are left. They are good walls. They will grow better over time. I trust that. It is airy and light in here.

I have deleted Don's phone number from my contact list. I have deleted all of our conversations. I have deleted him from my life. I have changed my AA schedule so he can go at the old times if he wants. That was the least I could do. But I don't think he is coming anymore. The other day, Marion said she hasn't seen him in a while, and she is here all the time. I didn't ask her. It was just a comment after the meeting. I haven't told anybody what happened. Not Robert, not AA friends. There is no need. It was just a bump on the road. An obstacle I had to scale to move on. A test of my resolve. They happen all the time. Every minute of every day, I am inching closer to myself. I don't need a man to help me do that. And I am not strong enough to carry someone else. Even if I was, I wouldn't want to. I can't jeopardize what I have become. Not for a man. Not for anyone. So I am making do with who I am.

Robert is good to have around, even with all his quirks and habits and stubbornness. I have come to the realization that he can't read my thoughts and feelings on my forehead, so if I want him to take them into consideration, I'm going to have to tell him about them in words he can understand. That is fair. I don't know if we are going to stay together or not. I do know I want to give him a chance to get to know me. Then we can take it from there.

I have also realized no one will celebrate my accomplishments or congratulate me on what I have done unless they know about it, and I would really like them to. It is not that these people in this circle right now are not important to me. They are. Immensely. But they are not my family. And I want my family to know. I am ready for that.

So I have invited all of them for lunch next Saturday. Here. They will have to stay at the Comfort Inn over the weekend—if they want to—because we don't have enough room and I need my space. They will have to figure it out. Ben is the only exception. Lily will have to ask him what he wants to do. It is Mother's Day on Sunday, but I won't promise that I'm going to act like one. I can only be me, and that will have to be enough. There are plenty of mothers in the family anyway. And we haven't celebrated Lily's birthday. At least I didn't.

I will cook something decent. I have been practicing baking pies over Easter. Everyone will be served sodas to drink. What they do on their own time is their own business, but I won't have any alcohol in my house, and that goes for Robert too. He was surprised I wanted it this way, but after he mulled it over for a day and a half, he kind of liked the idea, and I have caught him whistling a happy tune when he does not think I am listening.

It is going to be a good day. Every day is a little bit better.

"Hi, Olivia!" We all say.